Secrets of St. Vincent

Charles Farley

Pineapple Press, Inc.
Sarasota, Florida

Inquiries should be addressed to:

Pineapple Press, Inc.
P.O. Box 3889
Sarasota, Florida 34230

www.pineapplepress.com

Library of Congress Cataloging-in-Publication Data

Farley, Charles.
        Secrets of St. Vincent / Charles Farley. -- First Edition.
                pages cm
        ISBN 978-1-56164-612-8 (pbk. : alk. paper)
            1. Physicians--Florida--Fiction. 2. Murder--Investigation--Fiction. 3. Port Saint
Joe (Fla.)--Fiction. 4. Mystery fiction. I. Title.
        PS3606.A695S45 2013
        813'.6--dc23
                                                                        2012051587

First Edition
10 9 8 7 6 5 4 3 2 1

Design by Shé Hicks
Printed in the United States of America

Author's Note

Parts of the following story were inspired by Marjorie Kinnan Rawlings's 1938 classic, *The Yearling*, about a poor family trying to survive in the central Florida backwoods not too far in time and place from where this story takes place.

Savent les secrets de la mer.

(They know the secrets of the sea.)

— *Gérard de Nerval*

The frigid night air sent a shiver through his body. He had just rowed across the pass from St. Vincent Island to the mainland. He was soaked with sweat, and the ever-present wind across the water and through the pass froze him. He was about to wade into the dunes when he heard a car rumbling up the gravel road toward him.

He jumped behind a palmetto thicket and watched. An old man stopped the car at the end of the road, got out, and walked to the shore. It looked as if he wanted to jump in. But after a few minutes, he returned to the car, opened the back door, and dragged a burlap bag to the edge of the water. There, breathlessly, he heaved it into the sea.

And the sea gave up the dead which were in it; and death and hell delivered up the dead which were in them: and they were judged every man according to their works.

—*Revelation 20:13*

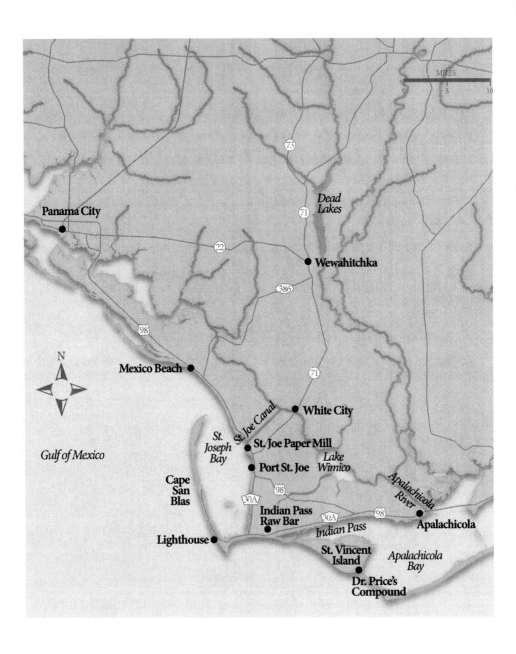

Chapter One

The doctor was dying. He was sure of it. Something was gnawing away at his insides. Maybe cancer cells like the ones that had killed his mother many years before. Or tuberculosis bacteria eating away at his lungs bit by bloody bit. He knew his heart must be tiring too, at his age. And some days he was certain he felt it failing, pumping feebly to an eventual, deadly halt. But he could not, would not heal himself. By this time, he was resigned to his fate, whatever it turned out to be. So he just kept on going, the best he could, day by day, one dismal day at a time.

This morning, as the sun seeped silently across his bedspread, he lay in bed missing Sally Martin and wondering exactly what to do about his friend and housekeeper Jewel Jackson. She was leaving him soon, and he would be here alone, or nearly so, in Port St. Joe, a quaint, quiet, mosquito-infested, little village on the Gulf of Mexico in northern Florida's provincial Panhandle—"the forgotten coast" some called it, never explaining who exactly had forgotten what. Truth be told, few people had ever known enough about it to have much to forget.

Dr. Van Berber was not looking forward to another day. He ached all over and, as usual, would have preferred to stay in bed. But he could hear Jewel downstairs preparing breakfast and could smell the grits and something fishy cooking, so he mixed up his usual morning cocktail of morphine and lukewarm water and braced himself for another day.

"You're finally up," Jewel greeted the doctor, as he sat himself down at the kitchen table.

"Yes, Jewel, I'm afraid so. Another day in paradise, as they say. What's new with you?"

"Ah, busier than a three-legged cat under a guava tree. How's shrimp and grits sound?" she asked, placing a plate of the steaming concoction in front of him.

"Hmm, smells good. Where'd you get the shrimp?"

"On the back porch this mornin'. Note says from Geraldine Anderson. Big and plump, ain't they?"

"Yes, yes indeed," the doctor said, as he liberally sprinkled Ed's Red Hot Sauce all over the shrimp and loaded his fork. "Her daughter Lila has been having some breathing problems lately, ever since that new mill opened up there on Blossom Row. Matter of fact, I haven't been feeling too chipper myself."

"Yeah, I've noticed that, Doc. Some mornin's the last couple of weeks you been lookin' like the back end of bad luck, but your breathin' seems okay to me. So I sorta doubt it's the mill that's botherin' you—God knows it can smell like a run-over skunk when the wind's in the right direction. Seems to me, though it ain't none of my never-mind, that you been particularly down ever since I told you about Sally Martin. What's goin' on with y'all, if you don't mind me askin'?"

The doctor did mind, but he didn't say so. Instead he took a sip of his coffee and looked at Jewel, standing there as immaculate as always in her starched apron and simple blue dress, leaning against the sink and drying her hands on a worn, white dish towel, with that shy, woebegone smile of hers. She was taller by half a head than the doctor and built as solid as a post oak chiffonier. Her shoulder-length, black hair was as straight as a stallion's mane and her smooth skin, as dark as the bark of a black tupelo tree. Anyone else in the world he would have told where to go, but Jewel held a special place for him. Sometimes, despite her comfortable familiarity, he had a hard time taking his eyes off her. She was one of the few people he cared for anymore and, if anyone did, she deserved an answer. But he was having a hard time forming one.

"Well," he finally said, peering into her searching, mahogany eyes, "we had a little talk, and what can I say? I guess it's over between us. I don't know what else to say to her."

"Do you still love her?"

"Geez, Jewel, you've got some hard questions for this early on a Monday morning."

The claustrophobic kitchen was already hot and exceedingly hushed. The doctor knew there must be some sounds out there somewhere, but all he could sense was a dull burn somewhere inside of him that he knew must be flushing his face into a crimson sting.

"Do you?"

The doctor couldn't think. He just hurt. And even though he could feel the tears welling up, he wasn't going to cry. He didn't want to let it all out yet. He wanted to feel the hemorrhage building inside him for a little while longer, like an artery fixing to burst. He wanted to keep wrestling with whatever the muddled mass of pain was that he had not yet been fully able to comprehend.

"No, Jewel," he finally muttered. "I don't think so. Honestly, I don't know what I feel anymore. Angry, sad, hurt, a whole mess of mangled misery that doesn't make a lot of sense to me right now. But obviously we're through and that doesn't feel good. So, yeah, I'm feeling kind of down, but, I guess like everything else, I'll somehow come to terms with it, and, who knows, maybe even get over it someday."

"I understand, Doc. I won't bother you about it no more, unless you wanna talk about it. I know you was really stuck on her. I'm sorry."

"Me too," the doctor said, staring at the remains of his breakfast, "me too."

A few months before when the doctor had started seeing Sally Martin, the widow of the hacked-to-death assistant lighthouse keeper, he had noticed how pale and flabby he had become over the years. So he had started walking to work in the morning to get some exercise and then back home at around noon to retrieve his old Ford to conduct house calls in the afternoon. It was no more than seven blocks each way, but it was better than nothing. He had also asked Jewel to cut down on the fatty foods that she was accustomed to preparing for him, but she hadn't paid him much heed. This deep into the Depression you ate what you could get and were plenty glad for whatever you got. The doctor's diet was therefore dictated primarily by what his patients gave him in payment, as Mrs. Anderson had this morning with the shrimp that her fisherman husband had caught, and what Jewel and the doctor's best friend Gator Mica brought from their gardens or from the sea. Fortunately, for everyone in poor Port St. Joe, the growing season was long and the sea still bountiful. Once wild deer, turkey, and waterfowl had been plentiful too, but with the lumber and paper mills' insatiable appetite for wood, hunting was becoming increasingly precarious as a dependable source of sustenance. Still, Gator shot a deer now and then and occasionally brought over a bluebill or bufflehead for Jewel to roast. They got by, but sometimes just.

In truth, the walk to and from work did more for the doctor's psyche than it did for his physique. It gave him a chance to think a little without anyone else around and to try to sort out what had transpired between him and Sally Martin. Jewel, as usual, was right about their breakup making him depressed. He had been in love with five women in his life and each relationship had ended badly. His first love, Rachel Manuelian, had died of polio when they were only twelve.

And while he had been very young at the time, he had also been very impressionable. So her death had indelibly marked him and imbued in him at an early age the gloomy view of the world and life that he continued to hold to this day. His wife of nearly thirty years, beautiful Annie, had mysteriously disappeared eleven years ago on a trip to visit her sister in Washington, D.C. To ease the pain of her absence and his increasingly painful arthritic aches and advancing old-age ailments, he had begun taking morphine on a daily basis. His next wife and faithful nurse, Carrie Jo, had died of breast cancer just four years after they had married. This had driven him into a deep depression from which he had still not entirely recovered. And his last wife, Jennie, had divorced him less than a year into their volatile marriage—an event which had ultimately prompted his move from Lynn Haven City to Port St. Joe three years before. By this time, he was sure he was finished with love. Enough was enough.

But then he had met Sally Martin when he was asked by Sheriff Batson to look into her husband's murder. In the process, the doctor had not only managed to get himself almost killed, but also to fall improbably for the charming widow who was at least half his age. And now he was paying once again. Not one of his previous loves could, in fact, match her physical allure: slim, crimson-haired, wide-eyed, sweet smelling, and all so effortlessly so. There was no doubt that the doctor was mesmerized by her beauty. But, once again, it had not worked out.

The doctor mulled all this over one more time, pondering how he had ended up in such a preposterous predicament, as he walked along Long Avenue toward his office in the center of this seemingly serene little village on this bright, breezeless Monday morning in mid-May. When his first wife Annie had disappeared, he had become confused and irrational, searching mindlessly for her along the train route where she had gone missing. And now that same feeling of panic and helplessness had overtaken him with this loss of Sally. He was distraught and couldn't think straight. Everything just seemed to be a perplexing mess. And who knows, maybe even a touch of senility had set in, because he just couldn't seem to let it go and move on.

Chapter 2

The doctor's rumination was interrupted by the blaring blast of a car horn that sounded like it was right next to his left ear. The doctor jumped and turned around to find the reddest, shiniest, longest Cadillac convertible that he had ever seen, now resting with its right front tire on the curb directly behind him. And there sitting behind the wheel in a starched white shirt and gray Fedora hat was none other Gabriel White, Jewel's handsome, blues-belting boyfriend. And next to him in a blue, pin-striped suit sat his sidekick, Reggie Robinson, both bluesmen beaming like Lincoln Perry and Ed Lee in their famous "Step and Fetch It" vaudeville routine. Gabriel gave another blast on the horn and the doctor's dejected look spontaneously turned into a laugh.

"Top of the mornin' to you, Doc," Gabriel called. "Care for a lift?"

"Why, Gabriel, Reggie, I'd be honored. This is undoubtedly the most beautiful machine I've ever laid eyes on."

Reggie hopped out and held the door open for the doctor so he could ease himself into the plush, tan leather backseat. Gabriel steered the new Caddie up Long Avenue until he got to Fourth Street, hung a wide left, and then drove a few blocks over to Reid Avenue, where he turned right and then rolled on halfway up the next block to where he guided the colossal creature of a car into a wide parking spot right in front of the doctor's downtown office. People on the sidewalk stared. It wasn't every day that they saw a pair of nattily-dressed Negroes and an old white man, wearing smiles wider than St. Joseph Bay, cruising through the city center of sleepy Port St. Joe in a shiny, new Series 75 Fleetwood Cadillac convertible that looked longer and redder than the town's single Ford fire engine and pumper truck that rested a few blocks away over at the City Hall garage.

"Come in, come in," the doctor said, as he held his office door open for Gabriel and Reggie. "This is Nadyne Wakefield, the best nurse and office manager in North Florida. No, in the entire state. Well, probably in the whole damn world."

Nadyne looked up over the top of her wire-rimmed glasses and smiled hesitantly at the three men standing in front of her narrow oak desk. "Nadyne," the doctor continued, "this pair of dapper gentlemen are two of the best bluesmen in all America, who, I assume, judging by their current means of conveyance, are about to be renowned throughout the entire radio-listening land."

"That's right, Doc," Gabriel said. "We've done signed a multi-show contract with the Richard Huey Players and the Mutual Broadcasting System up in New York City, and Mr. Huey done gave us enough advance on our salaries to put a down payment on that new Cadillac sittin' right out there."

"Oh my," Nadyne exclaimed, pulling back the chenille curtains that she had sewn herself and peeking out the front window at the gleaming, new automobile, "that is a beauty."

"You showed it to Jewel yet?" the doctor asked.

"No, not yet," Gabriel said. "We just got into town and was headin' over to see her at your place, when we seen you walkin' down the street like you was lost and lookin' for a friend. Where's your car anyway, Doc?"

"Oh, Gabriel, I'm trying to get some exercise, to be healthy in my old age. Come on now, let me show you around. It ain't much, so it won't take y'all away from Jewel more than a minute. Nadyne, any customers yet this morning?

"Not yet, but you've got appointments beginning in a few minutes."

"Okay, follow me, fellows. Through this door passes the sickest people in all of Port St. Joe, right into my own little shotgun shack of a medical center. On this side of the hall is an inside toilet and an examination room and on the other side an emergency operating room, not quite as well-equipped as the hospital's in Panama City, but okay in a pinch, and here's my messy office, which I won't let Nadyne touch, even when she threatens to set a match to it. Coffee? Want some coffee? How long y'all been on the road?"

"No thanks, Doc," Gabriel said, beginning to look ill at ease in the cramped confines of the little office. "We best be gettin' on. We started out yesterday from Eatonville, where our people are, and then we spent the night in Perry with my aunt, so we're fine."

"Yeah, don't worry 'bout us," Reggie added. "Gabriel can't wait to see Jewel."

"Reggie," the doctor said. "I have to tell you how sorry I am about what happened up there on Peters Street. I had no idea the sheriff would show up."

"I know, Doc. Gabriel explained it all to me. Don't give it a second thought. I'm just glad the sheriff's dead now, and I can come back with Gabriel to this little town again."

"Well, I appreciate your understanding, Reggie. Especially after I pretty near got you killed. We're glad to have you back. Gabriel sounds okay by himself, but he's even better when you're playing the guitar or one of those funny instruments along with him. So when you see Jewel tell her to plan a party for us to celebrate your radio show and y'all being back in town, okay?"

"Will do. Thanks, Doc." And with that, they were out the door.

He already had a headache thinking about Jewel leaving with Gabriel for New York City and was thinking about taking another little nip of morphine to soothe himself, but, before he could measure the amount, Nadyne was at his office door announcing another emergency out at the new St. Joe Paper Mill.

Chapter 3

Now the doctor had to figure out a way to get to the mill, since he had walked to his office this morning, or at least part way, until Gabriel and Reggie, who were now long since gone, had picked him up. It would take too much time to walk back home, so he summoned help, as he had become so accustomed to doing, from his daily anchor. "Nadyne," he hollered, as he gathered up his black bag and jacket, "I hate to do it, but may I borrow your car? I didn't bring mine this morning, and it sounds like I better hurry on up and get out to the mill."

"Don't worry, Doc," she answered. "I told Chief Lane that you didn't have a car this morning, so he's gonna stop by and pick you up on his way there."

Thank God for Nadyne. Fortunately, he had inherited her when he had moved to Port St. Joe. The only daughter of a struggling shrimp fisherman, her mother had insisted that she attend nursing school at the Florida State College for Women in Tallahassee. Thanks to a scholarship and lots of hard work, she was the first in her family of four boys to earn a college degree and, until the doctor arrived, was the only medical provider in town. There was a little hospital thirty miles northwest in Panama City, but Nadyne, and now the doctor, handled the rest. Now nearing middle age, Nadyne remained soft-spoken and cautiously shy, especially for someone who was so smart, well-organized, and competent. The truth was she kept the office going. If it weren't for her keeping his appointment book, paying the bills, supplying the medical histories of everyone in town, and ably assisting the doctor with any medical situation necessary, the doctor would be lost. If she had been a prettier woman, a man would have snatched her up long ago, but she was what they called "plain"—not pretty, not ugly, not slim, not fat, not charming, not dull—just plain. The doctor liked her like that and couldn't understand why other men didn't, but, to the doctor's boon, she remained single and dedicated to the doctor and their little town's health and well-being. Now she would once again cover for him and see to the morning's appointments until he returned from the mill.

Before he could walk out the door, the doctor heard the chief's car horn blaring in front of his office. "Thanks, Nadyne, sounds like the chief is here already. Hold down the fort. I'll see you later."

Port St. Joe's no-nonsense Chief of Police, John Herman Lane, was at the wheel of his late model, black and white Ford squad car, its single, round, red light pulsing like some sort of bacchanal beacon in the bright, broad daylight of the morning's brilliant blush. The doctor took the front seat beside the chief and, with tires squealing, they were off to the mill.

"What's going on out there now?" the doctor asked as the chief switched on the car's shrill siren.

"Not quite sure, to tell you the truth. We got a call from a foreman out there that said they had just fished a man out of a cooking vat, whatever that is, and that he wasn't breathing. So we may be too late, but, just in case, I'm gonna get us out there as fast as I can."

The chief sped down Third Street, as cars pulled to the curb to let him pass. The chief drove as fast as he dared through the town that was now becoming increasingly crowded with people moving in to work at the new mill. He swerved to miss Albert Cunningham who was hogging the road on his old Schwinn bicycle in front of Owens and Murdock's dry goods store. Albert waved nonchalantly as the chief honked and shouted out the car's window, "Out of the way, Albert! Move over, for Christ sakes!"

They passed several brick masons who were constructing the walls of D. P. Peters' new general store on Reid Avenue and sped past the carpenters who Cecil Clement had hired to build new homes for the mill workers on Eighth Avenue. Charles Lupton, the son of another San Blas lighthouse keeper who had retired a few years back, also had a crew who were up on ladders painting a new house on Bay Road. They drove past Mrs. Lawson's Rooming House on Second Street, that, according to Mrs. Lawson, who had been in the doctor's office the week before with a mild case of bronchitis, was now completely full, as was every other boarding house in town. This was a far cry from the sleepy, little town the doctor had moved to three years before, when the population had dwindled to eight hundred or so poor fishermen and turpentiners. Now, they were saying the mill would soon employ, when it geared up to full operation, up to a one thousand people, making anywhere from fifty cents an hour for common laborers up to one hundred dollars a week for experienced foremen.

Chief Lane was a short, thin man, with a full head of graying hair and sparkling blue eyes. He always dressed in the same plain tan uniforms as the other three Port St. Joe police officers, except, instead of the usual military-style uniform hat with its short, shiny visor, the chief sported a fashionable straw Panama hat with a wide black hatband. The doctor guessed he was in his late forties or early fifties, but that may have been because of his gray hair and the man's constant solemnity. He had a wife, Millie, whom the doctor had treated for irregular periods, and a sixteen-year-old son, Mathew, who was frail and afflicted with a mild case of chronic asthma. Millie had told the doctor that they were originally from

Tampa, where her husband had been a captain on the police force. But he had resigned in 1931, rather than obeying the orders of his superiors to tear down a lectern and arrest a lector who read newspapers and books to the workers while they rolled cigars in an Ybor City cigar factory. The orders, finally carried out by a more cooperative officer, had ultimately led to a major strike and the Lanes' decampment to Port St. Joe, where a law enforcement officer with his experience was roundly welcomed.

The doctor had never seen the chief crack a simple smile, let alone a joke, but he did like to talk, even with the siren shrieking so loudly the doctor could barely hear what he was saying. "You know, Doc," the chief yelled, as they passed the new houses on Parker Avenue, "even though this new mill's causing some accidents, it looks like it's bringing our little town back to life. It ain't like it was a hundred years ago when there was more than twelve thousand people living here—not yet anyway. Back then, they say it was one of the busiest ports on the coast. Lots of rich folks. Cotton growers and shipping big shots built themselves big, ol' mansions, more than twice the size of these new houses here, and, at its height, St. Joseph—that's what they called the town back then—was also called 'The Wickedest City in America.' Can you believe that?"

"I can," the doctor answered. "You don't by any chance attend the First Baptist Church in town, do you?"

"How'd you know?"

"Cause I've heard this sermon before."

"You have? I don't recollect seeing you in church there, Doc."

No, but I treat Reverend Babcock occasionally, and, since I'm not a churchgoer, he feels obligated to preach to me in my own office."

"I see. Well then, you probably already know that back then the waterfront had a bunch of hotels, bars, bordellos, and even the country's first horse racing track. According to the Reverend, the town was really wide open, with sporting types from all over the country coming here for all kinds of vice and trouble-making. I'm just glad I wasn't the chief back then."

"Yeah, it must have been something," the doctor hollered, as his head bounced up to bang the car's headliner when they sped across the Apalachicola Northern Railway tracks into North Port St. Joe. "Now the *Star* says that the boys over in Tallahassee have just passed a bill appropriating five thousand dollars for a big Centennial Celebration to commemorate all that this coming December here in Port St. Joe. Lot of money for a celebration of something that happened a hundred years ago, if you ask me."

"Well, it's a pittance to what this new Centennial Building over on Allen Memorial is gonna cost. If Roosevelt approves it, the Works Project Administration and the city are gonna cough up more than seventy-three thousand dollars for it. Now that's a lot of money."

"Well, I guess we have Andrew Jackson to blame for that."

"How so?"

"According to the *Star*," the doctor said, "Jackson was Florida's governor back then, and for some reason he wanted to have the territory's first Constitutional Convention right here in St. Joe. So St. Joseph, in all its decadence, was riding pretty high, I guess, and was even in contention to become the new state's capital."

"Yeah, well, those were the days," the chief said, as he switched off the siren and pulled in through the front gate of the new mill. "If you believe Reverend Babcock, the town paid dearly for all that wickedness."

"This sounds all too familiar," the doctor said.

"Yellow fever," the chief continued nonetheless. "The pastor claims that within a few weeks of the first case, sometime back then, can't remember exactly, when they buried a ship's captain who'd died of the disease, three quarters of the town was sick. The place went crazy. The reverend preaches that people were in such a hurry to escape the fever that houses were abandoned with dinner dishes still on the dining room table. He says it was so bad that, at one point, there weren't even enough healthy folks to bury the dead. Corpses were stacked up like cord wood on the shelves of abandoned stores."

"Yeah, like you, Chief, I'm glad I wasn't in my position back then."

"I should think not, 'cause accordin' to the reverend, God still wasn't satisfied, because the next year, there was this huge fire that swept from the forest through what was left of the town, destroying every building there in one big, hellish blaze. The final end came a little later, I think he said in 1844 when a big ol' hurricane, with one hundred and thirty mile an hour winds and a storm surge to match, carried whatever was left of the old town back out into the sea forever."

"Yep," the doctor said, "I guess those sinners got theirs, or so preaches the Reverend anyway."

"But just like that," Chief Lane said, "the whole damn town was gone. Can you believe it? I wonder if that could happen again today."

"No reason why it couldn't. We've got a vaccine for yellow fever now, but not for tuberculosis, influenza, polio, and syphilis. And nobody has yet come up with an antidote for hurricanes and fire. And if the Reverend is right about God's vengeance, you can bet He knows we still have our share of sinners just like they did back then."

The doctor also knew that to many old-timers the old town, St. Joseph, was still known as "The City of the Dead." Was it cursed by God, as Reverend Babcock contended? Or was it just fate? The doctor didn't know. Until recent events, he would have chalked it up to coincidence or bad luck; he was previously not too taken with curses or providence. But now, after the recent death he had witnessed and the distressing duplicity he had experienced, not to mention these horrid accidents at this new mill, he wasn't so sure. Maybe their little village by the bay *was* cursed.

Chapter 4

And the massive mill, now looming before them like an angry, belching volcano, didn't at all disabuse him of this determination. They drove past a two-story building that by itself was as big as downtown Port St. Joe. A long chute extended from the high tower of another building into the bay. An imposing brick smokestack emerged from it all, soaring up to meet and create the plant's very own dense, dirty, murky cloud cover. The dredging of the bay to thirty feet had been completed in February. Then a channel from the bay to the St. Joe Paper Company had been dug and a new half mile long dock had been built, where a steamer with "SS Ipswich" stenciled on its side was now moored.

Dr. Berber and Chief Lane were directed by mill workers to a wide door at the south end of the plant. When they hurried through the door, a heavy, mustached man in tan overalls, who introduced himself as Lyle McGregor, led them down a long, concrete walkway parallel to an idle black conveyor belt. After marching along the walkway for what seemed like a city block, they arrived at a group of six men standing helplessly around a prone figure dressed in dripping wet overalls and steel-toed boots. The doctor could tell by the man's sallow complexion that he was not well. He bent down on his knees and held the man's limp wrist, searching for a pulse—nothing. He grabbed the stethoscope from his bag, ripped open the man's overalls, and listened for a heartbeat—nothing. He looked at the man's pallid face, pried open an eye, and peered into his lifeless, dilated pupil—nothing.

"I'm afraid," the doctor said, looking from man to man in the group around him, "that we're too late."

"You have any idea what the cause of death might be?" the chief asked.

"No, not at this point. We'll need to take his body to Dr. Perron, the County Coroner in Wewa, to be examined. He's got a nasty bump here on his head, and it looks like he's been in that vat there. So my best guess right now would be either a head injury of some sort, brain hemorrhage maybe, drowning, or chemical asphyxiation from whatever might be in that vat. Or a combination of the three."

At this point, Chief Lane took over—thankfully. He asked the man named McGregor to cover the dead man and to bring any witnesses to some quiet place in the mill where he could question them one by one. He ordered that no one was to leave the plant until he had said so. McGregor led them all, except the man lying on the floor, to an office at the far end of the giant room. McGregor, Chief Lane, and Dr. Berber entered the cramped little room with a large window overlooking the plant floor. McGregor instructed the other men to wait in the canteen until he called them and closed the door. McGregor crumbled with a loud sigh into a chair behind his desk while the chief and the doctor sat facing him on new oak chairs on the other side.

"Now, first, please tell me what you do here at the mill?" the chief began, as he removed his Panama hat and carefully placed it on an open corner on the top of McGregor's desk.

"I'm the supervisor for this area of the plant," McGregor said.

"Okay, did you see what happened to the man lying out there?"

"No, I didn't, but I've talked to the other men who were nearby, and

I've managed to piece together what I think happened."

"Okay," the chief said, taking a miniature notebook and stubby, yellow pencil from his shirt pocket, "let's hear it."

"Well, apparently the man, whose name is Ridler, Robert Ridler, was doing a choke-up job.

"A choke up-job?"

"Yeah, he was unclogging the chipper feeder when too much wood got stuck in it. Happens fairly often. Anyway, he must have hit his head or somehow fell onto the conveyer belt that carried the chipped wood into the cooking vat where the chips are turned into pulp. That's where the men found him, floating in the cooking vat."

"Are wood chips actually being cooked there?" the doctor asked.

"No, not really," McGregor answered, "not in the usual sense of the word. There's no heat involved, only chemicals."

"What sort of chemicals?"

"Sodium hydroxide and sodium sulfide. What we call white liquor."

"Hence, the rotten egg smell," the doctor said.

"Yes, exactly," the supervisor answered, "but you get used to it after a while."

"Hmm," the chief said, "can the stuff kill a man?"

"No, not really," McGregor answered, as he pulled a pack of Pall Mall cigarettes from his shirt pocket. "Not any more than one of these," he continued, holding up one of the Pall Malls. "Care for one? No. Okay, well, the chemicals can be toxic to humans if mixed wrong or if they're breathed in too much, but we work in here every day, breathing in the fumes and, aside from an occasional headache, we seem to be feeling okay."

"What then would have caused the man to fall?" Chief Lane asked.

"Good question," the supervisor answered, lighting up the cigarette with a shiny steel Zippo lighter. "My best guess is that, as he was unclogging the feeder, he hit his head on the feeder machine and knocked himself out and then fell onto the conveyor belt. Or he could have fell on his head and knocked himself out then. At any rate, if he was still conscious when he was on the conveyor belt, he could have easily jumped off it before he landed in the cooking vat."

"How far is it from the feeder machine to the conveyor belt?" Chief Lane asked.

"Oh, maybe fifteen or twenty feet, not that far, so he would have to have landed pretty much directly on his head to knock himself out."

"Are there any guard rails around the feeder machine to keep a man from falling all the way down to the conveyor belt?" the doctor asked.

"Well," McGregor sighed, as he leaned his head back and blew cigarette smoke toward the ceiling, "not yet. They were supposed to be installed before we started operation, but they're not in yet."

"Why not?" the chief asked.

"I really don't know. Like I said, they were supposed to be installed by now. You'll have to ask the boss."

"The boss?"

"Yeah, Mr. Mitchell, he's in charge of the whole plant," McGregor said, stubbing out his cigarette in an overflowing ashtray on the corner of his desk, "the big boss."

Chapter 5

The big boss was indeed big. In fact, Michael Madison Mitchell, as the brass nameplate on his door proclaimed, bore a striking resemblance to W.C. Fields, whose latest moving picture, *The Big Broadcast of 1938,* the doctor had just recently enjoyed at the Dixie Theatre in Apalachicola. He had that flushed, potato nose, as well as a big, protruding belly and a receding gray hairline, but apparently not the comic's sense of humor, because this frowning man appeared in no mood for jokes when McGregor and Mitchell's prim secretary led Chief Lane and Dr. Berber into his spacious office located in a separate office complex across a dirt road from the main plant where the man, Ridler, lay dead.

The doctor had never met this big boss Mitchell, nor had he seen him around town that he could recall. He spoke rapidly with a gruff, Northern accent that was clipped and all business. "Please, have a seat," he said, rising slowly from his broad, brown leather chair. "Welcome to the St. Joe Paper Company. I'm sorry it's under such unfortunate circumstances. Susie, fetch some coffee, please. These gentlemen, and I, for that matter, have had a rough morning. Just bring a tray with a full pot and four cups, cream and sugar too."

"Thanks for your time, Mr. Mitchell," the chief began, as he placed his Panama hat on top of a file cabinet and sat down across the desk from the big boss. "I know you're a busy man, but this is the third death at your mill since you started construction, and I thought we should talk."

"Of course," Mitchell said, "I'm at your disposal, and you can be sure that I'm just as disturbed by these accidents as you are. The first, the kid from Baltimore, what was his name, McGregor?"

"Ross, Frederick Ross."

"Yeah, just a kid, only nineteen years old, fell from a scaffold, about fifty feet, as I recall, and fractured his skull. Just last year, before the plant opened."

"Right," said the chief, "and then there was the sheriff and then this man today."

"Right, so what can I do for you, Chief?" Mitchell asked, leaning dangerously backward in his leather chair while tugging with both hands on his black, elastic suspenders. To the doctor, he looked like he was merely acting concerned, and not sincerely being so, probably because the big man's uncanny resemblance to the wise-cracking, waggish actor made it hard for the doctor to take him very seriously, no matter how serious he tried to appear.

"Well," Chief Lane answered, "I'm not sure what you can do at this point. In retrospect, it would have helped if there had been guard rails on both the scaffold and on that feeder machine. And, who knows, maybe a little tighter security at night might have saved the sheriff."

Mitchell moved his pudgy hands to the arms of his chair, allowing his suspenders to pop against each side of his barrel belly in staccato unison. "Are you suggesting," he said as leaned forward to peer directly into the chief's eyes, "that the mill is somehow at fault in these accidents?"

The chief, it seemed, was in no hurry to answer this question, as if weighing carefully how to proceed at this point, but the doctor saw the policeman's face blanch as he stared silently back at the menacing big boss man. As they waited, it was so quiet that they could hear a clock on the wall behind Mitchell's desk ticking away and the doctor's stomach grumbling rudely.

"Let's put it this way," the doctor finally broke the silence in an attempt to drown out his noisy stomach and to help the chief out in what he knew had become a politically charged situation, "three men have died in less than a year, and I have personally treated at least a dozen others who have been injured here, some seriously, since your operation opened in March. So, I guess, if you're asking us if we think the mill is at fault, the answer would have to be yes. Yes, because there is no doubt that these accidents would not have occurred if your mill was not in operation. But given the fact that the mill *is* in operation, the real question becomes could they have been prevented? Perhaps. We don't know. We're just asking you to entertain the possibility to see if we can prevent future injuries."

"Doctor, you are a diplomat, I must say," Mitchell said with a forced smile, "but you have to understand that what we are doing here has much broader implications than a few accidents—not at all diminishing the pain and suffering that may have been experienced by a few individuals who were involved in them.

"Alfred duPont, regardless of what you may think of him, saved what little was left of this miserable little town. If it hadn't been for him buying up the declining properties around here, people would have starved to death during the worst of the Depression. You wouldn't have trees along your streets, new buildings downtown, improved schools and playgrounds. Your railroad, your port, and your telephone company would have all gone under. Even when he died back in thirty-five, he left a will that instructed that this mill be built to save this town, and that's exactly what his wife and her brother, Ed Ball, did, not to mention the formation of an institution to treat crippled children up in Wilmington, Delaware.

"So, yeah, like any big industrial complex, employing hundreds of people, we encounter a few mishaps. But, isn't it worth it, gentlemen, to save a dying town, to put poor, starving people back to work, to build an economically viable community that we can all be proud of?"

Chief Lane and Dr. Berber looked at each other. What could they possibly say to that? Despite looking like a movie buffoon, the man did make sense.

"Mr. Mitchell," the chief measured his words carefully, "we do appreciate your company's importance to our community, but Gulf County ranked fourth in the state in number of accidents last month, despite our low population, and that's not good. Unfortunately, this discrepancy is mainly due to the increasing number of accidents here at your plant. I'm afraid we just can't let this continue. I understand that we're all in this together, like it or not, but since a death has occurred here today, it's my job to investigate it and that is what I intend to do. So, if you will excuse me, Mr. McGregor will now show me more precisely where the accident occurred and introduce me to the men who may have witnessed it. Thanks again for your time."

The big boss man glared wordlessly at the chief and did not budge from his chair. He really didn't have a chance to before Chief Lane grabbed his Panama hat and, followed by McGregor and the doctor, was out the door, almost knocking over poor Susie who was on her way back into the office, balancing a loaded silver tray on both of her trembling hands.

The doctor, or more precisely his stomach, realized that it was getting on to noontime by now, but Chief Lane was not to be deterred, as he marched them all back to the main plant. There, the chief instructed McGregor to show him the chipper feeder where the man had been working, as well as the long, rubber conveyor belt that had carried him to the huge cooking vat filled with wood chips, water, and chemicals. The doctor followed along, since he had no other choice, but he really didn't see the point. Unless someone had actually seen what had happened, they would never know for sure how the man had ended up face down, like a lifeless lump of driftwood, in this toxic pool of pulp that smelled like rotten eggs.

So as McGregor and Chief Lane peered into the murky vat, the doctor wandered off on his own. Mitchell, the big boss, was, of course, right, as far as he went. The duPonts had, in fact, done a lot for the community and at a time—deep in the middle of this terrible Depression—when the people of their little town needed it most. But what Mitchell had failed to report, was the fact that the rich family's motives were not altogether altruistic. They had bought the town and surrounding countryside at extremely low prices, according to Sheriff Batson, whose father had previously owned much of it. But the new owners were initially unsure of exactly what to do with these vast holdings, until DuPont heard about a Georgia chemist named Dr. Charles H. Herty. This man had developed an inexpensive process to make pine into pulp that could be turned into high-grade newsprint paper, using acidic sulfite solutions to digest the wood, remove impurities, and increase the effectiveness of the bleaching agents.

When, according to the *Star,* the entrepreneurial DuPont examined this new process and discovered how much more economical and less chemically harsh it was than traditional paper-making methods, it immediately occurred to him that he could use it to take advantage of all of Port St. Joe's assorted attributes. He could use the railroad, that he now owned, to transport the remaining slash pine stands, that he also owned, to a mill, that he would build, in the port town, that was his as well, and ship the finished product to newspapers all along the coast via ships that sailed into the deep water port that would be at his complete disposal. Unfortunately, Alfred duPont died in 1935 before his plan could be implemented, but, as Mitchell had pointed out, his wife and her brother continued with the ambitious scheme. But, by the time the mill was finally completed earlier this year, 1938, the market for newsprint was so weak that it was decided at the last minute to convert the design of the plant to produce durable paperboard, using an older kraft process that required the use of much more caustic chemical combinations: the sodium hydroxide and sodium sulfide mixture in which the man Ridler had died. This decision, according to the now deceased Sheriff Batson, was resulting in hazardous wastes, like chemically treated tree bark, boiler ash, lime grits, and slag, being dumped into the bay and surrounding fields. And, until his untimely death, the sheriff had been doing everything he could to gather evidence of the new plant's destructive practices. So, ironically, the very process that had inspired duPont's initial idea for the mill was not ultimately employed, and with deleterious, hazardous results.

The doctor had no idea what the long-term implications of this dumping might be, but he did know that his workload had dramatically increased because of the new plant, both directly with a variety of mill accidents and indirectly with an assortment of new respiratory problems that kept cropping up like weeds in a Panhandle garden. So Mitchell was right as far as he went. The mill was helping a lot of people get back to work, but at what cost?

The doctor was not an economist, an environmentalist, or a sociologist, but, even so, he was uneasy with what was happening to his adopted town. At first, his move there had been a welcome respite from Lynn Haven City and his failed marriage to Jennie. With Jewel, Nadyne, and Gator, he had built a respectable practice and comfortable existence that he thought he could enjoy into old age, but then came Sheriff Batson and Sally Martin and now this confounding paper mill with all its attendant benefits and problems. He was not so sure anymore.

As the doctor wandered into what was labeled on the door as the mill's "Lunch Room," a big, cavernous room filled with long tables and benches, now occupied with men opening and eating the contents of brown paper bags and black lunch boxes, he found a pay phone on the wall. He searched his pocket for a nickel, found one, dropped it in the slot, and got Edna, the town's day operator, who connected him to Nadyne back in his office.

Nadyne gave him an update on his missed morning appointments and offered to rescue him from the plant so he could at least make his afternoon round of house calls. The doctor gladly accepted. He was already tired, hungry, and badly in need of the welcome reprieve that his mid-day morphine fix would bring.

Chapter 6

When the doctor finally arrived home at the end of the long day, he was glad to find that Jewel, along with her seven-year-old son Marcus, was still there. Sometimes Jewel would make him supper and leave it for him while she took Marcus to her house to have supper with her mother, but more often, if the doctor was not to be too late, Jewel and Marcus would stick around until the doctor arrived and have supper with him.

"What's cooking?" the doctor asked as he entered the sweet-smelling kitchen.

"Oh, hi, Doc," Jewel answered with her head still inside the oven and her ample backside pleasantly presented to him. The doctor loved Jewel's ass. Marcus caught him staring at it, and they shared a chuckle before Jewel withdrew her head, closed the oven door, and faced the doctor with a hint of perspiration dampening her dark forehead.

"What are you two grinnin' like a couple of possums for? Baked stuffed flounder, if you must know," she said. "Gator Mica came by this afternoon with a couple of nice flounder that he gigged on the sand flats out in front of his house and a coffee can full of crab meat, so I mixed the crab up with some chopped green onions and peppers from mama's garden, mayonnaise, egg, and cayenne pepper, put it all on top of the flounder fillets, with a little butter and lemon juice, and now I'm bakin' it all with some sliced new potatoes and a little rosemary that we borrowed from Miss Shriver's herb garden next door. Someone, don't know who, left a sack of turnip greens, on the porch, so they're cookin' down with some of that leftover hambone."

"Geez, sounds really good. I'm starved. Is Gator joining us then?"

"No, he said that he was too busy with his new job, but he said he wants you to go fishin' with him Saturday."

"Well, when you see him, tell him that sounds good. I need a break after today."

"Why, what happened?" Jewel needed to know.

"I'll tell you over supper. Just let me get out of this damn suit first," the doctor answered as he started up the stairs. He stopped on the second step and looked back at the brown-skinned boy in denim overalls sitting at the kitchen table with a thick textbook and a Red Chief tablet spread before him. "Marcus, you haven't said a word. Is that homework so important that you can't say hello to a tired old man?"

"Sorry, Dr. Berber, I didn't want to interrupt you and mama. Sorry you had a bad day."

"I'll live. How was your day? If I remember correctly second grade can be a lot tougher than most of my days."

"Yes sir," the boy said, shaking his head, "it can be pretty bad sometimes, but I like Mrs. Limburg, so most days are okay."

"Good. They'll likely stay that way as long as you do your homework and mind your teacher, so keep at it."

"Yes, sir. We only got a few more days till summer vacation, so I reckon I can make it. I can't wait."

When the doctor had changed into an old pair of dungarees and a clean, collarless, cotton shirt, he returned downstairs to find the kitchen table set and the platter of stuffed flounder and bowls of rosemary potatoes and turnip greens awaiting him. As he sat down, Jewel added a pitcher of sweet tea, salt and pepper shakers, and a bottle of pepper sauce for the greens. As was their custom, Jewel offered each dish one at a time to the doctor who then served Jewel and Marcus, doling out the amounts according to their requests, and then serving himself.

"Jewel, I gotta say, this, as usual, is great," the doctor said, still chewing, after he had sampled each portion on his plate. "I know you've probably told me, but where in the world did you learn to cook like this?"

"From my mama, of course. I done told you she can cook even better than my grandma, but don't tell big mama that. She'd wring my neck."

Everyone was quiet for a while, as they savored Jewel's masterpieces. The doctor thought of how lucky he was to have her. When he had moved to Port St. Joe, Nadyne was already there waiting for him. And although she didn't have an office—she worked out of the front parlor of her parents' house on Woodward Avenue—Nadyne knew everyone in town and how the place worked. So she already knew that Jewel Jackson was unhappy taking care of an ailing, old white couple who had been abandoned by their son who had moved to Atlanta, often forgetting to send enough money to feed them, let alone to pay Jewel regularly.

So, when the old couple had finally been committed to the poor farm, Jewel had joined the doctor. She came every weekday morning after she dropped Marcus off at the shabby, one-room, colored schoolhouse in North Port St. Joe. She made breakfast for the doctor and then, after he had left for his office, she cleaned up, did the laundry and ironing, and grocery shopped for the doctor, as well as for herself, Marcus, and her mother.

Jewel's mother took in laundry and ironing from a few white families and kept a large garden at the back of her tidy shotgun shack on Avenue C in "Nigger Town," as the dingy ghetto of North Port St. Joe was called by most white people in town. Jewel's father was serving the last two years of a ten-year sentence in the state prison in Raiford, his harsh penalty for assaulting a white man who had tried to stop him from finding and killing Gabriel White who had got his only child, Jewel, pregnant. Although Jewel loved her father, both she and Gabriel trembled at the thought of what he might do to Gabriel when he was released. This shared angst hung over their relationship like the unholy heavens of an approaching hurricane, postponing, along with Gabriel's constant rambling, their marrying and settling down. Now, with Gabriel's new and seemingly more stable radio job in New York City, the doctor was afraid Jewel's plan was to take Marcus and move there with Gabriel. And while the doctor had once told Jewel that the couple had his blessing for this long deferred move, his heart was telling him otherwise, because he was not sure, without Jewel, that he could go on. Her daily smile, her grace, her support, her stability, well, just the sight of her were usually all that kept him going most days, one day after the next. Without waking up to her each morning, he was not sure there was much more reason to wake up at all.

"So what happened at the mill today?" Jewel interrupted his reflection.

"Oh my, I'm not sure you want to know."

"Oh come on, let's hear it. It's been about as dull as dish water around here today. Brighten our day."

"Well, I'm not sure fishing a man out of a vat of toxic paper pulp will brighten your day any, but that's what happened."

"Was he dead?" Marcus asked, his eyes bulging with expectation.

"As a doornail," the doctor said, as he polished off the last of the turnip greens on his plate.

"Oh my," Jewel exclaimed, "how'd he get in a paper pulp vat, whatever that is?"

"Don't know. It's a mystery. Chief Lane was questioning everybody around there when I left, but he had a bump on his head, so maybe he fell on a piece of equipment or just slipped and fell. There were no guard rails on the platform where he was working."

"I'll ask around," Jewel said. "I know a few folks who work out there now. I'll find out what happened."

"Jewel, it's none of your business. Let's not get involved in another mess, okay? Enough is enough."

"Well, it won't hurt to ask."

"Jewel!"

"Okay, Doc, whatever you say."

"What's for dessert?" Marcus asked.

"Good question," the doctor added, wiping a piece of crab meat from his mouth with his napkin.

"How does lemon meringue pie sound?" Jewel asked.

"Hmmm."

As Jewel rose to retrieve the pie from the windowsill, the doctor finally blurted out what he now realized had been bothering him all day since he had encountered Gabriel White and Reggie Robinson early this morning, "Jewel, how's Gabriel? He was looking awfully good this morning."

"Yes, wasn't he though," she said with a sly smile. "He's just about as proud as a dog with two tails cause of this new radio job of his. He said y'all talked about gettin' together while he's in town. How's Sunday night sound? He won't be workin' then, and we can have Gator over and have a little party, if it's okay by you."

"Well, I'll have to check my crowded social calendar, but Sunday sounds fine. But, more importantly, what's going on longer term with you two, now that Gabriel's got this new job?"

"We're talkin'," Jewel said as she sliced the pie and served a generous piece to each of them. "Gabriel's waitin' to hear when rehearsals for the new show are gonna start, probably any day now, and then we'll see."

"Cut that piece in half for me," the doctor said.

"We're talkin', but ain't nothin' been decided just yet."

"I see," said the doctor, no longer hungry, despite the fact that he was now confronting the crispy, browned crust on the best lemon meringue pie in all of north Florida.

Chapter 7

The next Saturday morning, the doctor was relaxing on his screened-in back porch, reading Hemingway's new novel, *To Have and Have Not,* about a fishing boat captain in Key West, Florida, during the Depression, when he heard the familiar sound of screeching brakes and worn tires sliding to a slow halt in his crushed shell driveway in the backyard. Gator Mica's 1927 Chevy Capitol pickup was loaded with Gator's glade skiff and was covered with a dense coating of mud, salt, and sand so thick that it was hard to distinguish the truck's original color. The doctor guessed black, but who knew anymore, probably not even Gator.

"Mornin', partner. How's life?" the smiling man greeted the doctor as he bounded up the back porch stairs.

"Not too bad, I guess. At least it's Saturday and we're goin' fishing so it could be a lot worse."

"All right then," Gator laughed. "Let's do it. I thought maybe since it's so damn hot and humid this mornin' we might go out in the bay a little ways to see if we could catch a sea breeze. Whatta you think?"

"Sounds good to me," the doctor answered. "What about those clouds over to the east? You think anything's brewing over there?"

"I doubt it," Gator said, peering into the sky, as they walked to his truck. "There was a pretty heavy dew this morning and no red sky, west winds, but the humidity is so high that the pine cones are all closed up and, like you say, you never know what might happen when those harmless-looking clouds start gatherin'. We'll keep an eye on 'em though. Hopefully, they'll just keep us from gettin' sunburnt."

They drove north out of town on Parker Avenue toward the mouth of the new canal that connected the St. Joe Paper Mill and the usually calm waters of St. Joseph Bay. By now, Ed Ball and the St. Joe Paper Company had acquired every waterfront property in Port St. Joe, except one. As they drove past Fred Maddox's new house near the busy downtown dock, the doctor pointed it out to Gator. Maddox was a ship's pilot, and the doctor had occasionally treated him and his family for minor ailments and injuries. According to Captain Maddox, the St. Joe Paper Company had claimed his land, but he had refused to sell it at any price and had hired a couple of lawyers to fight the mill in court to retain his house and the property that had been in his family for generations.

Gator Mica shook his head. The fact was Gator was living rent-free on duPont's property about ten miles southeast of Port St. Joe without the family's knowledge or consent. But now, somewhere in his mid-fifties, the doctor guessed, Gator had no living family and nowhere else to go. He was a head taller than the doctor and nearly twice as broad at the shoulders—a big, hulking man who was as weather-beaten as his truck, due to the fact that he spent most of his waking hours outdoors. According to Gator, he had learned his way around the Florida wilderness from his father, Halata Mica, also known as the "Alligator King," and the boxing ring from his fighting mentor, Jess Willard, former heavyweight boxing champion of the world.

Gator's father was the last of the Seminole chiefs to be moved in 1858 from Florida to Indian Territory in Oklahoma, where Abraham "Gator" Mica was later born to the chief's Caucasian wife, Eliza Clinton. From an early age, Gator's head was filled with stories of his father's beloved native land in Florida, and, at the age of sixteen, Gator set out to return to the place he had never seen but heard so much about. In the Everglades, Gator learned to live in the swamps on his own, to fish, to hunt (mainly alligators, hence his nickname), to garden, to do anything he had to, to get by.

But before he had left Oklahoma, he had also learned to fight from Jess Willard, one of the largest, tallest, and most courageous boxing champions in the world. The man who, in 1915, had knocked out Jack Johnson in the twenty-sixth round, thus gaining the nickname "The Great White Hope," had been raised in Pottawatomie Indian country in Kansas and later moved to Oklahoma, where he retired briefly and worked with a few local Indian boys who wanted to learn to box. And while Gator never fought professionally, he was a skilled boxer who was afraid of no man when it came to a physical struggle and had proved it more than once to the few who had been foolish enough to cross him.

When the U.S. Congress authorized the creation of a new national park in the Everglades in 1934 and when Gator had killed a rival in a bar fight in Florida City that same year, he had wandered north, finally squatting on an empty snatch of Alfred duPont's dunes near Indian Pass, a narrow, natural ocean pass leading from Apalachicola Bay to the Gulf of Mexico. The doctor had treated Gator a couple of years ago after a fist fight at the Indian Pass Raw Bar and the two had been fast friends since: fishing, hunting, drinking, and eluding together, whenever they found the time, the widespread penchant for provincialism of their sedate, sedentary, little town by the bay.

Just before reaching the canal, Gator turned off the main road onto a narrow dirt trail, bordered by a thick scrub thicket of long leaf pine, sweet gum, and wisteria. At the end of the trail, he pulled the truck onto a flat, muddy beach, where the doctor and he wrestled the glade skiff out of the truck bed and into the murky shallows of the wide canal. The boat was built of cypress for fishing and alligator hunting in the Everglades, about five yards long and a yard wide and only about a foot deep, but it was the only boat Gator owned and he used it not only in the area's shallow marshes and streams but also in deeper lakes and even in the bay when its waters were calm. By the time they loaded Gator's rifle, two cane fishing poles, and the usual five-gallon lard cans—one filled with crickets and minnows for bait, another with waxed paper–wrapped sandwiches and cod balls, and the third with bottles of cold Spearman beer and big chunks of melting ice—the skiff rode dangerously low in the choppy waters of the canal. It sank even lower, with just inches between the surface of the water and the top of the gunwales when the doctor carefully crawled to his usual perch at the bow of the boat, and Gator pushed off and hopped into his spot at the stern. There he adjusted the gas feed of the little Briggs engine that he called a "hothead" and then repeatedly pulled the starter cord until the engine finally sputtered to life with a blatant belch of white engine smoke and an irregular clatter.

Gator guided them down the middle of the canal and then northward up into the bay's entrance at the end of St. Joseph Peninsula. There, in a quiet inlet, Gator cut the engine and dropped anchor, a coffee can filled with concrete connected to a hemp rope. They were only a few yards from the peninsula's broad white sand beaches and imposing dunes. The doctor watched a bald eagle slowly circle the tip of the shore, as Gator baited their hooks and then passed him a pole and a bottle of cold Spearman beer. The sky was a deep azure expanse interrupted only by the high cumulus clouds gathering inland to the east, somewhere this side of White City, the doctor guessed. They cast their lines, sipped their beers, and silently waited. When, after a while, there were no bites forthcoming, the doctor asked, "How's the new job, Gator?"

"Well, I've only been at it for a couple of weeks now, but it's okay, I guess."

"You guess?"

"Well," Gator said after a long swig of beer, "it's different, gettin' up every morning at the same time and havin' to show up at a certain place, out there at the Thirteen Mile Oyster House that Dr. Price bought. I ain't never done that before."

"So what is it exactly that you do once you get there?" the doctor asked.

"Right now my job is to teach all of Dr. Price's employees who used to make whiskey how to harvest oysters all up and around St. Vincent Island—Big Bayou, Indian Lagoon, St. Vincent Sound—round where I live. They ain't use to bein' outdoors in a boat all day, so there's a bunch of grumblin' goin' on most of the time."

"'Spect they'll get used to it?"

"You know, partner, I ain't so sure. Right now I'm thinkin' that when Dr. Price closed down his moonshinin' operation to go into the oyster business, he offered his employees a job oyster fishin' just to be nice; this bein' a Depression and all, and jobs so hard to come by. I told Dr. Price the other day that I expected most of 'em, especially the white ones, would leave when, if ever, they found somethin' more to their liking."

"Probably just as well."

"Yeah, to tell you the truth, I'd just as soon they was all gone. I'd be able to gather just about as many oysters on my own, I expect, if I didn't have to mess with all of 'em. But, then again, I know where Dr. Price is comin' from. Those people, most of 'em, have families and all, so it'd be mighty rough if they didn't have a job."

Since they weren't getting any bites, Gator pulled anchor after a while, and they let the boat drift slowly out toward the mouth of the bay. Gator handed out bologna sandwiches and cod balls and they drank more beer. The clouds from the east were approaching, but they looked harmless enough against the wide blue sky.

"What about you, Doc?" Gator asked as he reeled in his line to check to see if the cricket was still on the hook. "You still seein' that widow out on Cape San Blas?"

"No, I'm afraid not."

"What happened?"

"Well, it's sort of a long story."

"We got all day, partner."

So, drifting along serenely in Gator's skiff, the doctor told his friend how Sally and he had parted and how miserable it was making him feel. Gator, as always, listened intently and let the doctor reveal for the first time some of those muddled feelings he had been grappling with for the past few weeks.

"Damn, partner, I sure am sorry it didn't work out."

"Yeah, me too."

"Oh well, sometimes these things are for the best."

"Maybe so," the doctor sighed.

"So what next?"

"I don't know, Gator," the doctor answered as he stared at the red and white bobber bouncing on the gray waves. "I don't know. I've been trying to figure that out."

Gator didn't respond. Instead he reeled in a nice, three-pound yellowtail snapper that he detached from his line and tossed in the lard can with the beer and ice. "Well," he finally said, opening another bottle of beer, "it ain't none of my business, but it sounds to me like you're well rid of her, even if you do still love her, which it sounds like you do."

Gator, as usual, had grasped the situation and was able to sum it up in simpler terms than the doctor himself fathomed it. So they silently continued to fish. The doctor soon hauled in a pan-sized grouper and a small gray triggerfish, and Gator caught a big black sea bass. Then the fish stopped biting and the two napped, as their tiny boat drifted farther out of the bay and into the broad expanses of the Gulf of Mexico.

The doctor was awakened by the boat's restless rocking and the wind that had now increased and shifted from the west to the east. As he looked up from the boat's bottom where he was lying with his head resting on a ragged towel, he saw the bank of high cumulus clouds that was previously resting harmlessly over White City now directly above them, but with a dark flat base that shut out the sun and lay alarmingly close to their heads.

"Gator," the doctor called, raising himself up to see Gator lying at the other end of the boat fast asleep, "wake up. We got an issue here."

"What?"

"Look up."

Gator peered sheepishly into the black cloud above and then sprang upward, bumping his forehead of the top of the wooden shelf he ordinarily used as a seat at the skiff's stern.

"Holy shit," he shouted as he rubbed his head. "Let's get outta here." He sat up and grabbed the starter cord and pulled. Nothing but a sputter. It began to sprinkle. Gator adjusted the choke and pulled the cord again. The engine coughed like a wounded manatee and belched a whiff of white smoke that stank like burnt rubber. Gator pulled again. The engine sighed helplessly.

As Gator fussed with the motor's choke, the doctor saw behind him a dark funnel forming in the cloud mass overhead. Gator looked up and followed the doctor's alarmed gape, and they both watched as the funnel descended from the huge cloud and attacked the sea a few feet behind them with a senseless vengeance. Waves suddenly kicked the boat into a rollicky roll as the funnel spun toward them.

"Hold on tight, partner!" Gator yelled, just before he yanked the starter cord one more time and fell backward into the spiraling wind that picked the big Indian up and launched him abruptly into the sea. Even as the doctor tried to locate Gator, he did as instructed, clinging to the bow line with all his strength, as the skiff whirled madly in the angry sea.

The doctor was not sure, because his eyes were closed most of the time and when they were opened, filled with stinging, winging saltwater, but the boat seemed airborne, flying through the spout like a dead leaf in a wanton whirlwind. And then the rains came, pouring in heavy sheets all around him. But he was still in the boat—alone. He looked all around into the ocean for Gator, but there were only waves, bouncing higher and higher, their white tips gleaming in the premature dusk. The boat was no longer spinning, but instead bobbing helplessly up and over the mounting breakers. All he could see were the waves, one after another, incessantly battering the boat and filling it with water. What would he do without Gator? Would he even have a chance to find out? At the top of the next surge, he hung on tight, but saw the bleak black of still another larger wave, massive and roaring now in his ears, smashing toward him. As the surge lifted him and the boat, he thought surely they would flip, but at the wave's crest, he saw below a head and arms flailing in its trough.

The doctor, soaked and scared, continued to hold tight. The waves finally slowly subsided and the rain let up, but the boat was nearly filled with water by then. He began bailing with the one lard can that had miraculously survived the waterspout, looking feverishly for Gator in the enveloping sea. Can after can of water, until the doctor's shoulders were sore and weak. He could see land in the distance now and the clouds seemed to be drifting out toward the horizon, the sky above brightening. He sat in his seat at the bow of the boat exhausted.

And then there he was, just a few yards away, waving his arms as if he were herding an errant calf. The doctor put his hands into the sea and paddled, paddled with all his might, as fast as he could. Gator finally reached up and threw his right hand over the boat's slippery gunwale.

"Request permission to come aboard," he gasped with a tired smile.

"Permission granted," the doctor said extending his hand. And then the afternoon sun began to peep shyly through the dissolving clouds.

Chapter 8

The doctor dreamt of sea serpents and his own drowning that night. In his dream, a grotesque ocean monster had swallowed him, and he had tried unsuccessfully to catch his breath, until finally he had been belched from the monster's dark stomach onto the beach, gasping and crying. When he awoke, the doctor was worn out. He could barely move because he was so stiff from the previous day's struggle, so he lay in bed and stared at the ceiling until he finally realized he was not going back to sleep. At that point, he reached for his bottle of morphine, mixed it with the water that he had poured into the glass on his bed stand the night before, and drank, then waited until he gradually felt his body relax and his mind wander.

Yesterday, once the doctor had somehow wrestled an exhausted Gator, along with a few gallons of salt water, into the glade skiff, Gator had tried repeatedly to start the drowned Briggs engine, but, even after he had removed and done his best to dry out the motor's soaked spark plug, the "hothead" would not mutter a moan. Everything had just been too drenched. So they had knelt in the pool of cold water on the bottom of the boat and paddled with their hands toward shore. It had taken more than an hour of hard work before they had finally beached the boat on a stretch of desolate sand somewhere between Port St. Joe and Mexico

Beach. Gator had lost his shoes to the sea and looked even more water-logged and bedraggled than the doctor. He had been angry and grumpy, because he had not only lost his shoes, but also all his gear, including his fishing tackle and favorite rifle. They had both lain on their backs on the beach and tried to dry out in the late afternoon sun. They had been too exhausted to do anything else.

But with night approaching, they had to do something. So, since it was not a good idea for a barefoot Indian to be hitch hiking, especially at night, the doctor, still damp and weary, had traipsed inland over the dunes to Bay Road, where he had caught a lift with a timber truck driver who drove him back to Gator's truck, still waiting beside the canal where they had left it.

When the doctor had driven back to the dunes, he had found Gator sprawled sound asleep on the sand. He had awakened him, and then Gator had rigged up a long rope tied at one end to his skiff and the other to the bumper of his truck. Then he had driven down the road until the boat appeared over the top of a dune and then had slid effortlessly down it to within just a few feet from the pavement where they could load it onto the bed of the truck. It had been dark by the time they were through, and they had both been so drained that they had rode back into town in silence.

Now, since it was Sunday, Jewel was likely at church with Marcus and her mother, maybe even with Gabriel and Reggie. He remembered tonight was the night that Jewel had arranged the little party for them, and he dreaded the thought of her announcing her intention to move north with the bluesman. There wasn't much he could do about it now, he knew, so he just lay there and said a silent prayer, for what it was worth, to a God he believed did not exist.

Fortunately, the day passed without major mishap or emergency, but it was unusually hot and humid, even for north Florida. The doctor dozed on the back porch between chapters of *To Have and Have Not,* sprawled in front of an electric fan that he had rigged up with an extension cord to a socket in the kitchen, but all it did was move around the hot air. He was drenched in sweat when Jewel's old Ford pulled into the driveway and woke him up. He was glad to see her and Marcus. They were still dressed in their Sunday best as they walked across the lawn, and Jewel looked particularly pretty in a form-fitting blue dress that the doctor had never seen before. He roused himself and stretched his aching muscles before Jewel and Marcus joined him on the porch, each toting a brown paper bag in their arms.

"What have we here?" he asked.

"Yo' supper, what else? Open that door, will ya? 'Fore I drop this on my toe."

The doctor opened the door to the kitchen for them and followed them inside, where he helped them unpack the bags. Marcus's bag was filled to the top with green ears of sweet corn from Jewel and her mama's garden, and Jewel's contained a warm sweet potato pie that her mother had baked for them.

"What y'all catch yesterday?" Jewel asked, as she placed the pie on the windowsill.

"Oh my," the doctor sighed, "maybe a cold. That's about it." And he told her and Marcus the whole story of his and Gator's adventure in the waterspout.

"My goodness," Jewel exclaimed. "You must be as tired as a boomtown whore today."

"Well, I've felt better, but I've been napping this afternoon, so I'll be okay. I'm just not ready to go fishin' again anytime soon, I'll tell you that."

"I should think not. Sometimes I don't know about you and Gator. Y'all git together and act like little kids, always gittin' in some kind of a mess or another. Too soon old and too late smart, I swear."

"Speaking of which," the doctor said, as they heard Gator's truck slide to a stop on the crushed shell driveway in back.

Gator too was moving slower than usual this afternoon, taking his time climbing the back stairs and trudging into the kitchen with a burlap bag slung over his shoulder.

"Well, if it ain't the ancient mariner hisself," Jewel greeted. "You look like you been rode hard and put up wet."

"Yeah, and you look like a million bucks, Miss Smartass," Gator replied, as he gave Jewel a big hug and then began emptying his bag on the kitchen table.

"What you got there?" Marcus asked.

"Something especially for you, little man. Look at this here watermelon, first of the season, directly from my garden. And some swamp cabbage I cut down a couple of days ago and some mullet that I smoked on Friday, since everything we caught yesterday got away. And, of course, a jar of cane liquor for yo' mama and the good doctor."

"Were you scared, Mr. Gator," Marcus asked, "in that big ol' waterspout that Doctor Berber told us about?

"Me? Hell no, boy, you know better than that. Take more than some fool waterspout to spook ol' Gator. Besides that, my partner here caught up to me and pulled me out of it like a big ol' floppin' fish."

"Okay, boys, enough with the fish stories," Jewel instructed. "Out on the back porch and shuck that corn. I got work to do in here, and I don't need none of you underfoot."

The doctor excused himself to take a quick shower, and Gator and Marcus took the bag of corn to the back porch as they were told. By the time the doctor had showered, dressed, and downed a dose of morphine, Gabriel and Reggie, each with a glass of moonshine, were laughing with Gator and Marcus on the back porch. Instead of joining them, the doctor eased up next to Jewel at the kitchen sink and poured each of them a glass of Gator's cane liquor. Jewel handed him a paring knife and told him to dice up some watermelon and put it in an empty green-glass bowl waiting on the counter.

"What's that cooking there?" he asked, pointing his knife at a large cast-iron pot simmering on the oven top.

"Swamp cabbage, what you probably called hearts of palm up north. Here, have a piece," Jewel said, handing him a creamy white bit of the plant. "That'll cook up too bitter, but it ain't bad raw is it? Gator must be cleanin' up around his place. It's a lot of work to cut down a palm tree and hack the boots off and then chop it up like this. I just sliced and peeled off these bitter bits of skin here and then sliced up the heart and now it's simmering in salt pork and water with a little sugar, salt and pepper, and a squeeze of lemon so it'll keep its color. Should take no more than half an hour."

"And here?" the doctor asked, pointing to the chopping board in front of Jewel.

"An experiment," Jewel answered. "You make do with what the Lord provideth, and since He ain't provideth that much today, 'cause you and Gator didn't bring me no fresh fish, I'm makin' a salad with your diced watermelon, slices of Gator's smoked mullet, some pickled ginger and soy sauce that I found in the larder, and then, at the end, I'll have Marcus run over and borrow some of Miss Shriver's cilantro and I'll chop it up and mix it in with some salt and pepper. What do you think?"

"Sounds good, as usual. I don't know how you do it, Jewel. I believe I'd starve to death if it weren't for you."

"I doubt it. Grab that big ol' pot from under the sink there and fill it with water for the corn, will ya? We need to bring it to a boil and then drop the corn in for no more than six or seven minutes.

"Marcus, git yoself in here with that corn now and git me some cilantro from over at Miss Shriver's and then set the table real fast. You hear me?"

"Yes, ma'am," Marcus shouted from the porch.

Regardless of its humble origins, the meal was a great success. And, after everyone had helped themselves from the passing bowls, the doctor raised his glass to propose a toast. "To your new radio show, gentlemen," he said, as they all raised their glasses. "May y'all become America's next Amos 'n' Andy. Now, let's hear all about it."

"Well, it's gonna be called 'The Sheep and Goats Club,' like in the Bible," Gabriel began. "A fellow by the name of Richard Huey put it all together. I met him up in Harlem. Man was once a redcap for the railroad, but now he's an actor who's got his own theater group, and runs a fine barbecue joint called Aunt Dinah's Kitchen up on 135th Street."

"What's the show about? Farm animals?" Marcus asked.

"Well, it's sort of a variety show," Reggie spoke up for the first time. "It's got an all-Negro cast and an all-Negro studio audience. See, on one side of the stage they have folks singin' spirituals and givin' sermons and what not—they're the sheep—and on the other side they got the goats who be singin' and dancin' and boogie-woogiein'. That's where we come in. We be the goats, singin' the blues and whatever other popular tunes they want us to."

"How about we get a little preview then," Gator suggested.

By this time, Jewel and the men had emptied the entire bowl of watermelon/mullet salad and most of the corn, which they had liberally slathered in butter, and were now emptying their glasses and pushing back from the table. Marcus had turned his nose up at the swamp cabbage, but everyone else had helped themselves to seconds.

"My belly's tighter than a tick," Jewel said.

"Yeah, me too. I'm just gonna have to wait on that sweet potato pie, Jewel," the doctor said, patting his stomach. "I'm stuffed. How about we move out to the back porch, so Gabriel and Reggie can entertain us now?"

As Gabriel and Reggie got out their guitars, Gator refilled everyone's glasses, except Marcus's, who had been banished to the kitchen to wash the dishes. The two bluesmen declined, but the doctor and Gator lit up Cuban Partagas cigars that Gator had brought. When Marcus finally returned, Gabriel and Reggie were already into their fourth song, as Gator twirled Jewel around to a mid-tempo jump blues called "Talking in Sebastopol." Gabriel had a high tenor voice on most tunes accompanied by a variety of open guitar tunings, finger picking, and slide acrobatics. Reggie played along on rhythm guitar, harmonica, jug, hambone, whatever the song called for. He accompanied himself on guitar and sang a tune called "Po' Boy, Long Way From Home," while Gabriel danced with Jewel—a little too close, in the doctor's opinion. For some reason, the doctor did not know why, he loved these mournful melodies—the blues, Gabriel called them; they somehow touched him and made him feel grounded and melancholy at the same time.

Eventually, after they each had downed a slice of sweet potato pie, Marcus fell asleep curled up next to his mother on a white wicker rocking chair in the corner of the porch. Gator passed out on the hardwood floor next to Gabriel's guitar case, the burnt-out stub of a Partagas cigar still lodged between the index and middle fingers of his right hand. And, as the doctor downed his last glass of whiskey, Gabriel and Reggie serenaded him nearly to sleep with a slow, loping blues that resounded starkly across the lawn and into the night, and then, as clear as a clarion, into the ears of Chief John Herman Lane, who had just pulled his squad car into the doctor's dark driveway behind them.

Chapter 9

The chief, dressed as usual in his tan uniform and Panama hat, strutted purposefully across the back lawn, now wet with dew, to the screen door of the doctor's back porch. Gabriel and Reggie stopped playing, and the cacophony of cicadas returned. The sweet scent of honeysuckle from the vines hanging on the porch permeated the night air. The doctor was suddenly sober and wide awake.

"May I come in?" the chief asked as he tipped his Panama hat to Jewel.

"Of course," the doctor said, hauling himself out of his chair with a groan. "What brings you out so late on a Sunday night, Chief? Have we been making too much noise?"

"No, not at all. In fact, y'all sound mighty good, if you ask me. No, the fact of the matter is I've got an arrest warrant here for your friend, Mr. Robinson," the policeman said, pulling a crinkled envelope from his back pocket.

"What for?" the doctor asked as he shot a quick look at Reggie and thought that he had never seen a colored man as pale as the light shade that the slight bluesman had now turned. No one moved as they waited breathlessly for the chief's answer.

"Murder, in the first degree, of Sheriff Byrd 'Dog' Batson," he said, as he released a pair of gleaming handcuffs from his belt.

"No, that can't be," the doctor protested. "Reggie wasn't even in town when the sheriff was killed. You're mistaken, Chief. I'm sure of it."

Gabriel was standing now with an angry scowl on his face, hovering above the doctor and the chief, while Reggie shrank into the corner of the porch and Jewel began crying softly with Marcus still sleeping peacefully next to her. Gator was snoring, rather loudly now, flat on his back on the floor, through it all. Then Chief Lane eased carefully past Gabriel and the doctor and slowly approached Reggie who was now slumped, like a defeated fighter, in the dim shadows of the porch. Jewel had told the doctor that both Gabriel and Reggie carried pistols when they performed to protect themselves from drunks in the rowdy clubs where they often worked, but he had never seen one in his house. But when Gabriel made a quick movement toward his guitar case, the doctor blocked his way, and then in one seamless motion the chief had turned the deflated Reggie around and snapped the handcuffs on his wrists behind his back.

"Sorry, Doc," Chief Lane said, as he pushed Reggie in front of him toward the door. "I gotta take him in. Come on down to the station in the morning, if you want, and I'll explain everything, but tonight he's goin' to jail."

Gabriel's wrath was palatable, even though he didn't utter a word. But when he took a step toward the chief and Reggie, Jewel whispered a sharp "no," and he halted.

The next morning, clear and crisp, the doctor drove to Bob Huggins' house on Constitution Drive. He had phoned the lawyer after the chief and Reggie had left last night and arranged to pick him up today, even though it was Memorial Day and Huggins had planned to go boating in the bay with his family. Huggins was a pugnacious war hero, stocky and cocky, with slicked back black hair and wire-rimmed glasses, who had successfully argued, at the doctor's behest, for Gator Mica's acquittal when he had killed a man in a brawl at the Indian Pass Raw Bar a few years back. Today the lawyer was acting grouchy, instead of displaying his usual Southern gentility that routinely charmed judges and jurors alike and facilitated, along with his uncommonly sound common sense, favorable judgments for his clients, regardless of their transgressions, whenever he argued, ever so gently, on their behalf.

"Alright," he grumbled, as the doctor drove toward the jail, "why do you think they're holding this Negro?"

"Well, beats me. As I said on the phone last night, Lane said he was being arrested for murdering Sheriff Batson, but I know for a fact that he wasn't even in Port St. Joe when the sheriff was killed."

"A fact?"

"Well, that's what both Gabriel and Reggie told me, and I believe them."

"So you didn't actually see him somewhere else. Did Gabriel?"

"Well," the doctor said as he turned off of Constitution onto Fourth Street, "I don't know for sure. I just know that Reggie left town the night before Easter and never returned until this week."

"And how do you know that?" Huggins asked, squinting over the top of his spectacles at the doctor.

Here the doctor had to think. What part about that night should he tell or not tell? The only people who were there that rainy Easter Eve, besides himself, were Gator, Reggie, briefly, and the sheriff, who was now dead and buried. The doctor tried to decide what was pertinent to proving Reggie's innocence and what was not.

"Well," he began tentatively, "I had a visit from Jewel and Gabriel that night, the night before Easter, and they were all upset because Reggie was acting crazy and saying he was going to leave town because he had seen a white man dump a body into Lighthouse Bayou the night before when he was fishing out there and he was afraid about it. They convinced

Reggie to hang around and talk to me, since, as the only white man they could trust, maybe I could help clear things up. So I said I would. Then I called the sheriff since there was apparently a dead body now out in the bay somewhere, and then I picked up Gator and we drove up there in a storm to the colored section and found him in a little shack at the end of Peters Street near the tracks. So as not to spook Reggie, I had Gator lie down in the backseat of my car until I could figure out what was going on with the poor guy. Well, when he finally let me in, I found him scared to death and, as it turned out, for good reason, because the man he said he had seen dumping the body was none other than Sheriff Batson himself. Then, surprise of all surprises, the sheriff shows up and pulls a gun on Reggie, and Gator comes in to see what's happening, and Reggie jumps out the window and is gone before the sheriff can get off a shot at him. And I haven't seen him since, until a couple of days ago. Gabriel says he somehow made it back to Eatonville where they're from, and he hid out there until he heard about the sheriff's death."

They were now parked in front of City Hall, and Bob Huggins was shaking his head. "Damn, Doc," he said. "You sure do get into some messes, and I've got about a million questions for you about this one, but I guess we better go in and see about Reggie right now. Let me do the talking and don't say a word about what you just told me, cause if you think I've got a lot of questions, you can bet Chief Lane will have even more. Okay?"

"Sure," the doctor said, relieved that he didn't have to try right away to explain it all again to anyone else.

Chief Lane was waiting for them in his cramped office at the rear of the building's first floor. He pushed a pile of official-looking papers to the side of his desk and extended a hand to the doctor and the lawyer and motioned them to sit in the two hard, uncomfortable oak chairs facing his desk.

"Coffee, gentlemen?" he offered.

"No thanks," Huggins answered for them. "It's Memorial Day and I promised my wife and kids we would go boating today so I want to make this as quick as we can, if you don't mind, John."

"Not at all. I'd just as soon be at home myself. What can I do for you?"

"Tell us about what you have on Reggie Robinson. As you know, the doctor here is a friend of his and would like to find out what's going on."

"Okay," the chief said, leaning forward to clasp his hands and rest his elbows on his desk. "Here's the story. Before the sheriff was killed out at the mill, he received from Judge Denton up in Wewa a warrant for Reggie Robinson's arrest."

"Arrest for what?" Huggins interrupted.

"Yeah, I'm gettin' to that. The warrant said for threatening a police officer, attempted assault on a police officer, and resisting arrest. What wasn't on the warrant was the whole story that Sheriff Batson told the judge, his deputies, and apparently anyone else who would listen, that is that when he was out searching for a suspect in the Martin murder case he ran across this colored boy, Robinson, who he thought was trespassing and fishing, he assumed without a license, out near Lighthouse Bayou. And when he questioned the boy, the boy pulled a gun on him and then took off into the woods, where he took a shot at the sheriff when the sheriff gave chase. But apparently the sheriff was more interested in catching the Martin murderer than Robinson, so he didn't pursue the boy any further. But the sheriff, being the sheriff, didn't forget about him. So later he finds out the boy's name from the colored girl who works for Mrs. Ramey. She, this colored girl, had apparently told Robinson he could fish out there without even asking Mrs. Ramey."

"So how do we get from threatening and attempted assault and resisting arrest to murder?" Huggins asked.

"We got a dead sheriff," the chief answered.

"So?"

"Well, the sheriff made it plain that Reggie was out to get him, for whatever reason. So he told all his men to arrest him if they ever saw him again. The truth of the matter, and don't quote me on this," Chief Lane said, looking around as if to make sure someone hadn't sneaked into his office to listen, "but, use your head here, Bob, guess who's up for re-election right now?"

"Judge Denton."

"Right, one and the same, and who's announced he's gonna run for sheriff to replace Batson?"

"Mel Roberts."

"Right again, and that lazy deputy, Roberts, who's in charge of the department now, and who wants to be the next sheriff, hasn't been able to come up with a single goddamn clue since the sheriff was killed, not that I've done any better. Truth is a lot of folks think the murderer did us all a favor. But none of that matters in an election year."

"I see," said Huggins. "Bail?"

"Denton says no."

"Can we see him then?"

"Sure, follow me," the chief said, rising from his chair and pulling a large key from a wooden peg on the wall behind him. "Although I believe you know the way, Bob."

"Yeah, I'm afraid I do."

The jail was in the basement of City Hall, a dank, windowless cavern that smelled like mold, stale urine, and dirty laundry. There they found Reggie Robinson, lying on an uncovered mattress in the corner of the first of four, otherwise empty cells. Just like in the moving pictures, the doctor thought, steel bars, gray walls, open toilets, and all. All it needed was a sad man playing a mournful tune on a harmonica. But instead all they found was a sad man, without a harmonica, curled in the corner of the cell in the fetal position in the same clothes he had worn the night before.

"He's all yours," the chief said, as he pushed the cell door closed and locked it behind him. "I'll be back in thirty minutes, so make it snappy."

Reggie slowly raised himself off the mattress and stood before the two white men. Despite his blue, pin-striped suit, he did not look good. His hair was matted perversely, his eyes were bloodshot, and his hands were shaking like a man with Parkinson's disease.

"How they treating you, Reggie?" the doctor asked. "This is Bob Huggins. He's the best lawyer in Gulf County, and he's going to help you."

Reggie nodded, and the three stood there quietly in the middle of the cell, listening only to dripping water somewhere nearby and the distant echo of sporadic traffic far away outside.

"As you know, they're holding you for the murder of Sheriff Batson. Do you know anything about that?" Huggins began.

"No," Reggie muttered, shaking his head back and forth. "The last I saw of the sheriff was when he was trying to shoot me up on Peters Street."

Well, the case against you does not appear to be strong," Huggins continued. "That's the good news. But the bad news is . . ."

"I'm colored," Reggie finished for him and then dropped his head and peered silently at the gray concrete floor.

"Yes," Huggins admitted, "that's the bad news. But if we can establish a firm alibi for your whereabouts on the night the sheriff was killed, then we have a chance. Okay?"

"When was it?" Reggie asked.

"Uh, good question. Doc?"

"Let's see," the doctor thought, "a couple of weeks ago, just before Mother's Day. The Friday before, I think. That would make it the sixth, wouldn't it? The sixth of May."

Reggie continued to stare at the floor, the other two men still standing, waiting.

"Reggie?" the doctor finally prompted.

"I was still hid out then," Reggie whimpered.

"Where?"

"On the north side of Lake Bell, in the swamp."

"In Eatonville?"

"Yes sir."

"Did anyone see you there?" Huggins asked.

"No, not that I know of," Reggie whispered, as his whole body began to shake and tears rolled down his cheeks.

Chapter 10

The doctor thought he had seen the last of Sally Martin, but now he needed to see her again—fast. He didn't know how long Reggie could last down there in the clammy bowels of Port St. Joe's City Hall. The doctor knew that Sally was supposed to move into a rented house on Sixth Street on June first, which was the day after tomorrow, so, after he had dropped Bob Huggins off at his house, he drove down Sixth Street and past the white bungalow, with a sprawling magnolia in front, that she had pointed out to him a few weeks before. There was no sign of life there, so he continued south out of town on the familiar, palmetto-lined gravel road toward Cape San Blas.

The doctor knew he should be figuring out what to say to her, but all he could think of was how beautiful she was and how much he wanted to see her again despite all that had happened. He would just have to wing it and try his best not to crumble into a blathering blob of pathos. But first he had to find her.

There were two identical white clapboard cottages at the base of the San Blas Lighthouse, each with shiny tin roofs and wide covered porches that looked out over the white sand beach and the expansive sea before them. Parked next to the first house was an old rusted, faded-white Oldsmobile convertible touring car with a bald spare tire mounted on the back bumper next to a broken tail light whose few remaining sharp red shards shimmered in the summer sun. At the other end of the car, under the car's open hood, was Harvey Winn, the head lighthouse keeper, a mustached, middle-aged man with an unlit pipe in his mouth.

"Hey, Harvey," the doctor greeted, as he pulled his old Ford to a stop next to the Oldsmobile. "Car trouble?"

"Oh, hi, Doc," the keeper said, as he extricated himself from under the hood and wiped his hands on a dirty red rag. "Yeah, somethin's wrong with the brakes, either that or my legs are gettin' weaker in their old age. You gotta stomp like hell to stop this ol' buggy anymore."

"Well, I wish I could help you, but what I know about cars you could fit into a radiator cap. I didn't think I'd find you here today."

"Yep, I'm still here. Ain't found nothin' in town yet. Everything's pretty near all filled up what with all those mill workers movin' in. What about you? Long time no see. Where y'all been hidin'?"

"Harvey," the doctor said, as he eased out of his car, "I have to tell you, all those folks moving into town to work at the mill and all those accidents out at the mill have been keeping me busier than I wanna be. I hardly have time to turn around. How about you? How's your new job at the mill?"

"Can't complain. Bein' a night watchman is different from bein' a lighthouse keeper, but that's okay. After all those years out here, I'm ready for somethin' different."

"Yeah, I bet you are, but you're still protecting, helping folks, so that must be in your blood, right?"

"Oh, I guess so. Never given it too much thought, to tell you the truth. I just do what I have to do. Try not to worry too much about blood."

"Which reminds me," the doctor said, as he walked over to face the former lighthouse keeper, "you know that night when Sheriff Batson was killed. You said you were on duty at the mill, right?"

"Yeah, I was."

"And you said before, if I recollect correctly, that you didn't see anything unusual that night, that right?"

"Yeah, that's right," Harvey said, as he tapped a wad of tobacco from a can of Prince Edward into the bowl of his pipe. "It's a damn big place, you know, and it's only me, and one man at the gate and another on the docks, to keep an eye on the whole thing, most every night."

"Well, a friend of mind, a colored fellow named Reggie Robinson, was arrested last night for murdering the sheriff, so I was wondering if you saw a strange colored man around the mill that night?"

"No, like I told you before, I didn't see nothin' or nobody. It was real quiet that night, the best I can remember."

"Harvey, I have to ask you then, do you know anybody who'd want to kill the sheriff?"

The night watchman stared out to sea for a moment, as he leaned against the Oldsmobile's fender and lit his pipe. "That's a good question, Doc," he finally said. "As far as I know, the man didn't have a lot of friends, but then again I don't know of any enemies that'd want to kill him neither."

"You said a couple of weeks ago that Sally and someone else would sometimes meet up late at night after Sally's kids had gone to bed. What do you think was going on there?"

"Doc, like I told you then, that's about all I know about it. I never brought it up to nobody but you, for that matter. Wasn't none of my business. I shouldn't have even told you, but I knew you was gettin' sweet on Sally, so I figured you needed to know. But if you're suggestin' that Sally had somethin' to do with the sheriff's murder, then I'd have to say you was plum crazy. As you've no doubt noticed, the lady is as sweet as tupelo honey. Yeah, she's got a mind of her own at times, but she wouldn't hurt a fly. You know that, Doc."

"A mind of her own?"

"Well, yeah, if she don't like somethin' she'll let you know about it."

"Hmm," the doctor said, not being able to recall witnessing this outspoken quality of Sally's personality. "Is she home, by the way?"

"Oh yeah," Harvey answered. "She's over there packin' up a storm. I'm gonna borrow Carl Meadows's old truck in a little bit, and we're gonna start movin' her into town."

"I think I'll drop by and pay my respects then," the doctor said, "before she's all moved out."

"Okay, Doc. See y'all later." And just as the doctor was almost out of earshot, he was stopped abruptly by the sound of Harvey's voice. "Oh, by the way," he called casually, "did they ever find the sheriff's head, do you know?"

The doctor turned and peered back at the slight man, now puffing away on his pipe as he slouched nonchalantly against the front fender on his old Oldsmobile, without a hint of irony on his face.

"No, not that I know of," the doctor finally answered, as he tried to fathom further his questioner's intimation. "Why do you ask?"

"Just wonderin', that's all. Just wonderin'."

"Hmm," was all the doctor could conjure, as he turned once again toward Sally Martin's familiar cottage, wondering one more time why someone would slice off the sheriff's head and leave the headless body next to a circular saw at the St. Joe Paper Company.

The well-worn, sandy path from the head lighthouse keeper's cottage to his assistant's cottage could not have been more than fifty yards, but the doctor was sweating and a bit short of breath by the time he had traversed the distance and climbed the porch stairs to Sally Martin's back door. Once there, he took a handkerchief from his back pocket and wiped his face and tried to calm himself. He still didn't know what he was going to say to her or how he was going to say it, and he felt his stomach knotted with anxiety. A light breeze blew in from the ocean carrying the fishy smell of low tide. The ubiquitous squall of seagulls sounded from the beach. He knocked and waited. And soon there she was before him again, as striking and seductive as ever, behind the screen door.

"Well, hello there," she said, as she pushed an errant lock of red hair away from her face. "I thought I'd probably seen the last of you."

"Me too," he said, "but something serious has come up that I have to talk to you about."

"Okay, the kids are upstairs packing, and it's hotter than the devil in here. So do you want to sit out there on the porch?"

"Sure," he said, as he opened the door for her and followed her to the two rocking chairs facing the blue-gray waves of the Gulf of Mexico. Her long red hair was in a ponytail, and she wore a faded pink gingham shift that clung to her slim figure like a furled sail to a mast. As she came into the sun, he could see tiny droplets of perspiration on her forehead. He felt the old urges surface again.

They both sat quietly for a few moments, the doctor trying to figure out how to begin. Finally, he said, "Sally, this is hard for me, but I have to ask you something important. Do you remember me telling you about Gabriel White, Jewel's boyfriend, and his partner, Reggie Robinson?"

"Yes, I think so," she said.

"Well, Reggie was arrested last night for the murder of Sheriff Batson."

"Oh my, I'm sorry to hear that, but what do you expect me to do about it?"

"Well," the doctor said, as he looked into her misty green eyes, "I'm not sure, but we both know he didn't do it, don't we?"

She did not answer, but he heard a girl and boy upstairs in the house arguing about something he couldn't quite catch, something about who owned something or other. And he suddenly felt very sad and wished again it had all turned out differently with Sally Martin and him.

"Sally, it's not fair that he's locked up," the doctor said, trying as hard as he could to focus on Reggie's release and not on what could have been. "He's not a strong boy to begin with, and I'm really afraid for him in there."

"What do you want me to do?" she whispered again.

"God, Sally, I don't know. I was hoping you'd have an idea, I guess."

They stared out to sea, sparkling in the afternoon sun, as if it might hold an answer that would satisfy them both. The doctor wanted to go to her and hold her and bury his fingers into the thick curls of her crimson hair until it was all okay again.

"Do you want me to tell the police who the real murderer is?" she asked finally. "Is that what you want?"

"I don't know. All I know is that an innocent man is suffering, because of my, and your, our silence."

"Are you going to tell them, Van?"

"I don't know," he answered truthfully.

"I understand," she sighed.

"Look, just tell *me* who actually killed the sheriff. That's all I'm asking. You don't have to tell the police anything."

"I'm not going to say any more about it, Van. You know too much already."

The doctor didn't know what else to say or do at this point. He didn't know exactly what he had expected, but he had in mind something more definitive. As he was about to get up to leave, Sally turned to him and said, "If it would make you feel any better to tell the police what you know, go ahead. I halfway expected you would have done that by now anyway, so I'm prepared."

Chapter 11

Gator Mica was sometimes a hard man to find. He didn't own a phone or a conventional sense of time. He adhered to his own schedule, and only Gator was privy to what that schedule was. Maybe this insouciance had changed since Gator now held down a real job. But since it was Memorial Day and he was almost there anyway, the doctor figured that Gator's house hidden amongst the dunes and scrub forests of Indian Pass was as good as place as any to start his search.

So he drove back off of Cape San Blas onto Sand Bar Road, past the Indian Pass Raw Bar, which he was surprised to see open on Memorial Day, and right onto the dirt road that led to Indian Pass, the quarter mile channel that split the mainland from St. Vincent Island and joined Apalachicola Bay and the Gulf of Mexico. Before he arrived at the Pass, he took another right on an unmarked dirt road and then soon found himself among the dunes and slash pine woods of Gator's hideaway. Gator's place was so well hidden that the doctor had to slow almost to a stop to spot the red-rusted oil drum in the ditch that marked the final turn to Gator's camp. At the end of the sandy path sat Gator's house in a dense grove of scrub dune forest. Well, it wasn't really a house; it was instead a discarded houseboat that Gator had bought and hauled and propped up on six-foot cypress stilts to keep out the snakes, alligators, and flood waters. Luckily, Gator's truck was parked in its usual shady spot under a live oak tree covered with Spanish moss a few yards from Gator's house. The doctor honked his horn to alert Gator of his arrival, and, before the doctor could get out of the car, Gator was at the front door, in bib overalls and a ratty t-shirt, sipping a brown bottle of Spearman beer.

"Hey, Gator, I hate to disturb you on Memorial Day, but I need your help," the doctor said as he walked over to the house.

"What's up, partner? Need a beer?"

"Well, as a matter of fact, I could use one. Thanks."

Gator went inside and returned with a cold bottle for the doctor. "Anything new with Reggie?" he asked, as he popped the cap off the beer bottle.

"No, not really. That's the problem," the doctor answered. "Bob Huggins and I saw him this morning, and unfortunately he doesn't have an alibi, and Judge Denton won't let him out on bail, so he's suffering down at the city jail for the time being.

"Sounds like we got a problem," Gator said.

"You're right about that. And if we don't figure out a solution soon, Reggie is gonna shrivel up and die in there. He's not taking it too well, and I can't say that I blame him. That jail is a real hell hole, and it looks like Chief Lane, Judge Denton, and everyone in the sheriff's department are ready to send Reggie to the electric chair right now, since they don't have a clue of who really cut the sheriff's head off."

"So what do we do?"

"Well, first off," the doctor answered, as he downed the last of his beer, "let's get something to eat. This beer's going straight to my head, since I haven't had a bite to eat since breakfast. The Indian Pass Raw Bar is open, so I'll buy us lunch. Then I'll phone Jewel and Gabriel from there and ask them to come to my house tonight so we can put our heads together to see if we can figure this out."

"Sounds good to me. I'll meet you at the Raw Bar in a few minutes. I'll drive my truck, so you won't have to drive me back here."

The Indian Pass Raw Bar was located at the corner of Indian Pass Road and Sand Bar Road, only a few miles from Gator's camp. It was a long, clapboard structure, surrounded by a crushed oyster shell parking lot, with two Gulf gasoline pumps in front. The doctor drove up next to the pump marked "Regular," and a young man dressed in a crisp, khaki uniform, with the name "Harold" stitched above the shirt pocket, and a cap with an orange Gulf logo on it, dashed from the door and asked the doctor whether he preferred regular or ethyl gasoline.

"Fill'er up with regular," the doctor instructed. The man then inserted the pump's nozzle in the tank, and, while it was filling, washed the car's windshield and asked the doctor, who was standing shaded under the pumps' broad, white canopy, if he wanted him to check under the hood. The doctor told him to take a look, and the attendant opened the car's hood and ceremoniously checked the levels of both the engine oil and the radiator water, as well as the fan belt and the battery cables. "Looks good," he said. "Oil's about half a quart down. Tires?"

"No, they should be okay," the doctor said.

"That'll be a buck-sixty-five then," the attendant said, removing the nozzle and replacing it on the pump.

As the doctor fished in his pocket for some change, he asked the helpful attendant, "Say, Harold, you wouldn't know where a man could get a bottle of moonshine around here would you? All the liquor stores are closed up for Memorial Day."

"Well," he answered, "there used to be a fellow who sold out of the back of a white panel truck behind here in the parking lot, but I ain't seen him for some time now."

"Do you recall his name?" the doctor inquired.

"Yeah, was Lucky. Never knew his last name."

"You don't know where I could find him, do you? I sure am thirsty."

"Well, like I said, he ain't been around for some time now, but, at the end of an evenin', he always drove off in that direction," he said, pointing toward Indian Pass and St. Vincent Island, "to where I don't know."

"Thanks," the doctor said as he paid the man, "I guess I'll just have to settle for beer inside today, but much obliged anyhow."

The doctor drove away from the pump and found a parking spot near the front of the building. Then he relaxed on a wooden bench on the front porch and waited for Gator. As he watched the attendant fill up another car, he spotted a phone booth at the corner of the canopy and remembered that he needed to call Jewel.

"Edna," he said into the receiver, after he had dropped his nickel in the slot, "this is Van Berber. Could you connect me to Jewel's house, please. Thanks, sweetheart. Say hey to your mama for me, willya? How's she doin'?"

Jewel's phone rang and rang, and finally she answered breathlessly.

"Jewel? Hi, this is Van. Listen, I'm out at the Indian Pass Raw Bar having lunch with Gator. Could you and Gabriel come over to my house this evening? Judge Denton won't set bail for Reggie, so we have to put our heads together and figure out a way to get him out of there. Okay?"

"Sure," Jewel answered. "Gabriel and me been out back weedin' the garden in this damn heat, so we'll be more than ready for a break by then."

"See y'all at around six then. I'm bringing Gator."

And there was the big Indian just now pulling into the parking lot, brakes squealing, and tires sliding, as usual. They entered the roadhouse together, and the owner/cashier, Sadie McIntire, who had been so suspicious of him on his previous two visits, waved to Gator, removed the cigarette from her mouth, and shouted out a welcome over the juke box which was blaring out Roy Rogers' "Hi-Yo, Silver" into the smoke-filled room. The place was not nearly as crowded as before, and the two easily found a table in the corner away from the juke box where it was not quite as noisy.

"What'll it be, boys?" a pretty waitress in a low-cut blouse asked before they were even settled.

"Two Spearmans," Gator answered, as he stared at her breasts peeking flirtatiously from the top of her thin, white blouse. "We'll figure out what to eat before you get back with 'em.

"Pretty little thing, ain't she?"

"Yes," the doctor had to agree, as she wiggled off to fetch their beers.

Their choices were written in white, chalk letters on a blackboard on the wall behind the bar, which ran the length of one side of the room: raw, steamed, or baked oysters; steamed or stuffed shrimp; and seafood gumbo. Key lime pie, cheesecake, or ice cream for dessert.

When the waitress returned with their beers, Gator ordered a dozen raw oysters and a bowl of gumbo, and the doctor opted for the steamed shrimp.

"Well," Gator said, "I thought we was out of the investigatin' business when we left the sheriff up there on Peters Street, but I guess we're back in it again now."

"Yeah, Gator, I don't know if we have any other choice. I think Chief Lane's an okay guy, but, in the end, he's not really gonna care that much about poor old Reggie, I'm afraid. And I'm thinking that Judge Denton cares more about his re-election than he does about Reggie and that both he and Mel Roberts, who's running for sheriff, will welcome the favorable publicity they're likely to get for convicting a colored man. I'm afraid Reggie doesn't stand much of a chance. He's colored and he doesn't have an alibi, so I'd say he's headed for the electric chair, unless we can figure something out. But don't say that to Jewel and Gabriel, not just yet anyway."

"What about Bob Huggins?" Gator asked. "He got me off, and I'm an Indian. Not much difference in the eyes of most people around here. Nigguh or Injun—all the same to them."

"Well, maybe so, but we had a couple of witnesses that heard the man call you a half-breed son of a bitch before you took umbrage and laid into him."

"That's true," Gator said, as he squeezed a half a lemon over his oysters.

"Speaking of truth, Gator, you always seem a pretty good judge of what's true and what's not. What do you think? Do you think the sheriff was telling us the truth when he told us about this nut Lucky Lucilla killing Martin and then him killing Lucilla?"

"Hmm, you know, partner, that's a damn good question. I never did trust that sheriff further than I could throw him, so I 'spect he was lying, but I don't for the life of me know which part he was lyin' about and which part he was tellin' the truth about. But I guess we'll never know for sure, unless, of course . . ."

"Of course, what?" the doctor asked, stopping in mid-peel of the fat, pink shrimp in his hand.

"Unless Lucky Lucilla is still alive. His body ain't never been found yet, as far as I know, and it just might be that the sheriff told us he had killed him, so we wouldn't go lookin' for him no more."

"You think?"

"I don't know, partner, but I do know we ain't got a lot of time to figure it out, 'cause those crackers ain't gonna waste much time fryin' poor ol' Reggie now that they got him caught."

"I'm afraid you're right about that. So what next?"

"I think," Gator said, "we better find Lucky Lucilla. If he's still alive."

Chapter 12

They all sat on the doctor's screened-in back porch as the sun set and the tree frogs began their noisy nocturne. It had been a long three-day weekend for the doctor, and it was not over yet. Jewel had left Marcus with her mother, and she now rested next to Gabriel on the low, wicker love seat on the house side of the back porch. Gator was pouring drinks from a jug of moonshine he had brought along. And the doctor, buried in the soft cushions of his chair, was nonetheless still aching all over from his latest adventure with Gator and trying to think how and where to begin.

But he didn't have to think long, because Gabriel began for him. "Look," he said, "we all know Reggie didn't do nothin' wrong, so if that's the case, why don't we just let the doctor's lawyer friend Bob Huggins git him off?"

"Well," the doctor said, "as much as I hate to say it, and as good as Huggins is, I'm not sure he can pick a jury in Gulf County that'll *not* convict a colored man, especially when he doesn't have an alibi."

Faced with this sad truth, everyone nodded, and Jewel, after another sip of her drink, asked, "How 'bout the law then? Do y'all agree with me that the authorities ain't gonna help us here? The judge and the deputy wanna convict someone, looks like Reggie, so that they'll git elected, and Chief Lane, as nice as he is, don't care enough about Reggie to save him.

And Bob Huggins ain't got enough evidence to prove Reggie is innocent. Right? We all agreed on that too?"

They all nodded, and Jewel concluded, "As I see it then, we need to find out who actually cut the sheriff's head off. That's our only hope. All right then, any ideas?"

Before anyone could say anything else, a car the doctor did not recognize pulled into the driveway behind the doctor's old Ford and Gabriel's new red Cadillac. Gabriel reached in his pants pocket and pulled out a small, steel-gray pistol, but, before he had time to cock it, the car's back door opened and a small Negro boy about Marcus's age came trudging across the lawn with his arms loaded with a cardboard box with Crisco printed on its side. When he reached the porch's door, the boy carefully placed the box on the top step, smiled shyly, and then ran back to the car as fast as he could, without a word. As the car backed out, Gabriel put his pistol back in his pocket and went to the door and brought in the box.

"It's got a note on it," he said, as he sat the box on the wicker coffee table in front of them. "Says this here's for us and Mr. Robinson." Then he started pulling out towel-covered bowls and waxed-paper wrapped packages. There was a pan of fried chicken, a bowl of potato salad, a plate of corn bread, and a deep dish filled with what smelled like apple pie, still warm from the oven.

"Well, that sure smells loud. It looks like we got us some friends after all," Jewel said. "I'll be right back with some plates and utensils. No use anyone movin' inside since we're all settled out here now. Might as well have a little picnic, just as long as we save some for Reggie."

When she had returned and was passing out the food, Gabriel repeated her question. "Okay," he asked, "who do you think killed the sheriff?"

"Well," Gator said, "as I said before to the doctor, it could be that the sheriff was lying about him killing Lucky Lucilla, and he's still out there alive some place."

"Yeah, that sheriff was such a liar he probably had to git somebody else to call his hogs for him. But why in the world would this Lucky want to kill the sheriff?" Jewel asked.

"Good question," the doctor said, as he licked fried chicken grease from his fingers.

"Well, the only way we're gonna find out for sure is to find the man, if he's alive," Jewel said, "so I'll start askin' around to see if anybody's seen him."

"Chances are he's left town by now, if he is alive, but it's worth checking," the doctor said, "and Gator, I talked to the gas station attendant at the Indian Pass Raw Bar this afternoon, and he said he thought Lucky might live on St. Vincent Island or somewhere around there. So could you ask those folks that you've been training if they've seen anybody or anything that might suggest the man's still around?"

"Sure, partner," Gator answered with a mouth full of cornbread. "What about that lighthouse keeper, what's his name?"

"Harvey," the doctor said. "Harvey Winn. I talked to him this afternoon. He claims he didn't see anything out of the ordinary the night of the murder, but I'm not so sure I believe him. Why he'd have any reason to cut the sheriff's head off, I don't know, but I'll ask around at the mill to see if anyone else saw anything or if they know anything about Harvey knowing how to operate a power saw."

"That reminds me," Jewel said, "I told you before that there was likely some colored men who know how to run one of them saws and that maybe one of them wanted to make the sheriff pay for beatin' up them whores. What if one of them whores paid one of them to clean his plow for her?"

"Could be," the doctor said. "Check it out. Ask around. Also, now that we've all made pigs of ourselves with all this food, Gabriel, could you take what's left to Reggie tomorrow? I'll arrange it with Chief Lane first thing in the morning to make sure he'll let you in. He'll probably want to search you, but it wouldn't hurt for you to go over again with Reggie exactly what happened that night he saw the sheriff dump that body in Lighthouse Bayou. Maybe he'll remember something that could help us, and I think he'd be glad to see you."

"Sure," Gabriel said. "We ain't never really talked about the details of what happened that night, so I'll talk to him about it."

There was some kind of commotion in the front of the house. The doctor thought he heard a car stop, and the dog next door at Mrs. Shriver's house was barking like he'd gone mad. The tree frogs had stopped their bellowing and an unusual smell was wafting from the front yard. But before the doctor could get up to check, Gator said, "You know, I kind of hate to bring this up, but there's one other person who might stand to gain a lot by the sheriff's death."

"Who's that?" Jewel asked.

"Well, my new boss, Dr. Price, that's who. If the sheriff was telling the truth that Price was paying him protection money, then Price just might be happy to be rid of both Lucky and the sheriff. And it would be just like Price to want to tie up all the loose ends of his moonshining operation completely before he went legit by goin' into the oyster business."

"Hmm," the doctor said, as he drained his glass and pushed himself up out of his chair, "Maybe it's time we paid another visit to the good doctor."

"Oh no you don't," Jewel interrupted. "Don't tell me you ain't disremembered what happened the last time you two went over there. Goin' over there again would be like slappin' a hungry bear."

"What's that smell?" Gator sniffed.

"And why's that damn dog havin' a conniption fit next door?" Jewel asked, as she followed the doctor into the house.

By the time they reached the parlor in the front of the house, acrid, black smoke and the odor of gasoline were filling the room. Jewel screamed and covered her face with her apron, as the doctor continued through the smoke, and out the front door onto the porch. And there, not more than a few feet before him on the front lawn, stood a high, crude wooden cross burning fiercely and swaying awkwardly in the evening breeze.

"Get back in there and call the fire department," the doctor yelled to Jewel, just before he saw the cross pitch backwards and then suddenly fall and crash with a dull thud onto the roof of the porch a few inches above his head. Sparks flew everywhere, and the doctor did the only thing he could remember to do in a case like this; he dove off the porch as far away from the blaze as he could and began rolling over and over again on the dew-covered front lawn. He didn't stop until he felt himself drenched in cold water. Then he looked up and saw Gator Mica towering above him with an empty bucket in his left hand and his right hand extended to the doctor who grabbed it and was pulled swiftly upward off the wet grass.

"I'm getting too old for this shit, Gator," the doctor said, as he brushed himself off and checked for any burns. They heard a siren in the distance growing louder as they watched the blaze flicker on the sagging porch roof.

"It looks like it'll burn out before the fire department gets here," Gator said.

"Where's Jewel and Gabriel?"

"They're in the back yard. Safe. Jewel's got a flashlight, and she's searchin' in the shed for a garden hose."

And here they came, Jewel and Gabriel, with a big, black roll of garden hose in Gabriel's hands. Gator ran over to help him, and the two men hooked up the hose to the outside faucet next to the porch and soon had a steady stream flowing onto the porch roof. The doctor put his arm around Jewel's shivering shoulders and watched. By the time the fire truck arrived, the flames were gone and the roof shingles were only smoldering and admitting a pungent stench of soaked, scorched asphalt. The three firemen, one of whom, Raymond Harrison, the doctor had treated last year for a badly burnt foot, further watered the roof with a thick hose connected to a tank on their truck. They sprayed the entire porch roof for about ten minutes, until the smoke had disappeared, and then rolled up their hose, said goodnight, and vanished into the night.

Finally, some time near midnight, after Jewel had cleaned up the back porch, and when everyone had gone home, the doctor slowly climbed the stairs and opened the door to his bedroom closet. He took out his twelve gauge Remington Sportsman shotgun from the top shelf, loaded it, and placed it under his bed. He then undressed, poured himself a dose of morphine, and promptly fell to sleep.

Later, he awoke from a bizarre dream in which a headless Sheriff Batson had doused Jewel in gasoline and set her ablaze. The doctor was attempting to extinguish the fire by throwing himself onto her to smother the flames, when he awoke with a jolt and heard her downstairs preparing his breakfast. He closed his eyes again and rested, spent, but relieved. Before he joined her in the kitchen, he went out onto the front porch to survey the charred cross that still rested peacefully against the roof, exactly where they had left it the night before, and where he vowed to leave it, a sad symbol of his repugnance, until this entire ordeal was over.

Chapter 13

The doctor knew he was presenting an easy target by strolling back and forth to work in broad daylight, but he didn't care. He had survived this fiasco so far without getting killed, so he might as well continue doing what he wanted to do and hoping his luck would somehow hold. Besides, there could be worse ways to go than being gunned down on a beautiful summer morning like this one, what with the sun as bright as a new dime and the air as fresh as a sassy child.

As he walked down Long Avenue, he weighed the wisdom of just calling Chief Lane and telling him the whole story and letting him figure out what to do next. But by now, the doctor's head was beginning to clear enough that he could construct the likely scenario if he were to do that. And he had concluded that by telling the chief, by telling anyone, the person who was really responsible for the keeper and the sheriff's deaths, it would not help matters. It would not result in Reggie's release, and it would just hatch a whole host of other unpleasant problems that would unnecessarily hurt a lot of innocent people. No, the course they had set last night, to locate the one who had actually committed the murders, still seemed, in the morning's bright light, the most sensible, if not the most forthright, choice open to them.

When the doctor arrived at his office, the small waiting room was filled. He should have expected it since the first day after a long holiday weekend was always busy. So he quickly conferred with Nadyne to make sure there were no emergencies and then hurried to his office to phone Chief Lane before he started seeing patients.

"Good morning, Chief," he began when he had Lane on the line, "three quick questions and I'll let you get back to work. First, how's your prisoner doing?"

"Reggie? Well, he's not doing too well, hardly eating a thing and not saying a word," the chief answered.

"Well, that brings me to my second question. Would you mind letting his friend, Gabriel White, come visit Reggie today? It's bound to make Reggie feel better, and some folks brought over some homemade food for him last night that maybe'll tempt him to eat."

"Yeah, I guess that'd be okay," the chief said, "but I'm not gonna let him stay too long. I got some sore, out-of-work rednecks 'round here who haven't got nothin' better to do than ramble rouse about this thing. They're poor and starving half the time, so seeing these Negroes riding around in a brand new Cadillac convertible doesn't set too well with them. They'd just soon string up Reggie right now and be done with it, if for no other reason than his uppityness. So I'm not gonna do anything to make 'em more agitated than they already are."

"Okay, Chief, which brings me to my third question. Did you know that some of those rednecks took it upon themselves to try to burn my house down last night—while I was in it?"

"Yeah, Raymond Harrison told me he and a couple of the boys were out there last night with the fire truck. Got any idea who did it? Did you see anybody?"

"No," the doctor answered. "I suspect your guess is as good as mine, maybe better, but I didn't see anybody, or I would've called you last night. By the time I figured out what was going on, they were long gone."

"Yeah, that's the usual way with these fools. Even if you had seen them, they likely would've had their heads covered in hoods anyway. But let me ask around. Like you say, I got my suspicions, and I'll let 'em know that I'm not gonna tolerate this bullshit in Port St. Joe."

"Thanks, Chief, I appreciate that."

"Don't mention it, Doc, but be careful. I can't watch these crackers every minute of the day and night, and some of 'em are so hard up they'd welcome the chance to go to jail if they'd be sure to get three meals a day and a chance to get at ol' Reggie as well."

"Okay, Chief, I've got my shotgun loaded."

Then the doctor asked Nadyne to start sending in the people waiting in the waiting room. Six year-old Mary Watkins had the pointed end of a fish hook lodged in her cheek, as a result of her big brother's careless cast. When her daddy had tried to remove the entire hook with a pair of pliers, it had broken off and the girl had slept with the barb in her jaw. Sarah Stearn's entire right leg was covered with festering poison ivy sores. Art Hamlin had slashed his left palm clear to the bone while attempting to fillet a fresh red snapper that he had caught in Shipyard Cove. Rachel Duncan, who lived down wind of the new paper mill, was wheezing and gasping and unable to catch a full breath. Ernest Perkins couldn't put any weight at all on his right ankle ever since he'd planted it in underwater hole in Butlers Bay, where he had been scalloping. Marvin Webster had bright red burn blisters on his right forearm that he had sustained from a rusty, but still hot, exhaust pipe that he was trying to repair. And eighty-one year-old Charlotte Reynolds sported a long gash over her right eye suffered from a fall onto her dead son's grave marker in front of which she was genuflecting to place a bouquet of flowers.

When the doctor had finally emptied out the waiting room at 12:30 that afternoon, he walked over to French's Restaurant and had a quick lunch: a roast beef sandwich and mashed potatoes drowned in brown gravy and washed down with iced tea, unsweetened, and no dessert, in his new-found deference to his waist.

Then before making house calls in the afternoon, he called Bob Huggins and, hoping to arouse a greater sense of urgency in the man, told him about Reggie's deteriorating condition in the city's jail and about the unexpected gift on his front lawn the night before.

"Well," Huggins said, as nonplussed as ever, "I'm not sure I know what you expect me to do about it. It's like when we got Gator off; we need witnesses that either proves Reggie was not there the night the sheriff was killed or that saw someone else do it."

"We're working on it," the doctor said. "I'm going to talk to some folks at the mill who might have seen something the night he was killed, and Jewel and Gator are checking some other possibilities."

"Good," Huggins said. "I'll talk to Reggie tomorrow and see what more he can tell us. Meanwhile, y'all be careful. You wouldn't think in such a quiet little town, there'd be so many crazy fuckers, would you?"

"Tell me about it," the doctor said.

Next, he phoned Lyle McGregor, the supervisor at the St. Joe Paper Company, whom he had met when the Ridler man had fallen into the cooking vat last week. He figured McGregor would be more cooperative than the big boss, Mr. Mitchell, who struck the doctor as being too protective of the plant's reputation to offer much new information. The doctor was surprised not only to find McGregor in his office, but also available to see him right away. So before starting on his afternoon house calls, the doctor walked back home to get his car. Since Jewel wasn't around, he retrieved his loaded twelve gauge shotgun from under his bed and placed it under the front seat of his car. Then he drove out to the new mill to meet with the supervisor.

He found him in his office overlooking the big production floor, the rotten, rancid smell permeating everything like an undiscovered Easter egg. He was smoking a cigarette and poring over a high stack of papers when the doctor entered.

"Welcome back," he said, offering his right hand after he had snubbed out his cigarette in the overflowing ash tray at the corner of his desk. "What can I do for you? I think I've told Chief Lane about everything I can think of about Bob Ridler's accident."

"Well, I'm not here about his death this time. Instead, I'm hoping to find out more about Sheriff Batson's death a few weeks ago. A friend of mine has been accused of killing him, and I'm trying to help him."

"That colored boy?"

"Yes," the doctor answered. "I'm pretty sure he didn't have anything to do with it, so I'm trying to figure out what really happened."

"Well, I'm not sure I can help you, Doc. I'm responsible for this part of the plant, but not for the sawing and timber handling that goes on outside. That'd be Dwayne Moss. He's in charge of all that."

"Okay, but maybe you could tell me one thing. Do you know who knows how to operate that big circular saw that presumably cut the sheriff's head off?"

"Well, not right off hand. Come on, let's go find Dwayne," McGregor said, rising from his chair. "He'll know for sure, and I won't have to guess."

So the doctor followed McGregor out of his office, past the expansive cooking vat where the dead man had been found, and out the door next to the lunch room. Above the plant's mammoth smoke stack, the sun was trying to shine through the yellow cloud that hung over them like a soft sulfuric tent, but with little success. It had rained the night before so the yard was wet and muddy. They slogged past a tall stack of logs and found a slight man with short-cropped dark hair in tan overalls reading something on a clipboard in his hands.

"Hey, Dwayne," McGregor interrupted him, "this here's Doctor Berber. He's looking into the sheriff's death a few weeks back, and he's got a question for you."

"Sure. Pleased to meet you, Doctor."

"The pleasure's mine," the doctor replied, as the two shook hands.

"What's your question? I think I told Chief Lane about all I know, but shoot."

"Well, my question is," the doctor asked, "who knows how to operate the saw that cut the sheriff's head off?"

"Me, Ned Beachum, Ralph Carmichael, and Lowell Prine."

"Were any of them here the night the sheriff was murdered?"

"No, at least, not that we know of. They all work during the day, and the saw is not used at night when the plant is shut down."

"Who is here at night, then?"

"Well, like I said to the chief, just three people right now, until we get the plant up to full production. There's a man at the front gate who's supposed to stay there to make sure that no one enters the mill, another man out on the docks to keep an eye on the ships being loaded and unloaded, and the night watchman who wanders around inside the plant."

"And none of them know how to operate the saw?" the doctor asked.

"As far as I know."

"So . . . how did it happen then?"

Dwayne Moss just laughed. "Beats me," he finally said.

The doctor was about ready to give up and leave at this point, but he was still curious about a weapon that could slice off a man's head as cleanly as the sheriff's had been. "Could I take a look at that saw, Mr. Moss?" he asked.

"Of course, it's right over here. Not being used right now, so you can look all you like."

The saw that Moss led them to was basically a large steel platform outfitted at one end with a circular saw, edged with sharp, jagged teeth, about a yard across. "This is the saw that was used to decapitate the sheriff," Moss explained. "It's driven by a big electric engine under the frame right here."

"Could you show me how to start it?" the doctor asked.

"Sure, but cover your ears, 'cause it's louder than hell. But first let me explain how all this works. Technically speaking, this is what we call a cordwood saw. It crosscuts or cuts across the grain, instead of with the grain. We use it for one purpose, not to make cordwood, but to size the logs that come in off the trucks, the trains, or the boats to fit into the debarker. These longer logs are hoisted up here on this platform, then secured in this cradle, and then slid across the saw to cut off the end. To start the saw, you first pull the switch on this fuse box over here. That sends power to the engine right here under the frame. Then you power up the motor by throwing—cover your ears now—this switch here." Moss then reached under the platform and a terrible racket echoed throughout the yard, like the roar of an approaching hurricane. "And then this switch," Moss yelled, "to start the rotation of the saw." A loud, incessant buzz, like a giant bee hive, was added to the roar. The doctor looked at the switch and was sure he saw smears of dried, brown blood still on it.

"Geez, that's noisy," the doctor yelled, with his hands over his ears. "Would you mind leaving that on for a few more minutes? Say about ten?"

"Sure," Moss answered. "I'll have a man start sawing right now, so we don't waste any electricity."

"Thanks," the doctor said. "Thank you both. You've been a lot of help."

Then he walked as briskly as he could back inside, through the big cooking vat hall, back to his car, then drove around the circular road that bordered, alongside a ten foot tall chain-link fence, the entire plant, and finally back out the front gate. And, sure enough, even with the other noises of the mill, no matter how far away he drove, he could still hear the roar of that big, buzzing, slivering saw.

Chapter 14

When the doctor arrived back in his office, he phoned Harvey Winn and asked him if they could get together again. The former lighthouse keeper turned night watchman was suspicious since he had just seen the doctor the day before. "It's nothing, Harvey, nothing to be concerned about," he lied. "I just talked to a patient who has a house for rent that might work for you, that's all."

"Oh, okay then," Harvey said. "What if I stop by your place on my way to work this evening?"

"What time do you have to be there?" the doctor asked.

"At six, so if I stopped at your office at around five, that would give us plenty of time, wouldn't it?"

"See you then," the doctor said and hung up.

That gave him only a couple of hours to make house calls, so he would have to move fast. First, he needed to check on Madge Fuller who was in her third trimester of pregnancy and was not feeling well. He had told her, when she had called, to get in bed and stay there until he arrived. Fortunately, when he did, there was no spotting, only some cramping, so the doctor suggested that she take a warm bath and then curl up with a hot water bottle and a good book for the rest of the day. Let her husband cook supper for once.

Next, he stopped at ol' man Radcliff's house to see if he was remembering to eat. The man had dementia and was losing more and more thought processes, and weight, every day. As far as the doctor could figure, the man had no family, at least none who cared enough about him to take care of him. A neighbor, Lillian Monroe, who had been in his office last week about her insomnia, had reported that she had found Radcliff wandering around the neighborhood in the middle of the night in his pajamas, without a clue to where he was. According to Lillian, Radcliff was a retired conductor for the Apalachicola Northern Railroad, whose family, a wife and two cocker spaniels, had left him for a traveling Bible salesman, when Radcliff had disappeared for several days one time too many. Today, the unshaved, old man was sitting in his parlor in his robe, listening to big band music on his radio. When the doctor entered, Radcliff looked up and said, "Simon, I told you to never come in here when I'm listenin' to my music. Now get the hell out of here and paint the fence like I told you." The doctor placed the waxed paper wrapped salami sandwich that he had bought at French's on the end-table next to the man and left.

The doctor had many times vowed to himself that he would never end up like ol' man Radcliff or the thirty or so dying residents of the Wesley Home for the Aged that he visited once a week. He would instead devise some quick and painless way to end it all before he was mired hopelessly in his own suffering or worst yet advancing dementia. So far he had ruled out drowning (too slow), exsanguination (too painful), jumping (too uncertain), but was still seriously considering poisoning (readily available), gunshot wound (fast and painless), or an overdose of morphine (a pleasant, never-ending sleep). When the time came, he would figure it out for certain, something sure and elegant that would make those who knew him chuckle and revel privately in his inventive dissolution.

Jerry Kearney's broken leg seemed to be healing fine, so the doctor left him a bottle of aspirin and told him to stay off the ladder at the top of which the doctor had found him, cleaning the gutter at the side of his old house on Cypress Avenue.

Finally, the doctor stopped again to see Walter Foley who, he was sure, was dying of lung cancer. He had repeatedly offered the man two pieces of advice: one, to see a specialist in Panama City, and two, to stop smoking cigarettes——neither of which the stubborn man had yet heeded. Now, even a trip to the outhouse left him gasping for breath and wheezing in pain. The doctor gave him a shot of morphine and stayed with him until he had fallen asleep, his chest heaving laboriously under his dingy sheets.

The doctor arrived back at his office just before five o'clock and went in to see what fresh new hell awaited him there. Surprisingly, only Nadyne was there, sitting at her little desk, carefully updating with pen and ink the cryptic charts that the doctor never seemed to get around to addressing. "Go home," he told her. "Enough is enough for one day."

"You're the boss," she said, as she closed the folder and began straightening her desk. "Oh, by the way, could you stop by Albert Cunningham's place the next time you're out near Indian Pass. He's too proud and too poor to ask for help, but Mom says he hasn't been around this week for his usual handout, so she suspects something's wrong out there. Meanwhile, you should go home too, Doc. You look awfully tired."

"I feel awfully tired, so I'll take your advice and head home soon. Just leave the door open when you leave. I'm expecting Harvey Winn to stop by any minute now, and I don't want to miss him. And I'll check on Cunningham the next chance I get."

"Thanks, Doc. Goodnight. See you in the morning."

"Goodnight, Nadyne. Thanks, as always."

Then he walked back to his office and waited. He tried to find an article worth reading in the jumbled stack of medical journals piled on the corner of his desk, but he ended up thumbing through a recent issue of *Life* magazine with a photo of Errol Flynn on the cover. When, at 5:30, Harvey had not arrived, he asked Edna to connect him to Harvey's home phone, where, after several rings, a woman's voice answered. "Is this Mrs. Winn?" the doctor asked.

"Yes, it is, who's this?"

"Oh, this is Doctor Berber. I had an appointment about half an hour ago with your husband here in my office, and I was wondering if maybe he had forgotten about it?"

"No," the fragile voice on the other end of the line answered, "he left over an hour ago to see you. Is he not there yet?"

"No, not yet."

"Well, maybe he had car trouble," she said, with a hint of worry creeping into her voice. "There's always something goin' wrong with that ol' Oldsmobile of his."

"Well, not to worry," the doctor said. "It wasn't really that important, but I'll tell you what, I have to drive out that way anyway, so I'll head toward your place from here just to make sure he hasn't broken down somewhere along the way."

"Oh, that would be terribly nice of you, Doctor Berber," she said. "Thank you so much."

So the doctor closed up the office and drove out toward Cape San Blas. He would have preferred to just go home and forget about Harvey Winn for at least that day, but there was something in his wife's voice and something far back in his own head—he wasn't sure what—that made him concerned.

Despite all the new people moving into town, the traffic on Constitution Avenue was light this afternoon, and the sun beginning to set out over Cape San Blas was brilliant and bright. Soon after he veered right onto Sand Bar Road, the pavement was tunneled by thick palmetto woods that blocked, at least temporarily, the encroaching sunset, until it emerged in a couple of miles at a bend, known locally as Dead Man's Curve, that directly paralleled the rocky shore only an arm's length away from the right side of his car.

As he was simultaneously admiring the sunset and trying to stay on the road, he caught sight of a red glint in the water. So he slowed down and then saw clearly rising out of the sea a few feet from shore a broken tail light, a bald spare tire, the rear end of what he now recognized as Harvey Winn's rusty white Oldsmobile convertible, planted nose first into the water at about a thirty degree angle. He slammed on the brakes and skidded to a stop inches from the waves lapping at the gray rocks that blocked the sea from the road. Fortunately, there were no cars coming from either direction and he was able find a narrow strip of sandy shore to pull over on. So he jumped out and ran to the edge of the water and squinted into the setting sun to see the partly submerged front-end of the car, its windshield shattered, its canvas top in tatters. There, before the steering wheel, he was horrified to see in the otherwise clear waters of the bay a red mass of shredded flesh where the driver's head should have been. And then he saw the fins, at least a dozen of them, thrashing madly back and forth, and their wide, white mouths, ivory teeth bared, flashing into the gruesome, bloody pulp, one after another, tearing it piece by piece into a crimson pool of unrecognizable gore. He had heard about the feeding frenzy of sharks but never witnessed it, and from this point forward never wanted to again, at least not with the food that they were here so frenzied for.

He stood there for a long time, gazing into the bay, as the water cleared and the sharks swam away. This was definitely not the way he wanted to go when the time came. There was nothing left in the semi-submerged vehicle before him, except a few shreds of what was left of

Harvey Winn's shirt clinging to the obscenely tilted steering wheel and the ghostly red tinge that cloaked the dashboard. He would never get to ask Harvey Winn why he had not reported the roar of the circular saw that he surely must have heard the night of Sheriff Batson's decapitation, but, as he watched the setting orange sun rays splash across the sea, he thought he knew.

Chapter 15

But the doctor didn't know exactly what to do next, whether to find a phone and report Harvey Winn's demise to Deputy Roberts and let him deal with the widow, or whether to summon the courage to continue on a few more miles to Cape San Blas and inform the man's wife himself. He was looking forward to neither.

In the end, he decided to save the deputy a trip out to the cape. Despite several visits to the Cape San Blas Lighthouse to visit Sally Martin, he had never once met Harvey Winn's wife Mary. He had seen her at a distance, a broad, stout woman in a white bonnet, stooped over in the sun, hoeing weeds in their backyard garden. But there she stood before him behind the screen door of her cottage with a questioning look on her harsh, round face. "I'm Doctor Berber," he told her. "We spoke on the phone."

"Yes?"

"I hate to inform you, but your husband has had an accident. I found his car in the bay only a few miles from here, where the road curves close to the water. I'm afraid he's dead."

He hated to be so blunt, but he had learned over the years that in such cases it was best just to blurt out the truth and get it over with. There was no way to sugarcoat death.

The woman looked at him in disbelief and then the tears and the screaming began. And then the children appeared, four of them, about the same ages as Sally's children, frightened of what this strange man had done to their mother. So he had to tell them what had happened to their father. It was a mess. The doctor tried to console them the best he could, but they were inconsolable, especially the mother.

Finally, after he had calmed the children and had given Mrs. Winn a dose of Mebaral, he asked to use their phone and then called Deputy Roberts and their church's pastor, Reverend Babcock. The doctor told them all that Harvey Winn had apparently been washed out to sea after his car had crashed into the bay, leaving them a false hope, he knew, that the body might be recovered some day, but he just couldn't bear to tell the children that their father had been eaten by sharks.

Then, as he was driving home, he remembered Jewel, so he drove over to the Indian Pass Raw Bar and used the phone booth there to call her and tell her to go home. Despite the fact that he remained shaken by what had just occurred, he did find himself growing hungry. And, since he was already there, he entered the roadhouse and found Sadie McIntire still at her cash register with a burning cigarette dangling between her wrinkled lips.

The place emanated its usual stale, smoky smell mixed this evening with the spicy scent of simmering gumbo.

"It's you again," the old lady said, as the doctor approached her.

"Yeah, it's me again. How's business?"

"Not too bad, as you can see, but it's early yet. Folks are just now gittin' off work."

"I see," the doctor said. "Well, before it gets too busy, do you mind if I ask you a couple of questions?"

"I told you before that I keep my mouth shut about my customers and what they do and say in here."

"Yes, I know you're hesitant to talk about your clientele, and I understand that, but I have a friend in jail who may go to the electric chair for a crime he didn't commit if I can't find out who killed Sheriff Batson. You see a lot of different people out here. Do you have any idea who may have killed the man?"

"Not a clue."

"What about the man who sold moonshine out back, Lucky Lucilla. Have you seen him recently?"

"'Fraid not."

"Do you have any idea where he lives?"

"Nope, but you remember what I told you before, don't you?"

"What was that?"

"Stay away from the man," the old lady warned, squinting through the gray smoke of her own cigarette.

"But why?"

"Just stay away from him. That's all I'm gonna say."

"Well, thanks anyway," the doctor said and walked to the nearest empty stool at the bar. He was becoming increasingly frustrated with this old woman's refusal to help him in any way. Nevertheless, he ordered a beer and a bowl of gumbo and listened to Cliff Bruner croon "It Makes No Difference Now" on the juke box. The gumbo was, as usual, very tasty, filled with spicy chunks of chicken, andouille sausage, and whole shrimp.

After supper, since there was still some light and he had promised Nadyne, he decided to try to find Albert Cunningham's place. No telling when he would be out this way again. Harold, the helpful gas station attendant at the Raw Bar said he thought it was down the third dirt road on the right off the main road, just on the other side of the inlet, going east toward Apalachicola. So the doctor drove in that direction.

There were a lot of Albert Cunningham's, or men like him, during this Great Depression. Men who had been beaten down by joblessness, poverty, and plain old bad luck. Nearly every day, Albert pedaled his rusty old Schwinn bicycle from an abandoned sharecropper's cabin near Indian Pass where he lived the ten or so miles to Port St. Joe. Along the way, he picked up and carried in the big wire basket mounted on the front fender of his bike discarded refuse that people had tossed out along the highway. He tried to sell it in town, usually unsuccessfully, so he more often ended up giving it away and lived mostly off the largess of local people who gave him a few cents or a sandwich to pull weeds in their gardens or clean out their chicken coops or tackle those other unpleasant tasks that they didn't want to do themselves.

He spoke little, and many people considered him retarded, but Nadyne had told the doctor that before the Depression, Albert Cunningham had been a rather successful sharecropper whose pretty wife sewed intricate quilts and bore six children who never went to school but nonetheless helped their father become one of the few who had actually eked out a decent existence by farming in the bleak coastal Panhandle. That was before the Depression descended, along with the hurricanes, and the duPonts, and the bottom falling out of produce prices— all at about the same time. His wife finally took the children and returned to her family in Valdosta, vowing to return when Albert got back on his feet. But he never did, sinking deeper and deeper, day by day, into loneliness, depression, and dispiritedness. It was enough to sink any man, the doctor thought.

As the doctor tried to find the right dirt road in the diminishing light and with his own failing eyesight, he remembered what Sheriff Batson had once told him. Most of this land along the Panhandle from Mexico Beach to Carrabelle had once been owned by his father, Jeremy Batson, one of the largest land owners in North Florida. The sheriff, well before he was dismembered, had bragged about his daddy's vast holdings and how he managed them. Most of the land was in timber and cotton, but the acreage was so extensive that there was no way the elder Batson could manage it alone. So, according to the sheriff, like his forbearers before the Civil War, his father used Negro labor to farm the cotton. They lived on his plantation, almost as slaves, in shabby dorms and cabins, but, in deference to their free status, were paid meager wages in addition to their room and board.

But here, on the coastal plain where the sandy soil was too salty and unstable for cotton, he either leased the timber rights to the mills or hired tenant farmers to try to extract a living from the gritty loam. If he made a little cash from them each year, it was better than nothing, but usually just barely.

For these sharecroppers and their families, mostly descendants of the slaves his granddaddy owned, Jeremy Batson formed a crew of carpenters who built rough cabins in the piney woods along the Gulf of Mexico. Batson assigned each of these tenant farmers a piece of land, typically forty acres, and provided him with one of these cabins as well as a mule, food, clothing, and the necessary seeds and farm equipment. When the crop—watermelons, sweet potatoes, peanuts, feed corn, whatever the farmer could coax from the sandy soil—was harvested, one of Batson's hired hands would take it to market and sell it. Then he would give half of the proceeds to the sharecropper, but only after he had deducted the so-called "furnish"—the cost of the items that the tenant had been furnished during the year.

By the time Alfred I. duPont had purchased all of Batson's holdings in 1933, at a few cents on the dollar, nearly half of all white farmers and most all colored farmers in the Panhandle were working under this landless arrangement. But duPont had other ideas. What little these sharecroppers produced was more trouble than it was worth to him. He was used to much larger business schemes and profits. And what with hurricanes, floods, droughts, and the ever-present natural pests, the entire tenant farmer enterprise seemed more of a bad bet to him than a wise business investment. So when the Agricultural Adjustment Act was passed by Congress in 1933 as a part of Roosevelt's New Deal, paying land owners subsidies *not* to plant a portion of their land, it spelled an end to most of the sharecropping in Bay, Gulf, and Franklin counties. According to Sheriff Batson, duPont evicted the farmers and left their cabins to rot in the damp, decaying, salty air. No one really knew anymore how many of these pine hovels were left or where they were. The only clues to their whereabouts were these narrow overgrown dirt roads that led from the main highways, U.S. Route 98 and Sand Bar Road, between Mexico Beach and Carrabelle, off into the woods. At their ends, there might be a dilapidated old cabin, or just a foundation, or nothing at all, just a dead-end pair of ruts to an overgrown field or the remains of a makeshift lumber camp.

The doctor turned right down one of these roads, where Harold had told him that Albert Cunningham lived, and slowly navigated his way down the bumpy path. At its end he found a crude pine log cabin listing precariously into a thick patch of wild sea oats and salt marsh morning glory, about equidistance, half a mile, the doctor guessed, from the main road and the sea. The tin roof was rusty, the porch rotted through, and the windows open to the evening air, with neither screens nor glass. Standing on a cinder block, the doctor sat down his black bag and flashlight and pushed aside a dilapidated screen door that hung by one hinge to knock on the cabin's front door. There was no answer, so he knocked again. Still no answer. He tentatively pushed the door to see if it was locked. It was not, so he pushed it open all the way. He shined his flashlight inside, and there in the middle of the dim, single room, he found Albert Cunningham. He lay in a pile of dirty, ragged quilts on an old iron bed, a slim, gray, withered figure, somewhere around the middle of a normal lifespan, covered in sweat, his eyes closed either in sleep or death.

"Mr. Cunningham," the doctor said softly, not wanting to startle the man, since he knew these backwoods squatters often slept with loaded shotguns in their beds. "Mr. Cunningham, can you hear me? I'm Doctor Berber. I've come to see if you're sick."

The man still did not stir, so the doctor slowly moved toward him. "Mr. Cunningham?" he said again.

When he was next to the bed, he saw that the man was still breathing, shallowly, but breathing nonetheless. But he smelled like dirt, decay, and death. He gently nudged the man's arm, once, twice, and finally his eyes opened and tried to focus on the doctor.

"Mr. Cunningham," the doctor repeated, "I'm Doctor Berber. I'm here to help you. Do you understand?"

The man nodded, hardly moving a muscle.

"I'm going to examine you, okay?"

The man nodded again. So the doctor opened his black bag and removed his stethoscope and thermometer. Through a series of tests and questions and nods, it didn't take long for the doctor to conclude that Albert Cunningham was suffering from malaria. As much from the constant swarming of mosquitoes in the open-air room as from the symptoms (fever, headache, sweats, fatigue, nausea, and vomiting), the doctor was pretty confident of his diagnosis. This was definitely not the way the doctor would choose for his own death, or for that of any other man for that matter.

The state of Florida's mosquito eradication program had cut considerably the number of malaria cases the doctor treated in recent years, but this damn Depression had forced the state to cut back on its efforts, leaving poor people like Albert Cunningham, who lived in swampy areas and could not afford window screens or ditching, at the mercy of the infected insects.

"Mr. Cunningham," the doctor told him, "I'm afraid you have malaria. You need medicine. I'm going to have a prescription filled for something called Resochin. You need to take a tablespoon full of it twice a day for two weeks. Do you understand?"

Again the man nodded.

"Do you have food?" the doctor asked.

Cunningham shook his head no.

"On my way back to town, I'm going to stop at the Indian Pass Raw Bar and arrange for the gas station attendant there to bring you something to eat twice a day until you're feeling better. Okay?"

Another nod.

"Rest and eat and take the medicine that I'll bring you. I'll check on you every few days."

The doctor found a working well in the back yard and pumped a bucket full of water. By the time he had returned to the cabin, the surface of the bucket's contents was covered with mosquitoes and Albert Cunningham was sound asleep. Nevertheless, he left the bucket and a dented tin cup next to the sick man's bed, packed up his bag, and headed for the door. As he was about to step back out onto the cinder block stoop, he heard a faint voice behind him.

"Thank you," Albert Cunningham whispered. "Thank you."

Chapter 16

The next morning, after Jewel had placed a plate of bacon and fried eggs before him, she sat down at the table and poured them both a cup of black coffee. The doctor knew when something was on Jewel's mind, since she seldom joined him at the table, so he asked her, "What's up, Jewel? Have you found the sheriff's murderer yet?"

"Not yet," she said, "but I do have some news. First off, I talked to Yolanda Brown. You remember her, don't you? She was one of them colored whores that got beat up by the sheriff. You treated her. She's a friend of Brenda Walsh, the mother of little Willie that's in Marcus's class at school. She got a tongue that's loose at both ends. Anyway I asked Brenda to introduce me and she did, and Yolanda and me had lunch together at my house yesterday. The woman's had a hard life, I'll tell you that. Said she's used to bein' beaten up by men, startin' off with her daddy that was most all the time drunk and beatin' on her mama and her seven sisters and brothers until Yolanda, when she got old enough to take care of herself, she took off and did what she had to, to keep alive, includin' whoring. Since she was just a baby, fourteen, she said. Anyway, she said she knows most of the other colored prostitutes around town and she ain't heard nothin' about killin' no sheriff. Some said he wasn't worth killin'. Said all the whores are glad he's dead, but she didn't think any of them had anything to do with it."

"I expected as much," the doctor said between bites of bacon. "If those prostitutes were going to do anything like that, they would have done it a long time ago."

"Yeah, just to make sure, I asked Lily Kate Williamson, whose 'bout a half bubble off plum, but whose husband works out there at the mill cleanin' up the bathrooms and such, and he told her that the only men they let near that saw that killed the sheriff was white men. All the colored men work as common laborers and janitors like him. The white men run the machinery and have all the good payin' jobs."

"That's what I found out too," the doctor reported, "when I was out there yesterday. Seems there are only four men who know how to run that saw. I didn't ask what color they were, but I'll bet you they're all white. As a matter of fact, I didn't see many colored people anywhere out there."

"What else did you find out?" Jewel asked.

The doctor told her about his visit to the mill, the roar of the saw, and his ill-fated attempt to meet with Harvey Winn, and the lighthouse keeper's grim demise in St. Joseph Bay.

"Geez, Doc, that's a tough way to go. So what do you make of it? You think someone arranged Harvey's accident?"

"Could be. Nothing surprises me anymore. I really can't say for sure, but I know he would've heard that saw anyplace he was in the plant, especially since it would have been the only machine running at night, and he told me he had not seen or heard anything unusual at all that night."

"Do you think he killed the sheriff then?" Jewel asked, as she re-filled their coffee cups.

"Well, I don't know. He was there, at the plant, when it happened. We do know that. The four men who knew how to run the saw were not, or were not supposed to be. The saw is not that difficult to operate; you just have to throw a few switches, so it's possible that Harvey could have figured it out. But I can't for the life of me understand why he would want to cut the man's head off in the first place. Why didn't he just shoot the son of a bitch? Why go to all the trouble to start the saw, place the sheriff on it, and then saw his head off, and make all that noise and bloody mess? It just doesn't make any sense."

"Well," Jewel said, "the trouble is we'll never know now, 'cause Harvey Winn's dead as a hammer."

"Yep, I'm afraid so. I think then that the only hope left for Reggie is that we go under the assumption—and I think it's a pretty good one—that Harvey heard the saw, but covered up for someone who knew how to operate it. Because, like I said the other night, in the end, I just don't think Harvey was the kind of guy who would decapitate someone. He might have had it in him to cover up such a crime—and I could be wrong—but I don't think he would've done it himself."

"Who then?" Jewel asked.

"Lucky Lucilla?"

"Not a bad guess, I'd say," Jewel answered, as she began stacking the dirty dishes on the table. "Let me tell you what else I found out. First off, it wasn't Lucky Lucilla that the sheriff dumped into Lighthouse Bayou, like the sheriff said."

"It wasn't?"

"Uh-uh, was a woman, a colored woman, according to Reggie that told Gabriel all about it when Gabriel talked to him in jail yesterday. Said she was all dressed up sleazy with a red dress on and high heel shoes, like a real whore."

"The one who washed up a couple of days later, I bet?"

"I'm guessin' yes," Jewel said. "And that ain't all. Then, since we ain't heard from Gator 'bout what's goin' on with Dr. Price's people, I called my friend Pearl. She's the one that's got a cousin, Tom Black, that works for Price and that lives out there on St. Vincent Island with his wife and three kids. He's like the butler, Tom is. Anyway, Pearl talked to Tom when he come into town to buy some supplies, and Tom, he told her that someone's been stealing chickens from 'em out there. Tom keeps chickens, you see. Says it ain't a fox or wild hog, 'cause there ain't no feathers or busted fences. So he's thinkin' that maybe someone is livin' out there on the island, 'cause them chickens keep comin' up missin' and other stuff missin' too, like some barbed wire and some old lumber and such, he says."

"So you're thinkin' this Lucky Lucilla fellow might not be dead after all and is hiding out there on St. Vincent Island somewhere?"

"That's what I'm thinkin'," Jewel answered. "That's exactly what I'm thinkin'."

"Well," the doctor said, as he gathered up the dirty dishes that Jewel had stacked and carried them over to the sink, "that's what we thought before; that's what Gator and I went over there for in the first place, because everything seemed to point in that direction. This guy Lucky worked for Price, and he was always seen around Indian Pass, either at the Raw Bar, or, like the filling station attendant said the other day, headed in that direction, toward St. Vincent Island. But then we thought the sheriff had killed him, so we sort of forgot about him, but now that we don't have a body and Reggie says it was a woman the sheriff was dumping, then, I guess, we at least have a feasible theory."

"I'm thinkin' it's more than that, Doc. It just seems to make sense."

"Then you won't mind if Gator and I pay Dr. Price another visit, will you?"

"Oh, I'll mind alright, after the last time, I'd think you'd never want to go over there again. That's about as dumb as a soup sandwich."

"Well," the doctor admitted, "it's not number one on my list of things I'd like to do, but I'm not sending Gator over there by himself, and, anyway, I think the doctor and I got along pretty well. I think he was pretty honest with me when we were there before."

"You do, do you? Well, just remember Gator's theory, which ain't a bad one either, that it could have been Price or one of his men that killed the sheriff and this whole business with Lucky Lucilla is a trap, just a way to git y'all over there so he can arrange some sort of boating accident or such. It sure 'nough wilderness over there, Doc, ignorant of the axe. And you know what everyone say, don't you, about moonshiners?"

"No, what?"

"You can't trust 'em; they's tougher than a two-bit steak and as slippery as a greased eel."

"Well, according to Gator, Price has gone straight now, so maybe we don't have as much to worry about."

"Maybe, maybe not, but I wouldn't bet on it."

"All right," the doctor said. "Let's do this, for the time being. Try to find Gator and see what he's found out from Price's people, if anything. Then I'll go up to Wewa and see if I can talk that worthless deputy Roberts into letting me see the file on Lucky Lucilla that the sheriff got from Tallahassee. The sheriff told me about it, but I never saw it, so I don't know if what he told me about him is true or not. I don't even know for sure if the file exists, but if it does maybe it will shed some more light on this character. At any rate, he seems like he's our only hope right now. Without him, Reggie is in deep trouble, I'm afraid."

"Yeah, Gabriel said he ain't doin' too good. I ain't sure how much time we got here, between Reggie's own self and them crackers wantin' to hang him."

"Speaking of time, when does Gabriel have to be back in New York for this radio job?"

"Well, they called long distance yesterday and said they wanted to start rehearsin' right away. Gabriel told 'em his mama was sick, so's to hold 'em off for a few more days, but that ain't gonna sassify 'em for long."

"Sounds like time's running out on a lot of things," the doctor said, as he headed out the back door.

"Oh," Jewel said, standing at the door, "one more thing. You know that Ridler fellow that fell in the vat of chemicals out at the mill. Come to find out, accordin' to Lily Kate's husband—the man's as common as pig tracks— the man in the vat was a union organizer, was tryin' to git all the workers out there to join a union."

"Well," the doctor said, as he headed toward his office, "I'll be damned. You ever think we'd have someone trying to organize a union down here in the middle of nowhere?"

"Who'd a thunk it? 'Bout the only two things you can git white folks to join around here are the Baptist church and the Democratic Party, and then when they do, all they do is gripe about 'em."

When the doctor arrived at his office, he found Gator Mica parked there in front in his old pickup, slumped in the seat, with his ratty straw cowboy hat pulled down over his eyes, snoring away.

"Wake up, Gator," the doctor whispered, as he nudged Gator's shoulder through the open window.

"Oh, hi, partner, good mornin'. What's up?"

The doctor tried as quickly as possible to fill Gator in on all that he and Jewel had found out in the last twenty-four hours, but Gator was well ahead of them on several fronts. "Well, what y'all found out jibes pretty much with what Price's people told me too. Stuff missin' and all. But what I found most interesting was one of them, a colored fellow name of Washington, said he had actually seen a tall curly haired guy creepin' around their compound one night, out back next to the tool shed where they used to make the booze. He ran him off and then he said he told Dr. Price about it, but the man didn't seem too concerned."

"Let's go find out why," the doctor said. "See if you can arrange another meeting with Price as soon as possible. Ask him if we can have a look around the island to see if we can find any sign of someone else living out there. I'll have Nadyne cover for me, if necessary. We're already running out of time here, and it seems like we just got started."

"You got it, partner," Gator said, as he started the truck's clattery engine and put it in gear.

The doctor was not looking forward to facing his patients today any more than he was to sailing again to St. Vincent Island, but in both cases he seemed to have no choice, so he entered his office to find it again filled with the incessant suffering of poor little Port St. Joe.

Chapter 17

Before he could see who all was there waiting for him, Nadyne stopped the doctor at the door and informed him that Bob Huggins was already there and waiting for him in his office.

"Any emergencies here?" he asked, looking around the crowded waiting room.

"No," she answered, "not yet, anyway. Go see the man and get it over with. I'll hold 'em off until you're done."

"Thanks, Nadyne, there's no doubt about it, you're a gem of the highest order."

"Yeah, yeah. Go," she instructed.

The doctor found the lawyer sitting impatiently, flipping through a medical journal, in one of the solid oak chairs in front of his desk. The aroma of Brylcream filled the cramped, little room.

"Morning, Doc," Huggins said, as looked up over his wire-rimmed glasses, closed the journal and returned it to the stack on the doctor's desk. "I was just reading about a new campaign called the March of Dimes that's raising money to fight polio. Sounds like a good idea. Sorry I'm here unannounced and so early, but I know that once both of us get started on the day, it's hard to stop, and I wanted to talk to you before I see Reggie this morning. Anything new to report?"

"Well, actually, quite a bit," the doctor answered and then filled Huggins in on all that they had learned about Harvey Winn and Lucky Lucilla.

"My, y'all have been busy," Huggins said when the doctor had finished. "It's too bad Winn had to end up in the bay. Sounds like he could have helped us. I don't know about this Lucky fellow. It looks to me like maybe we're grasping at straws here. Anybody could be stealing chickens out on St. Vincent Island, especially during these hard times. But it does seem strange that someone would go all the way out there to steal them, when we have perfectly good chickens to swipe right here on the mainland."

"Well," the doctor said. "I don't know where else to turn at this point. As far as I can tell, it's all we've got right now."

"Yeah, and Judge Denton isn't giving us much time. He's set the trial for June twenty-eighth, less than a month away."

"Geez, that soon? Even so, I don't know if Reggie's gonna last that long," the doctor said.

"Well, he's gonna have to. Tell you what, y'all keep trying to find this Lucky character, and I'll talk to Reggie and the two other men who were working at the mill the night the sheriff was killed. Then we'll get back together and see what we have."

"Okay," the doctor said wearily, "sounds like a plan, maybe not a great one, but a plan nonetheless. By the way, Bob, could you do me a favor, since you're going that way anyway? I told Chief Lane last night when I reported Harvey's accident that I would stop in there today and fill him in on what we had found out so far. Could you tell him what you think he needs to know? And could you ask him if he could call Mel Roberts at the sheriff's office in Wewa and ask him if I could take a look at the file they supposedly have on Lucky Lucilla? I think it might sound more official coming from you and the chief."

"I'll do you one better, Doc," Huggins said, as he stood to leave. "I'll call Judge Denton and ask him to be sure that file is ready for you to see this afternoon. If he won't set bail for Reggie, it's the least he can do, especially if he's expecting my vote in November."

"Thanks, Bob. I'm not sure how I'm gonna pay you for all this, but I'm sure we'll work something out."

"Not as long as everybody in my family stays healthy, Doc, but I'm sure some mishap or another will come up. It always does. Talk to you soon."

The doctor spent the morning seeing patients in his office, then had lunch at Dad's Café—liver and onions, red rice, and orange glazed carrots—and started his house calls, just as it began to sprinkle, in the early afternoon haze. His plan was to finish by mid-afternoon, so he could drive the fifteen miles to Wewahitchka to read Lucky Lucilla's file before the day was done.

First, he drove out to Albert Cunningham's cabin to deliver the Resochin. Cunningham was still semi-delirious, but the doctor roused him enough to get the medicine and some water down him. The doctor had stopped by Gulf Hardware and Supply earlier that day and bought a mosquito net to hang over Albert Cunningham's bed, since there were no screens on the cabin's windows.

Now all he had to do was figure out how to install it, since Cunningham was in no condition to do it himself. The cabin's ceiling was low but still well out of the doctor's reach. He looked around the room for some means to reach the rough-hewn, log beam above Cunningham's bed. Damn, the man had a minimalist approach to decorating. There was just that old iron bed with the sick man on it parked right there in the middle of the room, and not much else. But then he saw a simple, wooden chair in the shadows of one corner of the cabin. He dragged it over next to the bed and stepped up onto its seat. He was still unable to reach the beam where he wanted to screw in the steel hook he had bought, so he took one more step up onto Albert Cunningham's shaky bed, being careful not to step on the man. He immediately sunk into the lumpy mattress, but he was now close enough to twist the hook into the beam. Once he had secured it, he carefully descended the way he had come, took the top ring of the mosquito net and again climbed up onto the chair and then onto the bed to hang the net. Just as he finally had it connected, Albert Cunningham decided to find a more comfortable position, causing the old mattress to shift like a tremor beneath the doctor's feet. He lunged for the hook to balance himself, but it was too late. He was falling, right down to the bed, landing "cheek to jowl," as Jewel would say, next to his reclining patient. And did he smell bad—something akin to rotting fish and rancid pork. The doctor wondered when the man had last bathed, or brushed his teeth, or laundered the ratty quilt that he was wrapped in. The doctor rolled off the bed as fast as he could without ripping down the newly-installed net.

"Well, there you go," the doctor said, standing on the solid floor at last. "Stay under this net as much as you can. Okay?"

"Okay," the man moaned, looking a bit bewildered as he peered at the doctor through the new mesh net that now surrounded him.

The doctor washed himself at the well in the backyard, re-filled the bucket of water, and left it next to the bed, where Albert Cunningham lay snoring.

The doctor next visited Lila Cartwright to help her make arrangements to get to the hospital in Panama City to begin diphtheria treatments. While he was there, her son Pete came home from the new paper mill, soaked from the rain that was now falling steadily and the blood that was dripping through a makeshift bandage on his upper arm. The young man had a deep cut into his right deltoid muscle that had severed a few blood vessels. When the doctor had thoroughly cleaned the wound and was stitching it up, he asked the man what had happened.

"I fell onto a shredder," he answered, "or was pushed actually."

"Pushed? You mean someone pushed you on purpose?"

"Uh-huh, but I'm not sure who. I went down hard and by the time I was able to get up and turn around, there was blood everywhere and he was gone."

"But why did he push you?" the doctor asked.

"Good question. I don't know for sure, but my best guess is that it was by someone who doesn't want a union."

"And you do?" the doctor said, as he applied another thorough coating of mercurochrome to the stitches.

"Yeah, I do," the man answered. "That's the only way we're gonna get a fair shake from the people who own the place."

"Hmm," the doctor said, as he packed his bag, "since this wasn't an accident, I'm going to have to report it to the police, you know."

"You do what you have to do, Doctor, but I'll tell you right now nothing will come of it. The duPonts have the law in their pockets. The police won't do anything to upset them."

"There's a law against union busting," the doctor said.

"Ain't no union to be busted yet, and they're doin' their best to see that there never will be."

Chapter 18

By the time the doctor was on the narrow, two-lane road to Wewahitchka, the sky had darkened and was dispensing a heavy downpour which showed no signs of letting up any time soon. All the doctor could see was the single, six-inch windshield wiper trying, unsuccessfully, to keep up with the deluge, and the edge of the pavement, which he used to guide his car ponderously due northward, over the Intercoastal Waterway, through tiny White City, and on into Wewahitchka.

Wewa, as it was called by the locals, was the county's oldest permanent settlement, according to former Sheriff Batson who had, before his death, also informed the doctor that the complete name, Wewahitchka, was an Indian name meaning "water eyes," for the two lakes, Lake Julia and Lake Alice, that are in the center of town and said by the early residents to be looking upward toward heaven. The doctor surmised the reason for this ethereal explanation was because the residents were all eager to get out of there, even if it meant death, rather than to live on in this dreary, little town, or so it appeared today, at any rate, in this wretched rain. As if to hasten their journey, the doctor supposed the townspeople had built a pretty, white, Episcopal Church on his right as he entered the village, its spire pointing hopefully into the gray clouds above. Then he drove on a few more blocks to the imposing Franklin County courthouse. It was not much more than ten years old, a two-story pile of bricks, in the Classical Revival style, with bright, white trim and a high, four-columned porch giving it, despite its youth, a distinct, ante bellum feel. The sheriff's office and county jail were in the back of the building, where the doctor parked and made a run through the rain to the back door.

Deputy Mel Roberts, who Judge Denton had appointed as acting sheriff, until the next regular elections in November, had already carved out his own modest corner in Sheriff Batson's former office, although he did not yet look fully at ease there among his predecessor's imposing belongings: framed photos of the former sheriff and some other people whom the doctor did not recognize, four oak file cabinets topped with a volume of the *Florida State Penal Code* and a thick layer of drab dust, and two pine gun cases, armed with a battery of weapons, mounted on the wall behind him. Roberts was a fat, fidgety, pompous man of indeterminate middle-age whose gray uniform was immaculately pressed, unlike Batson's which had always looked sloppily slept-in. The doctor had heard his patients call the man "the toad," presumably because of his rotund shape and protruding lower lip. Why Judge Denton had appointed him was a mystery to the doctor; the man was not particularly liked or respected and would probably be defeated in the fall election if another half-decent candidate decided to run. Nevertheless, he greeted the doctor courteously and was ready with the file on Lucky Lucilla.

"It's a toad strangler of a rain out there, ain't it? Here you go," the toad croaked, loosening his collar and handing the rather slim, manila file folder to the doctor. "I'm not sure what you're lookin' for, but I doubt you'll find it in there. The man's obviously a nut, but apparently a hard-to-find nut as well. So good luck."

"Thanks. I'll take a look. What was Sheriff Batson's take on this Lucilla fellow, do you recall?"

"Well, he didn't say that much about him, 'cept he was somehow tied up with the murder of that there lighthouse keeper out on Cape San Blas."

"In what way?"

"He never did say for sure, but he just told us if we ever seen the man to bring him in, straight to the sheriff, for questioning in the matter. But nobody's seen him as far as I know."

"Okay. Do you mind if I sit here and read the file then?"

"No, not at all, make yourself to home. I gotta check on our prisoners anyway. Just let me know if you need anything."

Well, at least there *was* a file. That was a good start. The doctor retrieved a notepad and pencil from his black bag and placed them on the edge of the toad's desk. Then he put on his reading glasses and read.

First, there was a fuzzy carbon copy of a police report, written by two City of Tampa police officers. It read:

City of Tampa
Police Department
October 17th, 1933
Occurrence about midnight.
AX MURDER (LUCILLA FAMILY),
1707 5TH AVENUE

Call received at Police Station by Officer Tom Rigdon at Police Station at 11:45 A.M. that none of the members of the family that lived at 1707 5th Avenue had been seen to come out of the house all morning. The family's sawmill at the rear of the house was not operating as usual. This call was received from 1709 5th Avenue and the caller stated that they had heard a peculiar noise about midnight.

Officer Bell and myself answered the call in the Police Call Car. Upon arriving there we asked the neighbors at 1709 what the trouble was. They related to us about the noise they heard about midnight, but didn't realize what it was. We then went to the side of the house, 1707 and called for Anthony Lucilla and there was no answer. Then we tried to go in the back door, which was latched from the inside. The screen window to the right of the door was unfastened and the window was up. I climbed thru the window by using a ladder, nearby – unlatched the door and Officer Bell came in with me. We then went into the bath-room by opening the door to same and found Anthony Lucilla sitting in a chair with his hands to his head. We then asked him 'what is the matter,' and he did not answer. I went into the hall after the sister of Mrs. Lucilla had screamed and discovered there had been murder. I saw then in the rear bed-room, Mrs. Lucilla dead and her son, Franklin, 18, at her side in bed, still alive. I examined Mrs. Lucilla and found that she had been killed with some sharp instrument. Then I went into the center bed-room and found the daughter, Providence, age 22, and the little son, Joe, age 8, lying in bed apparently had been killed with the same instrument. Then I proceeded to examine the front bed-room and found Mike Lucilla, the father lying there dead on the floor, who had fallen off the bed and also killed with the same instrument. I instructed one of the relatives to call the ambulance to send Franklin to the hospital. Bell – during this time had the prisoner in his custody. Deputy Sheriff Ben Watkins assisted Bell and they took the prisoner, Anthony Lucilla to the County Jail.

F. T. Blounts ambulance picked up Phillip and carried him to the Municipal Hospital, while J. L. Reeds with the assistance of B. Marion Reeds carried the 4 bodies to J. L. Reeds morgue.

The following officers investigated: Sheriff's Office, City Officers, Bush, McMorris, Blanton, Mansfield, Dunn, Story, Beasley, Latture, Haskins, Vance & Bates.

L.C. Stewart   T.R. Bell

The doctor couldn't help but remember the scene when he had found Sally Martin's husband hacked to death with fourteen axe and knife wounds in a pool of blood in a shed behind their cottage on Cape San Blas. All that, times four. What kind of person could do such a thing? And the Lucilla family owned a saw mill—with a big, noisy circular saw, the doctor guessed. He read on.

Next was the bleary, carbon copy of a report from the Florida State Hospital in Chattahoochee, signed by a Dr. H. Mason Smith. It stated that Anthony Lucilla was admitted to the hospital on October 28, 1933. After a thorough psychiatric examination, Dr. Smith had concluded that Lucilla was suffering from dementia praecox with homicidal tendencies that was probably hereditary. Smith noted that Lucilla's parents were first cousins and a granduncle and two paternal cousins had been committed to insane asylums. Lucilla's younger brother, Franklin, had been diagnosed with dementia praecox the year before. In addition, the report indicated that the Tampa police had tried to have Anthony Lucilla committed almost a year before the alleged murder of his family, but withdrew the petition when the youth's parents insisted they could take better care of him at home.

The report also noted that Lucilla had been frequently observed being "overtly psychotic," but did not go into details. The report of the treatment performed on Lucilla was equally scant, indicating only that he should receive barbiturates, as needed, and be considered for insulin shock therapy, if and when the hospital determined to begin using the new treatment.

Then the report ended abruptly with a matter-of-fact statement that announced that Anthony Lucilla, on October 14, 1934, had killed another patient, unnamed, in the institution and was found missing the next day. And there the report ended, with the broad flourish of Dr. Smith's signature at the bottom of the page.

There was no mention of whether the patient was ever captured or what happened to him after his escape on that day almost four years ago from the Florida State Hospital in Chattahoochee, less than one hundred miles away from Port St. Joe via the Apalachicola Northern Railroad which connected the two towns.

The reports pretty much matched what Sheriff Batson had told him, but the doctor still had no irrefutable evidence of this Lucky Lucilla's personal connection to the sheriff or that he had been the one who had beheaded him. He only knew that if he were the murderer, and they found him, they were in big trouble.

"So, you find anything interestin'?" the toad asked the doctor when he returned.

"Interesting, yeah, but revealing, not so much. Do you know anyone who might have had it in for the sheriff?"

"Well," the toad pondered, "he wasn't the most loved man in the world, but I don't know of no one who could of killed him, if that's what you're gittin' at. Sounds to me like this colored boy that they got in jail in Port St. Joe is the most likely."

"How so?"

"The sheriff told us all, all his deputies, that this boy was dangerous and out to get him."

"I see," the doctor said. "Why's that?"

"Why's what? That the boy was after the sheriff?"

"Yeah, why'd the sheriff think that?"

"I ain't sure. I think he said the boy took a shot at him."

"But why?"

"Hell, I don't know. He's a stupid nigger. What do you expect?"

"I see. So I hear you're planning to run for sheriff in November to take Batson's place?"

"Yeah, I ain't no Byrd 'Dog' Batson, but I reckon I'll give it a shot. My daddy and his daddy were turpentiners around here, but that business has about dried up. I was an infantryman in the Army so law enforcement's 'bout the only thing else I'm good for, I guess."

"Well, we'll see what happens. Thanks for finding that file for me," the doctor said, as he started back to his car. Through some visual trick of caricature, the man did, in fact, look like a toad. A really big one, but a toad nonetheless.

The rain had finally stopped, presumably no longer strangling toads, by the time the doctor returned to his car, but the sun had gone down and a humid haze was rising from the pavement. The windshield fan on the old Ford was useless, so among the fog on the glass, the mist on the road, and the doctor's failing night vision, he was having a hard time staying on the pavement. He was concentrating so much that he didn't even notice the lights approach from behind until the car, traveling much too fast, was practically on top of his rear bumper. Then the bump came, forcing the doctor to skid as he tried to wrestle the steering wheel to a straight position. He managed somehow to stay on the road, but the next collision came too quickly and too forcefully, causing his hands to jump from the steering wheel and the tires to turn and screech in defiant strain. And the impact of his front bumper came only too rapidly as it plowed madly into the sturdy trunk of a solid longleaf pine tree that didn't budge an inch. The doctor's forehead bounced off the windshield and blood was soon streaming into his eyes. He instinctively reached for the shotgun under his seat, pumped it, and aimed it out the car's window. Then he saw, through the blood, the bleary lights coming behind him again—fast. This was not the way he wanted it all to end. He leaned out the window, aimed again, and when the car was dangerously close, he fired. The car's right head light blinked and went black, the car swerved, one hundred and eighty degrees. It finally stopped, and then reversed and was gone. Through the blood and the fog, the doctor could not read the car's license plate or focus on the driver, but he was able to see that it was not a car, but instead a white panel truck, like the one that Harold the gas station attendant had said Lucky Lucilla used to sell moonshine whiskey from, behind the Indian Pass Raw Bar. He reloaded his shotgun and waited.

Chapter 19

And waited, the doctor's chin resting on the open window sill, leaning against the butt of his shotgun, aimed into the darkness in the direction in which the panel truck had disappeared. The blood trickled, in a thin, steady stream, down his cheek and onto the gun's wooden stock and down the car's door toward the running board. He pulled a wad of gauze from his black bag and pressed it to the wound. He watched a wispy cloud of steam rise from his car's crumbled radiator. He was tired, very tired, and he may have drifted off, he wasn't sure. But he was sure when he heard the growing rumble of an approaching vehicle and suddenly saw its bright lights quickly bearing down on him once again. He was about to pull the shotgun's trigger when he heard the car's squealing brakes and saw its lights, two of them, slow, and then the familiar old truck sliding to an awkward halt just a few feet from his car's rear bumper.

Gator Mica haltingly emerged from the rusty hulk and raised his hands when he saw the shotgun pointed directly at him. "Partner, is that you?" Gator stopped and shouted, squinting into the night.

"Gator? What the hell are you doing here?"

"The better question is what the hell are *you* doing here? I came looking for you at your office to tell you that Dr. Price could see us on Saturday, and Nadyne tells me you've took off and gone to Wewa. So when you didn't show back up at closin' time, I figured I'd just go and check up on you. There's only this one road here between the two towns. You okay?"

"I've been better."

"What happened? Partner, you got blood all over you."

"Let's take a look," the doctor said, sticking his head out the window and trying to see his forehead in the little round mirror mounted on the upper, outside edge of the car's door. "Can't make out a damn thing," he muttered, "too dark and too blind. What's it look like to you, Gator?"

Gator leaned in close to the doctor's forehead to examine the wound. "Don't know, partner, all I see is blood. Y'all bleedin' like a stuck pig. I think we need to get you back to your office where there's some decent light and call Nadyne to come over and clean you up."

"Good idea, if I can just get this old thing started," the doctor said, as he clicked the ignition and turned on the gas valve, disengaged the spark lever, pulled the choke, and stepped on the floorboard starter button. The engine groaned, sputtered, and then died. The next attempt brought even feebler grumbling.

"It ain't gonna make it, partner," Gator pronounced, "sounds like a dying duck to me. Let's just haul her back to town and see if Wilbur Wells can save her." Gator then produced a thick hemp rope from the back of his truck and tied one end of it to the disabled car's back bumper and the other to his truck's rusty back bumper. The doctor hauled himself into the cab of the truck with Gator, and Gator started the engine. It took several attempts for Gator's truck to pull the doctor's car out of the mud and onto the pavement, but the old Ford finally busted loose. The doctor retrieved his shotgun from his car, just in case, and, after they had reapplied the rope to the front bumper of the doctor's Ford, they were on their way, slowly, but steadily back through the night to Port St. Joe.

On the way, the doctor told Gator about the attack by the white panel truck and what he had found out about Lucky Lucilla in the sheriff's office in Wewahitchka. Gator said he had talked to Dr. Price that morning and arranged a meeting on St. Vincent Island with him, the doctor, and Gator on Saturday morning at ten o'clock after which they could scout around the island to see if there were any clues to Lucky Lucilla's whereabouts.

The next morning, Thursday, from his office, the doctor called Chief Lane and Bob Huggins and reported what had happened to him the evening before, as well as Pete Cartwright's shredder incident at the new mill and the contents of the Lucky Lucilla's file in Wewahitchka. Chief Lane said he would report Cartwright's mishap to the federal marshal in Panama City, but he didn't know quite what to make of the doctor's information about Lucky Lucilla.

Huggins said that he had learned nothing new from Reggie or from the two men at the mill, neither of whom recalled seeing or hearing anything unusual on the night of May sixth. Huggins suspected that they were both asleep when the murder occurred or were just too lazy to investigate the noise from the circular saw, if, in fact, it had even awakened them. Huggins also said that he was concerned for Reggie's health, since he had looked ill and seemed to be withering away down in the dank, dismal basement of the City Hall jail. He said he had asked the chief to see if he could arrange for Reggie's transfer to the newer county jail in Wewa. The chief had agreed to talk to Judge Denton and Deputy Roberts to see what he could do.

As far as the doctor's health, his head wound turned out to be superficial, despite all the blood, but unfortunately his automobile had not fared as well. Wilbur Wells at the Port St. Joe Texaco Station reported the next morning that he could probably straighten out the car's bumper but its radiator and fan belt assembly, at least, needed to be replaced, and that he was calling area junk yards to see if he could find the necessary parts so that the doctor wouldn't have to pay for new ones. Meanwhile, the doctor would be without a car for the next few days until Wilbur could work his magic, but Nadyne had generously offered to loan him her old Chevy to conduct house calls until that was accomplished.

The doctor did not ordinarily make house calls on Saturday, and he wanted to make sure Nadyne had her own car available to respond to emergencies while he was on St. Vincent Island, so he was left with no way to get to Indian Pass to meet Gator on Saturday morning. He was not about to ask Jewel for a ride, since she would only give him more grief about returning to St. Vincent Island with Gator, so he phoned Bob Huggins and asked him to drive him out to Gator's camp. It would also give him a chance to talk to the lawyer about Reggie and discuss what else they might do to exonerate him.

Huggins was worse than Jewel. "You sure you want to go out there with Gator?" he asked as they drove out of Port St. Joe. "I can't see any good that'll come from it. If this guy Lucky is out there, how are you gonna find him? And this man Price. I think Gator may have it right about him. He may be more involved in all this than you think. Not to mention all the natural traps out there, what with mosquitoes, alligators, snakes, panthers, you name it. Why not just call Sheriff Duffield in Apalachicola and let him check it out?"

"Bob, you know no one in authority, including the Franklin County sheriff, gives a good goddamn about Reggie or any of this stuff. We're pretty much on our own here. And I know all this about Lucky Lucilla sounds pretty far-fetched, but I have a feeling we may be getting close to finding him, so I'm not going to give up now. It's either this, as unpleasant as it seems, or letting Reggie go to the chair, as far as I can see."

"I guess so," the lawyer sighed, "but I'm sure glad I'm not going with you."

The one thing the doctor could never get used to in the South was the light. When the sun was out, the world seemed to him to be ablaze. In the North, if his fading memory served him correctly, it was always dark. Here he seemed always to be squinting against the brilliance of the day. He had tried sunglasses, but he inevitably lost or broke them. But all this light was a blessing, he reminded himself, better by far than the short, gloomy winter days of New England. So sitting next to Bob Huggins in the lawyer's new Buick, the doctor closed his eyes against the sun's white reflection off the deep waters of St. Joseph Bay and nodded off as the attorney drove south out of town to Gator Mica's Indian Pass camp.

The doctor was roused by the deep ruts in the narrow dirt road to Gator's house and Bob Huggins's question, "You know I still have a ton of questions for you, Doc, about all this business with the murders of the assistant lighthouse keeper and the sheriff, but let me cut to the chase and ask you the one that's been bothering me the most."

"What's that?" the doctor asked.

"Well, if Reggie saw the sheriff dump a body into Lighthouse Bayou and the sheriff tried to shoot Reggie, why didn't you and Gator report this to somebody, Judge Denton or Chief Lane?"

The doctor was still groggy from his brief nap and tried to think fast how to answer this. All this subterfuge was becoming much too tedious. "To tell you the truth, Bob," he finally answered, somewhat stretching the truth, "the sheriff threatened us. He said he would kill us if we breathed a word about it."

"Hmm," Huggins replied, "and after the sheriff was dead?"

"Well, it didn't seem to matter then."

"This could help Reggie at trial, though," Huggins said. "If Reggie testifies that he saw the sheriff dump a body in the ocean and you and Gator testify that the sheriff admitted as much to you, then we can begin questioning the sheriff's veracity."

"But wouldn't the fact that Reggie and the sheriff had had this altercation lead jurors to think that Reggie might have a score to settle with the sheriff?"

"Could be," the lawyer admitted. "I need to think on it more."

All this speculation was too much for the doctor, so he was thankful when he saw the rusted oil can in the ditch near the path to Gator's house. "Here," the doctor said, "take a left down that little trail over there."

"Are you sure you want to do this?" Huggins asked again, as the doctor was getting out of his car.

"I sure as hell don't, but I'm gonna do it anyway. Don't worry. We'll be careful. And, Bob, thanks for the ride."

The fact was the doctor, if he had to choose, wouldn't discount dying on St. Vincent Island. It was beautiful out there and it would be for a good cause as well. What more could he ask, really?

So the doctor and Gator hauled the provisions for their excursion to Gator's boat: the usual five-gallon lard can filled with Spearman beer and chunks of ice, two Army surplus sleeping bags, a burlap bag with bologna sandwiches in it, Gator's rifle and two machetes, and the doctor's shotgun and his ever-present black bag. Through the dunes they trudged to where Gator had hidden his glade skiff. They wrestled it across the beach and down to the water, the doctor huffing and puffing mightily by the time he collapsed on his perch in the front of the boat, and Gator, with one hardy shove, launched the craft into the surf, then throwing himself stomach first across the bow as they floated quickly into the receding tide. Gator had overhauled the boat's little one and half horsepower engine after its soaking in the waterspout the week before, and it sputtered to life on Gator's first tug.

"This time, partner," Gator said, as he pointed the boat west, "we're gonna go around the island on the gulf side. There's not too much wind, not a cloud in the sky, and the tide is going out, so we shouldn't have any trouble. Once we're through the pass, we'll head along parallel to the shore southeast past Oyster Point Outlet along the Black Sough to Dr. Price's dock. Shouldn't take long. I know it's early, but throw me a beer anyway, willya? There's somethin' about being surrounded by water that makes a man thirsty."

Without stirring, the doctor looked at Gator, and Gator looked at the doctor, and in unison their eyes shifted to the lard can resting innocently in the middle of the skiff. Then they both began to laugh, somewhat nervously, as they remembered the last time on this trip when the doctor had tried to retrieve a beer from the lard can for Gator and had instead extracted a wriggling cottonmouth water moccasin—a trap set by Lucky Lucilla they had guessed.

"Well?" Gator snickered.

"Okay," the doctor said, "but no funny business, right?"

"Right. I'm pretty mean, but I ain't that low. Only beer and ice in there, I promise."

Sure enough, no snakes were perceptible this time, although they did spot, on the leeward side of their boat, the brown dorsal fins of a couple of fishing sandbar sharks just as they were coming out of the pass into the wide expanses of the Gulf of Mexico. So the two sailors sipped their beer in silence and enjoyed the sight of the long, white abandoned beach as they floated steadily down the shoreline. At first, beyond the dunes, they saw tall, upland slash pine stands, which gradually gave way to several fresh water lakes and sloughs surrounded by scrub live oaks, cabbage palm, and yaupon. Ospreys, kites, and wood ducks flew low overhead, as a pair of dolphins raced the boat along the island's coast. They cruised through a large school of redfish that made Gator curse himself for not bringing his fishing pole, and the doctor was splashed by a big tarpon that jumped high out of the water just inches from him as they were entering West Pass.

St. Vincent Island is shaped roughly like an isosceles triangle, its two nearly equal sides on the north and south of about nine miles each, meeting at their western tip at Indian Pass, and with a base on the eastern side of approximately four miles, at the southern end which sits Dr. Elmer Price's compound. Hidden behind high dunes, the four houses, a roomy horse barn, and a one-hundred foot long, cedar-shingle woodshed cannot be seen from the sea, the only indication of its presence being a long white-washed dock extending about thirty feet out into Apalachicola Bay, within a stone's throw from St. George Island, where they could see the tip-top of the Cape St. George Lighthouse peeking out above the pines far away in the distance. Gator and the doctor finally sighted the dock, and Gator steered the skiff in next to a big, bobbing, wooden Chris Craft that was tied up about halfway down the boardwalk. The doctor had the distinct feeling that they were being watched, but he did not see a soul, only a subtropical paradise that both fascinated and frightened him for all its wildness.

They trudged up the sandy path, bordered by thick, waist-high sea oats and lush goatsfoot vine, from the dock between two high dunes and on to the other side where a narrow sand road led to the compound that sat serenely in a green grove of live oak. A pair of bald eagles soared soundlessly high above them.

Two barking mongrel dogs greeted them as they neared the clearing. All four houses rested on five-foot high stilts even though they were at least a quarter of a mile from the sea. The first was the largest and was built with huge, hand-hewn pine logs. It had a cypress shingle roof like the other houses, but, unlike the rest, rose two stories high with large curtained windows on all sides. A wide screened-in porch surrounded the house on three sides. Several sturdy wooden rocking chairs sat empty near the front door. Behind this big house on the flat, sandy clearing rested three identical white cypress clapboard cottages, all with green trim and tall brick chimneys, and off to the side of them a long windowless barn and the tool shed where Gator said they made the moonshine. A wide set of concrete steps led down to a shallow creek that had been damned to form a swimming hole, partially enclosed by a tall cedar fence, where now only lily pads and a few wood ducks floated. A narrow, wooden bridge crossed the creek near the damn. A sixty-five foot windmill, its long blades rotating steadily, towered above it all.

In the shade of the live oaks, draped with Spanish moss, hanging like threads of thick tinsel, goats, chickens, and even some peacocks wandered, grazing peacefully and unafraid, as the doctor and Gator climbed the steps to Dr. Price's front door, with the two dogs still sniffing and dancing at their heels. "Well, here we go, partner," Gator said, raising his fist to deliver a loud knock.

"Yep, here we go," the doctor whispered.

Chapter 20

Tom Black, the dark, distinguished Negro butler who had answered the door on their previous visit was there again before them, dressed in his black suit and striped tie. He led them again through the house, smelling of fried bacon and freshly baked bread, to Dr. Price's office with its wide plate glass window overlooking West Pass.

"Gentlemen, gentlemen," the wrinkled, old doctor greeted them, hauling himself with some effort from his brown leather chair. "Welcome back to St. Vincent Island. How have you been?" he continued, extending his right hand.

Dr. Berber could feel the bones in the elderly man's hand, and he seemed older and more fragile than on their last visit only a few weeks before. Then, he had told them about his father's patent medicine business that he had inherited—the producer of Dr. Price's Pleasant Purgative Pellets, Dr. Price's All-Healing Salve, Dr. Price's Vaginal Tablets, Dr. Price's Favorite Prescription, Dr. Price's Golden Medical Discovery, among other questionable elixirs—as well as his expansion into the bootlegging business, and about his love and appreciation for his island paradise.

"Fine," said Dr. Berber. "And you, sir? I understand that you have now moved into the oyster business."

"Well, yes I have, thanks to nature's bounty here and Gator's knowledge of the best harvesting methods. I believe if we keep at it, we'll be making some good money soon. But Gator can tell you all about that. May I offer you a drink? It's perhaps too early for alcohol, but that's up to you. How about some coffee?"

Both Gator and Dr. Berber nodded their assent, and Dr. Price reached under his desk and apparently pressed some sort of button or signaling device, because before they were all seated—Dr. Price in his cushy leather chair behind his broad oak desk and Gator and Dr. Berber on the other side, sinking pleasantly into their own comfortably padded chairs—the butler reappeared, awaiting Dr. Price's instructions.

"Coffee all around," he ordered. "Bring something to eat too, some pastries or something. I'm damn near starved.

"So Gator tells me that you're looking for Sheriff Batson's murderer and you think it might be this man Lucky who used to work for me?"

"Yes," Dr. Berber answered, "and we have reason to believe, as we surmised in our last visit, that he may be hiding out here somewhere on your island."

"Right, so I understand. In fact, as you know, some things have come up missing around here and one of our men, Jed Washington, says he saw a man who fits this Lucky's description not too far from here. We've so far not mounted any search for him, but perhaps it's now time."

"We were thinking the same thing," the doctor said.

"I've generally not been too concerned about a missing chicken or two," Dr. Price continued. "These are rough times and if someone is so hard up that he has to cross the pass to get over here to steal a chicken, then I say more power to him. But Washington tells me that we're missing some other things: old lumber, a roll of barbed wire. He's even now found one of our steers half-butchered and being eaten by a flock of turkey vultures and a family of wild hogs. That's going too far, I'm afraid. And, if he is, in fact, the man who murdered the sheriff, then he is dangerous and should be captured."

"Yes," Gator agreed, "and we have a friend in jail right now who is being wrongly accused of killing the sheriff when we think it may have been this Lucky man. So we've got lots of good reasons to find him—if we can."

The butler returned and served them all coffee and some sort of sweet biscuit. As Dr. Price slathered his biscuit with butter and jam, he suggested that Jed Washington join them to discuss how they might track down Lucky Lucilla and instructed the butler to fetch him. "While we're waiting for Washington, let me tell you a little bit of what you're up against here, fellows. This island is quite large, in fact, one of the largest barrier islands in the Gulf, I've been told, over twelve thousand acres altogether. There are no roads, except what you see here around the compound. It's all woods and brush, for the most part. You'll be crossing a bunch of low dune ridges which were once actual beaches way back when, so you can see how the ocean levels have fluctuated over the millennia—quite fascinating actually. On the ridges themselves you'll see scrub oak, live oak, and a few magnolias. Between the ridges you'll see mostly slash pine groves. Once you leave the compound here, which we've cleared pretty well, you'll have to hack your way through a thick undergrowth of buttonbush and saw palmetto and other vines and brambles. In that undergrowth you'll find quite a habitat: snakes of all sorts, of course, opossums, armadillos, rabbits, raccoons, squirrels, rats, fox, oh my heavens, even weasels, wild cattle, and wild boars, some more than four hundred pounds, jet black, speedy, and truculent as hell. Just take a look at this old photo of my father with one of his trophy kills."

Dr. Price picked up a silver-framed photo from the corner of his desk and handed it to the younger doctor. There, peering into the camera, was a solid, stout man with a full beard and floppy hat, rifle in hand, next to a huge, furry beast, at least seven feet high, hanging helplessly by its long, dark snout. The hunter looked a bit surprised—maybe the

photographer had used a flash—but there was no doubt about the point
of the pose: they were entering a fierce and frightening wilderness that
bore no benevolence for interlopers like them. The doctor shuddered at
the thought of what lay ahead.

"But, as bad as that sounds, what's even worse are the insects," Dr.
Price continued. "There's generally a sea breeze and we've cleared around
the compound, so they're not so bad here, but out in the woods and
marshland there's a veritable witch's brew that'll eat you alive, literally:
scorpions, spiders, deer flies, and, of course, a special breed of St. Vincent
Island mosquitoes so vicious they'll make you cry for mercy.

"Tell them, Washington," Dr. Price prompted, as a tall, athletic-
looking Negro man in denim entered the room. "This is Jed Washington,
gentlemen. He's in charge of the domestic livestock here, our beef cattle
herd, the goats, chickens, peacocks, what have you. He tries his best to
keep them all contained and healthy, despite the panthers and hogs that
keep trying to eat them all."

Gator and Dr. Berber rose and shook Jed Washington's hand and
introduced themselves. "He's also a pretty fair hunter and fisherman,"
Price continued, nodding at Washington who remained standing near
the door, "not to mention, our resident educator and historian. Tell them
about the history of this place, why don't you, Washington. You know
more about it than I do."

"Well," Washington began in a baritone so deep that Dr. Berber's
limited hearing range could hardly decipher the words, "going way back,
there were Indians here, of course. We've found quite a few pottery
pieces that likely date back as far as Jesus' time. In 1528, the first Spanish
expedition stopped at an Indian village near here. It was led by an explorer
named Panfilo de Narvaez whose men were attempting to travel from the
Tampa Bay area to the Rio Grande River and Mexico. It took them eight
years to make that trip and only four survived it; one was a man named

de Vaca who wrote the account of the expedition and the other was a Moorish servant who was said to have started the fable about the 'Seven Cities of Gold.' Franciscan friars showed up in the early sixteen hundreds to save the Apalachee Indians, and they named the island St. Vincent in 1633, after a French priest who had been dedicated to serving the poor. Creek and Seminole Indians lived here in the mid-seventeen hundreds. A large Scotch trading house called Panton, Leslie and Company, and subsequently a group named John Forbes and Company, acquired from the Creek one and half million acres of Florida land, including St. Vincent Island, in 1803. This land grant was then passed to a group of Cubans led by Colin Mitchel around 1814, and they reorganized it as the Apalachicola Land Company in 1835, when the Supreme Court ruled that the land could be privately held. And this group then sold the island to Robert Floyd in 1858."

"Wasn't there some sort of fort here during the Civil War?" the doctor asked, vaguely recollecting one of Reverend Babcock's more boring in-office, history-based sermons delivered not too long ago.

"Yes," Washington said, "Fort Mallory, a small fort, apparently stood not too far from here to guard West Pass. Then, not long after the war, in 1868, a man named George Hatch, a banker from Cincinnati, and his wife, Elizabeth Wefing, a native of Apalachicola, bought the island at auction for three thousand dollars. This man Hatch was the mayor of Cincinnati during the Civil War. In 1862, with the Confederate forces threatening Cincinnati, he ordered all businesses closed and all able-bodied men to defend the city. And despite the mayor's protestations, the police-provost guards recruited many of the city's Negroes to form the Black Brigade of Cincinnati, which built fortifications and helped defend the city. Hatch was a Pro-Southern sympathizer who was ousted as mayor and moved down here in 1863. His grave is just west of here with a little fence around it still. His widow then sold the island in 1887 to the former Confederate commander of artillery under Lee, General Edward Alexander. You want to take over from there, Dr. Price?"

"Sure," Price continued between sips of coffee. "My father, Roy Price purchased the island from the heirs of General Alexander for sixty thousand dollars in 1908. At first, we used it mainly as a hunting preserve. My father sowed acres of wild rice, wild celery, smartweed, and potamogeton to attract ducks, geese, turkey, and quail. We'd come down for a few months each year to escape the harsh Buffalo winters and hunt deer, turkey, duck, and alligator. Later, my father imported some more exotic animals—zebras, elands, black bucks, pheasants, and Asian jungle fowl—but the only one that survived was the offspring of three does and a buck Sambar deer that we got from the New York Zoological Park in 1908. If you're lucky you'll perhaps see some descendants of these marvelous creatures. They're native to Asia, but seem to thrive here in the more low-lying, marshy areas and, unlike the much smaller native white-tail deer, grow to up to seven hundred pounds."

"That's a lot of deer," Gator said.

"My father eventually retired down here," the old doctor continued, "and gradually expanded the hunting camp to the more permanent complex you see now. Besides the windmill for pumping fresh water, we also generate our own electricity with a gas-powered generator out back. We've dug an artesian well that supplies a constant stream of warm sulphur water. And we have radio phone service to the telephone office in Port St. Joe. But for the most part we've tried to preserve it like God intended. The turpentiners, the lumber barons, and now these paper peddlers have all come looking to ruin it, but so far we've been able to hold them at bay. I don't know how long that will last, however, since no one else in my family cares a wit about the island. My wife did, but she's dead now. Some will come down to visit it occasionally, but most of them, including my three children, consider the place too wild and untamed to vacation in. They don't like the mosquitoes and snakes and all the hassle of getting down here. So when I'm gone, who knows what will become of the place. So enjoy it while you can. I'm feeling pretty well today, but, at my age, you never know about tomorrow."

"Well, we'll hope for the best," Dr. Berber said. "But with all this wilderness, what chance do you think we have of locating this Lucky Lucilla fellow if he is, in fact, hiding out here."

"Washington," Dr. Price answered, "What do you think? You know the island beyond our complex here about as well as anyone. What're the odds?"

"Good question," Washington answered still standing straight as a soldier next to the office's open door. "Gator knows the oyster beds around the island pretty well, and I know the interior west of here only fairly well. I occasionally chase a stray steer or do some deer hunting around the lakes at this end of the island, but I rarely venture much farther than that."

"Still, you know the interior better than anyone else," Dr. Price interjected. "If my father were here, he could help. He loved to fish and hunt all over the island, but he's long since passed."

"I'm sorry to hear that, Dr. Price," Dr. Berber said. "But you've raised a good point. And I sure hate to impose, but would there be any way at all we could borrow Mr. Washington for our search? Frankly, from what you've told us, I don't see that we would have much of a chance without him. Do you agree, Gator?"

"Yeah, I'm afraid so," Gator said. "Jed's right. I've fished a little around here, but I'm pretty lost beyond that."

"Well, I'm okay with it, if Washington is," Dr. Price said. "How long you figure to use him?"

"I want to be back in my office Monday morning," Dr. Berber answered. "So I thought we might take off from here this afternoon and return some time tomorrow, Sunday. If we can't find a sign of him by then, I guess we'll just have to figure out what to do next. Mr. Washington, what do you think?"

"Well, I'm glad to help. We've families with children living here and someone's been getting a little too close to them for comfort. So I believe it's time to see if we can find him. I've been thinking about it, and the way I figure it, if he were actually living on the island, he would need fresh water, so we could check the freshwater lakes. The eight lakes to the far north of us are brackish, but the ones to the east are fresh. There are six of them and, as I said, they're all at this end of the island. We could check on the ones just northeast of here first. They're connected by a creek that flows through our compound to the sea, but traveling by boat won't give us a very good view and limit too much where we can go. But traveling by horseback, we'll be able to go where we want and should be able to make pretty good time. And, with the horses, we can loop back around onto the beach and maybe get to the Gulf side beach by tonight. There are some fairly high dunes over there where we can get a good view of the southern lakes to see if we can spot any camps or fires. Then if we see anything suspicious, we can check it out tomorrow when it's light out. There's not much fresh water at the other end of the island, so I doubt he could last long there. So, who knows, we might get lucky."

"Get Lucky," Dr. Berber smirked.

And while this prompted laughter all around, it was more out of pent-up anxiety than it was for the humor of the unintended pun.

"All right then," Dr. Price said, rising slowly from his chair. "Good luck, men. Something tells me you're gonna need it."

Chapter 21

Dr. Berber had not a clue how to saddle a horse. In fact, he had never even ridden a horse before today. But here they were, Jed Washington showing him how to put his left foot in the stirrup and his hands on the saddle horn and then shoving him up onto a gentle palomino called Clover. Gator, taking up the rear, looked more at home on a big, black filly named Loco, and Washington led the way on his prized mare called, of all names, Frou-Frou. Following the three and tied to the saddle horn of Gator's horse via a hemp rope was a stout, unnamed mule loaded with all the gear they had hauled up from Gator's skiff, as well as Washington's provisions.

The doctor found the view from Clover's back to be exhilarating. It was like being tall. At five feet ten inches, the doctor had always wished to be taller. Now, as they headed for the woods, he had a good view of the rest of Dr. Price's compound: a small garden and fruit orchard, a dog kennel, a smoke house and butchering shed, and a steam boiler and engine for supplying power to a large circular saw used to cut wood for the fireplaces and cook stoves.

They soon entered a thick forest of slash pine rising high above them, smaller live oak below, and then, as they left Price's clearing and entered the woods on a narrow deer trail, closing in on them on both sides closer and closer, a dense ground cover of wire-grass, wild grapevines, brierberry, gallberry, myrtle bushes, and the ever-present saw palmettos, all casually identified by their guide Jed Washington.

The doctor did not have to do a thing but observe. Clover followed closely behind Washington's horse as they plodded slowly through the forest. The doctor noticed a long, jagged scar on Frou-Frou's hind quarters and asked Washington about it. "Alligator attack," Washington said. "Last year. I came close to putting her down."

Then, as they lost sight of Price's compound and pressed on out of range of the sea breeze, the mosquitoes struck. The men pulled down and secured their long sleeves, buttoned their shirts to the neck, and pulled down their hats. Finally Washington stopped their trek and produced from his big canvas bag on the mule three beekeeper's helmets, a bag of garlic cloves, and a bottle of something he called DMP. He instructed the men to eat as many garlic gloves as they could stand, as this would help repel the pests, and to rub their hands and any other uncovered skin with the DMP oil to further deter the little monsters. The beekeeper's helmet was simply a pith-helmet with a thin, circular mesh veil hanging from its top down its circular bill to the shoulder. The doctor had to laugh; all enwrapped like this, they looked more like some sort of kooky Klansmen than southern searchers.

Washington's determents worked, for the most part. But occasionally a mosquito or flea or some other biting little beast would find its way under or around the impediments and bite. Then, because of all the covering, it was hard to get at the pests to kill them or to even scratch where they had bitten. The big, black deer flies were undeterred, however. They bit through everything and hurt like hot coals. So the men tried to shoo them away with their swinging hands and the horses with their swishing tails before they had a chance to bite. It was maddening and miserable, and what had started as a pleasant adventure in paradise now turned into a forced march into hell. Still, Washington pressed on and Gator and the doctor followed.

By mid-afternoon, sweat-drenched and tired, they arrived at the northern lakes. The forest thinned and the underbrush turned to sandspur and sawgrass. The horses slowed as they sank deeper and deeper into the moist sand near the lakes. They passed a herd of about a dozen white-tail deer that just stood and stared at the men not twenty yards away. A great blue heron fished silently in the marsh choked with waving cattail stems. A black turkey vulture circled overhead—hopefully not a portent of things to come. An osprey nest rested in a dead pine high above, a big, thatch-work bundle of sticks balanced precariously in the highest branches. A brown and gray osprey circled and then landed in the lofty nest, a fish in its talons.

Suddenly, Washington raised his hand, and the little search party halted. On the bank of the lake on the narrow path before them, he pointed out a fresh alligator wallow—the mud packed smooth where they had rolled their crusty bodies. On the other side of the lake, blocking the trail were six, long, black alligators lounging in the sun. Washington dismounted and told the others to do likewise. Taking a rifle from his saddle's scabbard, he instructed them to tie their horses to a nearby magnolia. Then he crept to within a few feet of the wallow, grouching behind a buttonwood bush. Gator and the doctor followed. Washington removed his beekeeper's helmet, checked and cocked his rifle. In a few minutes there was splashing in the water near the wallow. A dark, black log floated to the surface. Two bumps appeared at one end, then the remainder of the log: a fifteen-foot alligator, its dark tail swaying serenely, the two bumps now surfacing as eyes. It submerged again, then raised up and pushed itself onto the bank. It crawled slowly to the wallow, heaved its bulk up and down on its stubby legs, flipped its tail and lay there silently, staring directly at them. Then one of the horses whinnied loudly behind them, and the alligator raised its head, sniffed the air, and suddenly charged directly at them. Washington carefully drew a bead. He fired. The long tail thrashed fiercely, but the alligator's black body sank helplessly to the mud. The alligators on the opposite shore splashed into the lake at the sound of the gun. Gator ran through the marsh grass to the shot alligator, its broad flat jaws now opening and closing automatically. Gator held them shut with one hand and grabbed a foreleg with the other. Washington joined him and together they dragged the body to firm ground. Gator stood up and wiped his forehead with his sleeve. "Just like back in the Glades," he said with a broad smile. "Nice shot, Jed."

The doctor tramped over and joined them. He was glad Washington had been so cool in the face of impending death. He had never considered being devoured by an alligator as one of his preferable methods of departing this world and was relieved to have the chance to experience another more agreeable means at a later date.

They all sat there on the banks of the dark lake and admired the dead beast before them. Presently Gator drew a knife from his pocket and began slicing out the alligator's tail meat, as well as some fat from its back. "We got too much baggage to carry him back," he said, "and not enough time to skin him here, but I'm at least gonna carry home some meat to smoke and share with Jed."

After Gator had packed away the meat on the mule's back, they continued on around the lakes. They saw a few more alligators sunning on their banks, but the search party kept its distance and was not bothered. They stopped on a sandy hammock overlooking one of the largest lakes, dismounted, and, resting in a sparse clearing, ate beef jerky and drank some of the Spearman beer, now warm, that Gator had insisted on bringing. They saw another herd of white-tailed deer near the edge of the woods. A red-bellied woodpecker tapped stubbornly on a pine behind them. There were all manner of birds darting among the branches of the thick forest: flycatchers, egrets, kingbirds, vitreos, crows, barn swallows, gnatcatchers, and tanagers. In addition to the trees and plants, Washington could identify them all.

"I want to make it over to the gulf beach before nightfall," he said, raising himself from the sandy soil, "so we best be going. Hopefully, we can catch a breeze over there and get a smudge pot going to keep these mosquitoes at bay. Otherwise, it's gonna be a long night."

It was more of the same as their horses trudged through the soft sand. The afternoon sun was exceedingly hot and the air was heavy with humidity. Bundled against the mosquitoes, they sweated until their clothes were soaked and their eyes bleary. If not for the intermittent shade of the pines and live oak, they would have sweltered to mush, the doctor imagined. By now his backside was beginning to ache and his shoulders were burning. The novelty of being up there on a horse had by now worn about as thin as the skin on his posterior felt bouncing constantly on the horse's hard saddle.

They had just forded a little stream and passed what Washington identified as the eastern tip of Oyster Pond—they could see the high dunes ahead now—when Washington's horse, Frou-Frou, came to an abrupt halt, causing the doctor's mount to stumble quickly to an ungraceful stop. Funny, the doctor had not seen Washington rein him in; it appeared that, without warning, the horse had just halted on his own. They all heard the rattle. Washington reached for his rifle, but he was too late. His horse gave a frightful, anguished snort, a sound like the doctor had never heard before, and was down on its front knees, heaving Washington over its head and into a palmetto thicket. The other horses jumped and backed away, as Washington's horse fell over on its side with a brutal crash, but Gator and the doctor were somehow able to hang on and quiet their mounts, finally. They dismounted and secured the horses to a scrub oak. The doctor hurried to Washington who was twisted on his side at an odd angle, deeply entangled in the palmetto spears. Gator ran to Frou-Frou, looked on the path in front of him, lifted his rifle and fired. The doctor jumped. The rattler just inches from his left foot coiled and writhed in its spasms. Its head now lay helplessly in the sand. Its contortions moved down the length of its diamond-covered back, its rattles now silent. The snake's coils flattened into slow convolutions, blood seeping, like a gulf tide ebbing.

Washington raised his head from the ground, wincing in pain. "He got Frou-Frou," he said. They all looked dully at the horse, lying on her side, panting onerously, her dark eyes wide with fright. They all saw the two puncture wounds in her ankle. A drop of blood oozed from each. Worse, a pink bone protruded grotesquely at the horse's knee, blood trickling down onto the ground.

"What do you think?" Washington asked the doctor.

The doctor just shook his head.

"Put him out of his pain, willya, Gator?" Washington said, still sitting helplessly on the ground. "That was some big rattler. And her leg is broken. No way she's gonna make it. Damn, I loved that horse."

Gator reloaded and raised his rifle again. The doctor and Washington turned away as its blast shattered their silence and echoed ominously through the woods. No one spoke for several minutes. Finally, the doctor asked Washington where he hurt.

"All over," he answered. "In my shoulder some, but most of all in my heart."

The doctor had nothing for the man's heart, but he did have a sling in his black bag to hold his left arm in place. Washington's shoulder blade was broken, the doctor was quite sure, but other than the sling to keep his arm immobile there was not much else he could do, except give him some aspirin to ease the pain. The doctor told him if the pain got too bad, he just happened to have some morphine in his bag, if Washington wanted it.

The doctor and Gator heaved Washington onto Clover, the doctor's horse, and with some effort both Gator and the doctor mounted Gator's horse. As the turkey vultures began to circle, they continued down the narrow path toward the dunes, the Gulf of Mexico, and the setting sun.

Just as they were emerging from the forest to the dunes, Washington pulled up Clover and pointed with his good arm to a grove of scrub pines about fifty yards to their right. There in the shadows of the dunes, along a little creek that drained out of Oyster Pond, grazed eight huge deer, the Sambar, that Dr. Price had described to them earlier. Even from this distance they looked massive, six feet high at the shoulder, upwards to seven hundred pounds on the hoof, chestnut in color, large muzzles and broad ears, and spreading antler racks on the bucks, of which they counted three. Gator peered at them wistfully and said, "Damn, ordinarily I would love to shot one of those, but what's the point. I'm too worn out to dress one out, and that mule's so loaded up that we ain't got no way to haul the meat out anyway. Besides they're too damn pretty."

When they finally came to the base of the dunes, they found a shallow gap, dismounted, and led the tired horses through the loose sand onto the beach. Gator found a high pile of driftwood to stake out the horses and the mule, and they sat up camp well above the high-tide mark and just below the rising dunes. Next to them was a ten foot high oyster shell midden, stretching down the beach for about a hundred yards. Washington explained to them that these were the left-overs of Indian mollusk hunters thousands of years ago, basically shell dumps composed mostly of oyster shells as big as saucers and other shell remnants that now supported a fine grove of high cabbage palm topped with green fronds waving gently in the ocean breeze above. Washington also pointed out a low, green bush covered with dozens of delicate lavender flowers that flourished on these middens but nowhere else in the world. He identified them as wolfberries or Christmas berries and said that in December they would produce red berries that tasted like spicy, salty, sweet tomatoes.

With the breeze and the driftwood fire that Gator had built, they were able to remove their beekeeper's helmets and relax, for the first time that day, it seemed. And as they were clearing the sand around the fire of sandburs and shells, Washington held up a piece of red clay pottery about the size of his palm, a remnant left by the island's first residents, he said, more than a thousand years before.

Gator had brought along some bologna sandwiches, and Washington handed out some more spicy beef jerky, and the doctor passed around warm Spearman beers. "Before it gets dark, let's hike to the top of that tall dune over there and see what we can see," Washington suggested. "I have some binoculars in my pack."

"I wanna see what I can catch surf-fishin'," Gator said. "I brought along some line and that gator meat should work as bait."

"Mr. Washington," the doctor said, "you stay here and rest that shoulder. I'll take your binoculars and climb that dune. Gator, you go ahead and start fishing. I sure could stand some fresh meat tonight."

It wasn't easy climbing the dune. The dunes here on the island were not nearly so high as those on Cape San Blas where he had walked with Sally Martin not so long ago, but this one was steep and loose, with only a sprinkling of sea oats and maiden cane to hold the sand in place. But it turned out to be worth the trip. Panting at the top, he had a panoramic view of the Gulf of Mexico and the empty nine-mile white sand beach, completely deserted and pristine, except for Gator fishing in the surf and Jed Washington napping next to the fire. Inland, he saw just how vast St. Vincent Island was, stretching as far as he could see, nothing but dense forest and sand, dotted with a few deep, dark lakes. He saw the flock of turkey vultures gathering in the sky and a black mass of them on the ground where the dead horse lay. He scanned the shorelines of the lakes with Washington's binoculars, but there wasn't much to see: maybe what could have been an alligator resting on a hammock near Oyster Pond, beyond that more woods, marsh reeds around another lake, and another, as he scanned east, then a gray something on its shore. He tried to focus the binoculars to make it out. Damn his eyesight; he well knew he needed something more than the reading glasses he had been using now for a few years, but he was too vain and too lazy to go all the way to the optometrist in Panama City. He squinted into the twilight and again adjusted the lens. I'll be damned, he thought, but there it was, what appeared to be a little lean-to hut on the shore of a small, round lake not more than half a mile west from where they had started out at Dr. Price's compound. There was no sign of human existence that he could see from this distance and he couldn't really tell how big it was, but there was no doubt that it was out of place in the verdant surroundings and that maybe, just maybe, their trek out here to this unforgiving wilderness had not been made in vain.

Chapter 22

When the doctor returned from his reconnaissance hike, worn out and sweaty, his lower pant legs covered in sandburs, Washington was asleep next to the fire and Gator, kneeling beside him, was shoving a cast-iron frying pan onto the red-hot coals. On the other side of the fire were three long sticks propped on driftwood stands hanging out over the flames. It smelled like home.

"What's cooking?" the doctor asked, leaning over Gator's shoulder to see what was in the pan.

"Speckled trout fillets in alligator fat," Gator answered, turning his eyes away from the spiraling smoke. "Little salt and pepper, some left-over garlic gloves, and I'll be damn if Jed didn't bring along a couple of lemons. And fresh alligator tail with Jed's homemade hot sauce roasting over there on them sticks. You might wanna turn them some, partner, if you don't mind."

"Hmm, sounds good." Washington rose up at the mention of his name and at the smell of the fresh fish and alligator. "I'm already tired of that jerky," he said.

"Yeah, and I'm tired of warm beer," Gator said. "Could you break out some of that moonshine I know you got tucked away in your pack somewhere, Jed? Sure would go good with this fish."

Washington fished through his big pack and pulled out a Kerr-Mason quart jar full of clear liquid. He opened it carefully, took a sip, and passed it to Gator, who sipped and declared, "Good god almighty, that's mighty good! I been sippin' that cane liquor all these years, almost forgettin' how good this here corn liquor can be. Smooth as silk. Damn!"

Gator passed it on to the doctor, who had to agree, although it didn't have much flavor, it sure did go down easily. They continued to pass the jar among them, as Gator flipped the fish and checked the doneness of the alligator. Finally, he declared their supper ready. Jed dug again in his pack and brought out three shiny silver forks and passed them out.

So there in the gathering darkness, the three stooped on their haunches in the sand around the frying pan, now off the fire but still sizzling hot, each with an alligator stick in one hand and a fork in the other, except for Washington who still had his left arm in a sling and had to switch between his fork and the alligator stick that he stuck in the sand when he was scooping a bite of the white, flaky trout from the shared pan. Why was it that everything tasted better cooked on an open fire, the doctor wondered. It tasted so good that they ate it all, the two trout fillets that had once nearly filled the entire pan and the crispy, chewy alligator tail that tasted, well, like alligator, hot and spicy with Washington's homemade hot sauce.

When they had finished, Gator took the dirty frying pan and their forks down to the seashore to wash them, Washington fed the two remaining horses and the mule, and the doctor gathered driftwood and fed it to the fire. Its smoke and the cool breeze from the sea fortunately kept the mosquitoes and sand flies at bay. And, as the day turned to night, and the cloudless sky filled with stars, the three men spread their khaki army surplus sleeping bags on the sand around the fire and passed around the jar of moonshine. Gator had also brought along some Partagas cigars that matched the moonshine in smoothness and richness and helped keep the mosquitoes away as well. As they relaxed around the fire, the doctor told them what he had seen from the top of the dune.

"Tomorrow we'll check it out," Washington said. "The old lumber that's gone missing was painted gray, so I suspect you've spotted something interesting."

They peered into the camp fire. It glowed reassuringly in the darkness. Black, darting Seminole bats flitted up from the dunes behind them and swept out over the open beach before them. The stars were so bright and plentiful this far from the lights of any town that they could see the sea glistening in their radiance. The air was finally cool. One of the horses stirred, and Gator pointed down to the shore, to a big, dark mass, larger than a washtub, emerging from the surf and pushing itself slowly with four wide flippers up onto the sand.

"A mother-to-be loggerhead turtle," Washington whispered. "My kids love to ride them after they lay their eggs."

The three watched in silence as the massive reddish-brown animal, like some prehistoric sea monster, moved toward them, making a strange blowing noise. When she had reached the dry sand, well above the high tide line, she began digging with her rear flippers. Slowly, methodically, she dug, and dug. Finally, after about an hour, the doctor guessed, she began to deposit her round, white eggs, about the size of golf balls into the nest. They continued coming, maybe a hundred of them, before she stopped, rested a moment, and then began to cover them slowly with the sand she had dug out for the egg chamber. And then she languidly returned to the sea. It was a fascinating and humbling sight.

"They return to the beach where they were hatched to lay their eggs," Washington said, as the giant turtle disappeared back into the gulf.

"Sort of like me," Gator added. "Coming back from Oklahoma to Florida where my daddy and all his ancestors were born and raised."

"Why'd you do that, Gator?" the doctor asked. "Leave your parents on the reservation and come all the way back here to live by yourself?"

"Same reason the turtle does, I guess. This is home. It's about all my daddy talked about when I was growing up. It was like I had no choice, really."

"And, you, Mr. Washington," the doctor asked, peering across the dying fire at the young Negro, "what brings you here to this wild, but beautiful island? Primordial instinct like the turtles and Gator?"

"No, I'm afraid not. If that were the case, I suspect I would be back in Africa somewhere. My history is a bit more confined and far less romantic. My grandparents were slaves here in Florida—in Leon County. My parents were self-educated farmers who barely scraped by, but somehow they saved enough for me to attend Florida A&M University in Tallahassee. With their help, a scholarship, and lots of menial part-time jobs, I finally became the first in my family to graduate from college, for what it was worth—not much, I'm afraid, in 1929 when the stock market crashed. I was left with a useless degree in agriculture and history at a time when farms, both colored and white, were failing left and right. No one would hire me, and I had no money to buy my own place. I got by doing odd jobs: priming tobacco, chopping cotton, shaking peanuts, picking peas, pulling corn, toting watermelon—anything I could find. I was shining shoes in the train station in Tallahassee when Dr. Price stepped off the train from up north one cold December day. I shined his shoes, not very brightly, I might add, and, through a few, convoluted conversational curves, we discovered we shared a love of nature and history, and I ended up working for him full-time. That was eight years ago. Now I have a good job, tending the livestock here and teaching the children who live on the island, including my own two little ones. Altogether we have two colored families and one white one, with eight kids now in my little schoolroom in the corner of the shed, the only integrated schoolhouse in the state of Florida, maybe in the entire South. I count myself very fortunate, but I'd like to have a little larger classroom someday, so I've applied for a teaching assistantship at Florida A&M while I work on my master's degree in history."

"That's great," the doctor said. "Does Dr. Price know he might lose you?"

"Yes, I've warned him, and he's not too happy. But he understands that the mainland offers a lot more opportunity for me and my family than a life here on this island. And you, Doctor Berber, what about you? What brings you to these parts? Are you returning or running away?"

"A good question. We're all either doing one or the other, aren't we?

"Sometimes both," Gator interjected.

"In my case," the doctor continued, "retreating would be the operative direction, I must admit."

"From what?"

"Many things," the doctor answered, as the fire's flames died down. "First, my mother and father and I fled Armenia in 1879, when I was only six, to escape persecution by the Ottoman Empire. Then, I fled constantly feuding parents in Watertown, Massachusetts, to go to college in Hamilton, New York. Later, my first wife and I left our little clinic in Nashua, New Hampshire, to move south to avoid the snow and harsh winters there. And just three years ago I moved here, well, to Port St. Joe, from Lynn Haven City to forget an unpleasant divorce and to start over still again."

"That's a lot of running," Washington said.

"Yes, too much," the doctor replied. "But hopefully I'm done with all that. This is home now, and I expect to live out my remaining days here."

"To home," Gator said, raising the jar of moonshine above his head and taking a long swig.

"To home," Jed Washington repeated, as he accepted the jar from Gator, raised it and drank.

"To home," the doctor said and then tipped the bottle back and drained the remaining liquor. "Thanks for bringing that, Mr. Washington. It was very good. Too bad Dr. Price is out of the moonshine business."

"Well, we still make a bit for our own consumption," Washington said. "Thank goodness."

"I wonder how it was that the law never came down on Dr. Price all those years he was making and selling his liquor?"

"I don't know, for sure," Washington answered. "I assume there was some sort of arrangement. We're pretty isolated out here, as you can see, and Dr. Price doesn't like anybody nosing around. If it wasn't for the doctor's fondness for Gator, I can tell you, we'd not be out here searching for somebody tonight."

"When you say arrangement, what exactly do you mean?"

"Well, let's put it this way," Washington said, "in my eight years here, I've never once seen a lawman on this island. Not once."

"How about this sheriff? The one in Gulf County. The one that was murdered. Did Dr. Price ever mention him to you?"

"No," Washington said. "I never heard the doctor say anything about the law."

"Well, if there was an arrangement, as you say," the doctor said, "perhaps something went awry with it?"

"Like I said, I don't know anything about the sheriff and his deal with Dr. Price."

"Moonshiners generally have a reputation for being particularly ruthless," the doctor said.

"I don't know, but if you're thinking that maybe Dr. Price had something to do with the sheriff's death, I'd say it was highly unlikely. Dr. Price is too old and too feeble to do anything like that himself, and I know everyone on the island who works for him pretty well, and not one word has been said to me about the sheriff or any other law enforcement person."

"Hmm," the doctor said. He had no reason at all to disbelieve this man who seemed as honest and straightforward as any man the doctor had ever met.

They piled more wood on the fire and returned to their sleeping bags. Washington, lying on his uninjured side and peering into the fire, asked the other two men if they wanted to hear a bedtime story before they went to sleep. Of course, they did. So Washington began, his deep baritone resounding across the fire. "One tale I didn't tell you this morning happened here a few years after Cortez conquered the Aztecs in Mexico in 1521. One of his followers, a man named Alvarez, returned to Spain after the conquest and organized an expedition of his own to this area. But when he tried to set up a camp here on St. Vincent Island, the natives took issue and chased the explorers back to their ship, pelting them with arrows and spears. Some of the explorers died here on these very beaches, but a few made it back to their ship. Still, the Indians continued their pursuit and attacked the ship and set it on fire, killing all that was left of its crew, except for one young adventurer named Don Rodrigo. He was badly wounded and about to sink with the ship when a beautiful Indian girl, named Suwanee, the daughter of an Apalachee Chief, came over the water in a canoe and saved him. Afterwards, he was adopted by the tribe and married his rescuer. A few years later another Spanish ship visited our island and found Don Rodrigo and his Indian bride. Don Rodrigo convinced his wife to return to Spain with him to live in his ancestral estate. Unfortunately, Suwanee did not have the necessary immune system to fight off the many diseases of her new country and died of influenza soon after the couple had moved there. But her spirit was restless in Spain and eventually it relocated here to her native land where, late at night, on evenings like this one, she is often seen to be roaming the beaches, searching and calling out for other wounded sailors who are drowning or in need of help."

"Very good," the doctor said. "I'll keep an eye out for her. Goodnight."

"Goodnight."

"Goodnight."

Soon Gator was snoring loudly. Washington was wriggling in his covers, apparently trying to find a comfortable position for his painful shoulder. The doctor's backside was sore from the unaccustomed saddle, but he lay on his back for a while anyway, enjoying the star-filled sky, then turned to his side to watch the fresh blaze for a few exquisite moments before he took a sip from a slim vial of morphine and fell asleep.

The fire was smoldering when the pressure on the doctor's bladder forced him to rise sometime in the middle of the night. He was stiff and sore but managed to pull himself out of the sleeping bag and slip into his shoes. Beyond the low glow of the fire, the sky was ablaze with stars, and a bright sliver of a crescent moon hovered above the dunes, drifting in and out of the high, dark clouds. He stood for a moment and admired them. Their brilliant light made it easy for him to see his way into the dunes and find a scrub oak on which to relieve himself. As he was doing so, he felt the spooky presence of something else.

He turned toward the woods and saw, resting on the top of a nearby dune ridge, a dark shadow, with a pair of wide yellow eyes staring at him, not more than ten yards away. Then he distinguished the rest of the form: a big, black cat, the size of a fawn, resting silently on its haunches, watching the doctor pee. The doctor froze, not sure what to do. He quickly considered the options. The panther could easily catch him if he decided to run. If he yelled for help, he might startle the cat into unwelcome action. If he stared back, the animal might take it as a challenge. The panther would be too fast for him no matter what he did. So the doctor slowly zipped up, averting his eyes from the panther, and tried to look as little and as inconspicuous as possible. The doctor's heart was pounding furiously, but he willed it to slow down. He knew that these predators could sense fear, so he did his best to quell it. He waited, hoping, praying that the panther would not spring into action. Although, now that he thought about it, this would not be the worst way to go, probably painful, but somehow poetic—death in the wilderness at the jaws of this beautiful beast. But it was not to be. Finally, after what seemed like hours, he saw out of the corner of his eyes, the cat move, lithely, loping gracefully back into the woods.

Chapter 23

The morning mist hung heavy over the sea. The doctor listened. The birds were waking in the woods, a seagull squawked in the distance, a mockingbird trilled. A predawn chill sent a shiver through his body. The moon had disappeared as the fog rolled in from the sea. The doctor, with his waning vision, saw the bleary figure moving through the haze far away down the beach. It was slowly coming his way, but he could not yet make out who or what it was. Gradually, the white wisp materialized into a long dress, batiste, he thought they called it. Then the straight, slim body, the long, curly, red hair, and the freckled face emerged from the mist. She raised her right arm and beckoned him to come to her. He did.

She extended her hand and he took it, and they walked wordlessly like that, hand in hand, together down the long white sand beach, crabs and sandpipers scurrying out of the way before them. Finally, she spoke in that small, sad, familiar voice. "I've missed you," she said.

"And I, you," he answered.

They continued strolling along the shore, the waves lapping gently.

"Shall we try again?" she asked.

"I don't know," the doctor said. "I don't know.

"Do you still love me?" she whispered.

"Yes, of course, but . . ."

"But what?"

"I no longer trust you," the doctor answered. "You lied to me."

"Only to protect you. I would never do anything to hurt you."

"But you did, by lying to me and by seeing the sheriff in secret while we were seeing each other."

"I was hoping you would never know. The sheriff was only there in transition. When I realized how much I cared about you, I left him. Please, Van."

The fog thickened around them, blotting out the morning sun and the dunes rising above them. She turned and kissed him, and he returned the kiss. Then she backed away from him and disappeared into the brume. The doctor stood there on the shore alone.

Until he was jarred awake by a hideous scream that echoed through their camp, across the dunes, and down the beach—a high-pitched, bone-rattling howl that sounded like a woman being murdered.

"Sally!" the doctor yelled, bolting upright from his sandy bed.

"Shh, partner," Gator said from his sleeping bag on the other side of the fire. "Ain't no Sally here. You must've been dreamin'."

"But that scream," the doctor exclaimed. "What the hell was that?"

"A panther," Washington answered, as he crawled out of his sleeping bag. "Or a Sambar deer. They sound about the same. Or a panther attacking a Sambar deer."

"Jesus," the doctor said. "What next?"

It was now morning, a little past seven o'clock by the doctor's pocket watch which he had carefully placed on the sand next to his sleeping bag. And there was not a cloud in the sky or on the ground, for that matter—no fog, no mist, no ghost from the past to be seen or heard. He walked down to the shore and stared out to sea, wondering about his strange dream. Damn if he didn't still love Sally Martin after all that had happened. What an old fool he was.

When he returned to the camp fire, it was again blazing, with a smoke-stained coffee pot already perking at its edge and Gator crouched over his cast-iron frying pan filled with the pork sausage that Washington had brought along. When Washington returned from the dunes with his binoculars still hanging from a cord around his neck, they ate their breakfast as the camp fire once again died down.

"Okay," Washington said, between bites, "I saw the structure that Dr. Berber saw yesterday. It looks to me like some sort of lean-to, like you said, not very big, and apparently unlived in, at least for the moment. I couldn't see anything else that looked suspicious, so I guess our best bet is to go over there and take a look at it. Maybe there's something inside or around there that might give us a clue to who built it and why."

"What's the best way to get there?" Gator asked.

"I'm thinking the fastest may be to head east on the beach from here," Washington explained. "The sand near the water should be solid enough to support the horses. And then when we come within sight of West Pass, we'll head inland again. If we don't get too lost, an hour or two should get us somewhere near that little lake that the hut's next to."

So they packed up everything and loaded it on the mule. Again, per the doctor's prescription, Washington took the lead on Clover with his arm in a sling, with Gator and the doctor uncomfortably crowded onto Loco, and the loaded mule in the rear. The march down the beach was not too uncomfortable. They had again buttoned up tight against the mosquitoes and sand flies, but the sea breeze kept the pests away from their faces so they didn't yet have to resort to the beekeeper's helmets.

About a mile or so down the beach, Washington reined in Clover and raised his good right hand and pointed inward near the dunes on their left. There, about fifty feet ahead, wallowed a family of six wild hogs, digging fiercely in the sand, their black backs covered with white sand and their stouts wet and gooey with the remains of a nest of sea turtle eggs they were in the processing of plundering. It was a ferocious and frightening picture of gluttony and power, as the huge animals fought each other and plunged their snouts greedily into the nest, snorting wildly, intent on ruination, oblivious to the approaching search party.

"My God," the doctor exclaimed.

"If they get anywhere near the compound, we shoot them and butcher them," Washington said. "They'll eat anything and like to dig around for roots, bugs, worms, and moles, anything in the ground. But that nest is already gone now, so there's not much we can do. Feel free to take a shot though, Gator, if you like."

"Naw, I ain't gonna waste the bullets on 'em. Let 'em have their fun."

"Well, just keep your rifle cocked, in case one of them decides to come after us, if you don't mind," Washington suggested. "We'll just try to ease on by while they're havin' breakfast and hope they don't pay us too much attention."

The largest of the hogs, the doctor guessed at around three hundred pounds, raised his snout and sniffed as they passed, then continued his digging, apparently unimpressed by the strangers.

About a half mile farther down the beach, Washington halted again and dismounted. "West Pass up ahead. I can see the lighthouse on Cape St. George," he said. "Let's walk these ponies through the loose sand and over that low dune over there and head inland for the lakes."

Once beyond the dunes, the mosquitoes struck again, and Washington passed around the beekeeper's helmets and DMP. The doctor insisted that Gator ride on Loco's saddle since he was bigger and was more adept at handling the horse, so the doctor's sore backside was now riding bareback behind Gator. With this arrangement, when a red fox bounded out of the brush beside them, Gator was strong enough to rein Loco in before he could bolt. The doctor almost fell backward off the horse's haunches when it reared up in surprise, but he somehow managed to hang onto

Gator's overalls and regain his balance.

It was slow going as the horses stomped through the sandy loam and thick undergrowth: scrub sweet gum and dogwood, ironwood and holly, thick buttonbush and the ever-present spears of saw palmetto, giant ferns and twisting vines of yellow jessamine, wild grape, bougainvillea, wisteria, Virginia creeper, poison ivy, and catclaw mimosa. Washington named them all like the teacher he was. Then, as they neared the lake, the forest gradually gave way to sawgrass almost as high as the horses. Washington halted and took out his binoculars and looked out toward the lake. "I see the hut," he whispered. "There's a door that's closed and no windows, at least not on this side. Let's tie up the horses and hike over to it. They'll sink too deep in this mud. Gator, you go over to the left. Doctor Berber, you go straight in. I'll come in from the right. That leaves the back end. Hopefully, there's no back door. So if someone is in there and he comes out, we'll sort of have him surrounded."

"How far?" Gator asked.

"About a quarter of a mile—mostly through thick sawgrass, rushes, and sedges" Washington answered. "A few more feet ahead is a dune ridge. When we get to it, you'll be able to see the place. Take your machete. The reeds are likely to get thicker as we get closer to the lake. And your rifle. Look out for snakes and alligators. Don't take any chances. Shoot first and ask questions later. Don't worry about making noise. We want him to come out if he's in there."

To see better they removed their beekeeper's helmets and left them next to the horses. Washington handed the doctor a machete, and the doctor loaded his double-barrel twelve gauge shotgun. Washington pointed in the direction he wanted Gator and the doctor to go. The doctor trudged forward through the sawgrass slough, his shotgun in one hand and the machete in the other. The ground was soft and the reeds at about eye level. The mosquitoes buzzed all around him in great swarms.

He kept his eyes on the ground in front of him, on the alert for alligators and snakes. He jumped as a fat, brown rat the size of a large house cat scurried past him through the cordgrass. When the doctor reached the top of the dune ridge, he could see Gator over to his left and Washington to his right and the lonely, gray hut about fifty yards in front of him. Washington waved them forward.

The doctor was sinking deeper and deeper into the mushy soil, but he slogged on, one step with his eyes to the ground, the next with his eyes on the hut. Out of the corner of his left eye, he could see that Gator was almost to the hut, his rifle raised. Then he was gone.

No, not gone, but suddenly a foot shorter. The doctor heard Gator's moan, before he realized that Gator must have somehow descended into some kind of hole. Gator continued to moan a low, angry, painful growl that he began interrupting with angry curses. "I'm coming, Gator," the doctor shouted, slogging as fast as he could toward him. "Hold on!"

"Careful, Doctor," Washington shouted, swinging his machete through the rushes toward Gator and the hut. "It looks like some kind of trap."

Sure enough, Gator couldn't seem to get himself out of the hole. As the doctor neared him, he could see him trying, trying frantically to raise his legs up and out of the pit. "Ah shit," Gator moaned. "Godamn, fuckin' shit!"

"Stop moving," the doctor ordered him, as he cleared the dry grass from around Gator's knees. When the grass was removed, the doctor saw the problem. Gator had fallen into a hole, or more precisely a trench about a foot deep that he now recognized by the pattern of dry grass that covered it circled the hut like a moat. "Hold up, Mr. Washington," he yelled, pointing to the ground. "There's a trench surrounding the hut. Come on around behind me."

And what was holding Gator helplessly in the trench, like a trapped weasel, were thick rolls of barbed wire. The more Gator pulled, the deeper the barbs dug into his pant legs and the flesh beneath them. "Don't move," the doctor again ordered Gator. Now that the doctor had removed the dry grass, Gator could look down and see his predicament and his own blood that was now seeping through his torn overalls. "Shit," he cursed. "Shit, shit, shit, shit!"

Washington knelt next to the doctor and surveyed the damage. "Don't move," he also ordered Gator. Then he removed his left arm from his sling, stepped over the trench, and marched toward the hut, his rifle on his good right shoulder aimed at the door. He raised his right foot and kicked the door as hard as he could. It sprang off its weak hinges and Washington rushed inside. The doctor and Gator then heard a loud crash. The doctor picked up his shotgun that he had dropped on the ground next to Gator, pumped it, and aimed at the door. He was about ready to pull the trigger when Washington reappeared, shaking his head. "Nobody," he said. "Just some old beat up pots and pans in the corner and a pine straw pallet."

Chapter 24

Extricating Gator from the coiled barbed wire was not easy. Shrouded in a cloud of mosquitoes and drenched in sweat, the doctor, working slowly and meticulously not to get entangled himself, cut away Gator's trouser leg with a scalpel from his black bag. Then with his arterial forceps he pulled the barbs from Gator's legs, with Gator cursing angrily through it all. When all the barbs were removed, Washington began cutting the wires with the cutter hinge of a pair of flat-nose pliers that he had found in his bag. The pliers were not designed for cutting the heavy double-wound wire in the trench, so Washington, down on his knees in the mud, his shoulder aching, had to squeeze and twist with all his might to get through each wire. By the time Gator could finally remove his legs, Washington's hands and wrists were covered with blood from all the accidental nicks from the sharp barbs. The doctor applied mercurochrome to both men's cuts and then wrapped them in gauze more to protect them from the mosquitoes than to stop the bleeding.

Then, after carefully traversing the trench, they examined the little hut which was no larger than the inside of the doctor's old Ford and a lot less luxurious. Just as Washington had reported, there was nothing there but a few blackened, battered pots and pans, a tin cup, a knife and fork, a rusty axe, and the pine straw pallet. In front of the hut were the remnants of a fire. Gator felt the black ashes and dug down in them a few inches with his hand. "Cold," he said. "Ain't been a fire here for a while."

"What do you make of this?" the doctor asked, as they walked around the outside of the hut.

"Well," Washington answered, "It looks like our wood and our barbed wire. Other than that, I don't know what to make of it."

"Ordinarily, I would say somebody had just set himself up a little hunting camp out here," Gator said. "Except for one thing, there ain't no good reason why a hunter would go to the trouble to build himself a barbed wire moat, especially this far away from the rest of the world."

"It's obvious to me that whoever built this is not living here permanently," the doctor said. "No roads. Hell, not even a trail. No clothes or anything that would indicate someone was staying here. Maybe our man Lucky comes out here to hide when he needs to, all I can think of."

"Jed, what's the chances that we missed something here," Gator asked. "Could he be hiding out somewhere else on the island?"

"Oh, he could be, but we've checked the most likely spots. He couldn't live long though without fresh water and we've checked the freshwater lakes and this is all we've found. The other end of the island has no water, except when it rains, unless he dug a well or brought it in, both a lot of trouble. My bet is that he's just not here. Maybe, like Dr. Berber says, he hides out here sometimes and steals our chickens and such just to survive until he thinks it's safe to return to wherever he really lives."

So they slogged back to their horses. Washington stepped on a thin black snake about five feet long that he identified as a harmless black racer, but everyone jumped, and the doctor's heart raced, harmless or not. Riding back through the brush—wet, bedraggled, puffing, perspiring, and wasted—they watched a pair of bald eagles soaring over one of the lakes. When one of them dove and then swooped back up with a fish in its talons, they all finally had something worth smiling about.

But their smiles were no match for those of the two young children who greeted their father when they rode into the Price compound later that afternoon. Washington dismounted, slung his sling aside, and scooped them up in both arms, with the two mongrel dogs romping and whining around them. As Washington began telling them about his adventure, Gator started unsaddling the horses, and the doctor trudged over to Dr. Price's house to report to him what had happened to two of his best men and one of his horses.

Predictably, Dr. Price was not pleased. He sat there behind his big oak desk with a scowl on his face as Dr. Berber told him all that had occurred.

"Well, at least the horse died and not the men, although Washington probably would've preferred the other way around," he growled when Dr. Berber had finished. "He loved that horse."

"I'm so sorry," Dr. Berber said. "It was obviously a foolish pursuit, particularly since we didn't find the man we were looking for. I'll be glad to compensate you for the horse and Mr. Washington's time when I can."

"That won't be necessary," Dr. Price replied wearily. "I agreed to your search and offered Washington's assistance. I understood the risks— probably a lot better than you. And I let you go. So, live and learn, as they say. What's next in your quest?"

"You know, Doctor, I don't have a clue. Not a clue."

Washington invited the men to stay for dinner, but they declined, eager to get off the savage island and return to the comforts of home. Washington walked with them down to the dock, leading the mule that was still loaded with their gear. When they had transferred everything from the mule to the skiff, the doctor turned to Washington and said, "Mr. Washington, I am sincerely sorry about your horse and your shoulder and your hands and wrists. Had I known that it was going to end up like this, I would never have asked for your help. If there is anything I can do to make it up to you, please let me know."

"Not to worry, Doctor. I'll heal soon enough. And the horse, well, she could have been bitten by a rattlesnake anytime. It wasn't your fault."

"Well, thanks for seeing it that way. Thanks! For everything. It's been a pleasure getting to know you. At least take this bottle of aspirin," the doctor said, digging in his black bag, "and keep that sling on for a couple of weeks."

"Okay, Doctor. Have a safe trip, fellows," Washington said, as Gator and the doctor climbed into the boat.

Gator steered the skiff back the same way they had come, parallel to the wide, white, sandy beach on the southwest side of St. Vincent Island. Despite the morning's sun, the clouds were now gathering in the west, gradually coalescing to deliver one of the frequent afternoon showers so commonplace this time of year. They tried to identify the spot where they had camped the night before, but after a while it all looked very much the same: pristine barrier beach, cabbage palms swaying in the breeze, gulls, sandpipers, and oystercatchers patrolling the shore. At one spot, they saw a flock of over a hundred big brown pelicans resting at the water's edge. As they turned into Indian Pass, the boat's little engine struggled against the current, as strong as four or five knots, Gator estimated. Then, near the middle of the pass, they saw two, large gray masses, just below the water's surface, off the leeward side of the boat. Gator steered the boat a few feet from them. They looked like huge, swimming pigs at first, but then they saw the flippers, their whiskered, wrinkled faces, and their paddle-shaped tails. Gator turned off the boat's engine and whispered, "Manatees."

First one, then the other's back rose to the surface and then their heads. They heard the expiration and then the inspiration of the air through the nostrils at the ends of their whiskered snouts. Then their nostrils closed and they sank just below the surface and slowly resurfaced to repeat the breathing exercise again. Afterwards, Gator and the doctor watched as the manatees sank deeper and deeper into the murky water until they were completely out of sight. What secrets of the sea must they know, the doctor thought.

The doctor felt the wetness in his shirt before he felt the pain or heard the abrupt pop, like the crack of a whip, in the distance. He put his hand to his side and watched the blood ooze between his fingers. This was it, he thought; surely he was going to bleed to death right here and now in the middle of Indian Pass. He looked to Gator for explanation, and found the big Indian diving toward him. They both were suddenly lying side by side at the bottom of the boat with all their supplies. Gator, still lying flat, somehow twisted his body around, extended his right arm, and pulled the starter rope on the engine. It sprang to life, with Gator steering them toward shore, while still lying on his back. They hit the sand at full speed, which wasn't very fast, since the engine only had one and half horsepower and the tide was going out, but the jolt of the sudden stop threw the doctor's right side against the solid, cypress wale of the boat. Then the pain began, like a sharp knife slashing through his bleeding side.

Gator cut the engine that was straining to drive the skiff up onto the sandy shore and pulled the boat out of the water with the doctor and their gear still in it. "Can you walk, partner?" he panted as he grabbed the doctor under his armpits and lifted him out of the boat. The doctor felt weak and unsteady, but with Gator's help, he was able to stumble across the beach and between the dunes to Gator's truck. The doctor remembered Gator wrapping a sheet around his waist to stop the bleeding. And then somewhere between Gator's camp and Port St. Joe, as a late afternoon shower darkened the day, the doctor blacked out.

He awoke looking at the ceiling of the operating room of his own office. He raised his head and saw Gator standing on his left side and Nadyne swabbing mercurochrome on his right side. "Stay still," she ordered. "You've been shot clean through your right, external oblique muscle, what is more commonly called a love handle. In your front side and out the back. Clean as a whistle. Small caliber, I'd guess. Lucky for you."

"Don't make me laugh, Nadyne," the doctor said.

"Oh, you won't be laughing for a while," she said. "Once that morphine I gave you wears off, you'll be hurting too much to smile."

Nadyne continued cleaning and bandaging his wound, as Gator looked on, and the doctor lay there helplessly.

"I have one question for you, Gator?" he said.

"Yeah, what's that?"

"Could you tell where the shot came from?"

"Yep."

"Well?"

"The mainland. No doubt about it."

Chapter 25

If the doctor thought his adventures on St. Vincent Island were rough, it was nothing compared to the level of wrath that Jewel rained down on him when she arrived Monday morning. Apparently Gator, Nadyne, or one of her contacts on St. Vincent Island had filled her in on what had happened there over the weekend.

"If you didn't already have a hole through your side, I swear I'd put one there myself," she scolded, as the doctor eased himself down on a chair at the kitchen table. "You and Gator, like bad little boys. Every time you get together, you get in trouble. It's a wonder you got back alive. Goin' over there into that wilderness. Well, that's dumber than a box of rocks. What was you thinkin', Doc?"

"Okay, Jewel, you've made your point," the doctor said wearily. "I already feel bad enough without you adding your insult to my injury. Instead, why don't you help me figure out what to do next?"

"Here, eat," she ordered, plopping a plate of steaming bacon and grits in front of him. "I swear, you make me madder than a snake. Will you just listen to me for once. No more adventures with Gator Mica, okay?"

"Okay."

"Here's where we're at," Jewel sighed, pouring each of them a cup of black coffee and then sitting down across from the doctor at the table. She looked fantastic when she was angry, the doctor thought, eyes all ablaze and her dark skin reddening. He was wise enough not to share these sentiments with her, however.

"Bob Huggins got Chief Lane to let Gabriel see Reggie again," she began, "and Gabriel says Reggie ain't doin' too well in jail. He's really down in the mouth, accordin' to Gabriel. He ain't eatin' and he ain't talkin' much. Just lyin' there, Gabriel says, miserable and sad. In the meantime, Richard Huey up in New York City been callin' Gabriel on the phone at mama's house tellin' him he better git up there right away cause they done started rehearsals now. Says early don't last long. And, as far as I can see, we ain't got no closer to findin' this man Lucky or whoever killed the sheriff than we was when we started. So what're we gonna do, Doc? I tell you between worryin' about Reggie gettin' the 'lectric chair, and Gabriel goin' to New York City, and you and Gator tryin' to kill yoselves, I'm about fit to be tied."

"Okay, Jewel, let's figure this out. First of all, I'll talk to Chief Lane today to see what we can do about Reggie. Bob Huggins has already asked him if we can get him moved to the jail in Wewa. It's in the new courthouse and has to be a lot more pleasant than that hell hole down there in the city hall basement.

"I don't know what to tell you about Gabriel. Sounds to me like, as much as I hate to say it, that he best be heading to New York City, if he wants to keep this job. And with jobs the way they are, I'm sure he does. He'll just have to trust us to somehow get Reggie freed.

"As far as finding Lucky Lucilla, I've been thinking. I'm pretty sure he's not hiding out on St. Vincent Island, but I do believe he may be somewhere near there, around Indian Pass. The gas station attendant out there said he always headed toward the pass when he left the Raw Bar. I assumed he was crossing the pass to go to St. Vincent Island, but I think he may be staying somewhere on the mainland close to Indian Pass, judging from where the bullet that hit me came from. I'll talk to the toad, I mean Deputy Roberts, in Wewa to see if we can mount some sort of search for him in that area. You talk to your contacts to see if they know anyone out there who may have seen this Lucky guy."

"Okay, Doc," Jewel said, refilling their coffee cups, "I'll git on it, but I ain't feelin' too good 'bout all this. Seems like, so far anyway, we just been poundin' our heads against the wall."

"Maybe so, Jewel, but that's all I know to do right now."

The doctor was genuinely surprised that his side did not hurt more than it did, but with a little extra morphine he didn't feel too bad at all. Fortunately, the doctor's old Ford was faring better as well. Wilbur Wills had repaired it and delivered it back to his house sometime over the weekend, so he didn't have to walk to work. So much for his new exercise regimen. He would have to get over to Wells' Texaco station and settle up with Wilbur sometime today.

Nadyne looked surprised to see him when he walked in at his usual time. "How're feeling, Doc?" she asked.

"I've been better, but I'm gonna live, I guess. Thanks for patching me up."

"You're most welcome. Let me know when you want me to change your bandages, but . . ."

"But what, Nadyne?"

"Well, it's none of my business, but it seems like every time you and Gator Mica get together something bad happens. Now I don't have anything against the man, but I would think you'd start wondering about why that is."

"You're as bad as Jewel. But to answer your question, maybe it's because Gator cares enough about me to always be there when I really need him. Like you, Nadyne. Or maybe it's just coincidence. Whatever, I'm glad he sticks around. Now let's go over today's schedule. I've already got a list."

Nadyne did not entirely approve of Gator Mica. Never had. She never said as much, but the doctor suspected that she thought he could do a better job of picking his friends—someone with a bit more class than the unrefined Indian.

"Let's see," she said, squinting through her wire-rimmed glasses at her appointment book, "Mabel Dilly thinks she's pregnant. Gee, I sure hope so. She and Charlie have been trying so hard for so long. She'll be here at nine. Frank Reynolds cut his leg with a saw yesterday and wants you to take a look at it. A fellow named Dorman who works out at the new mill says he was shot in the leg last night. Millicent Connors says her daughter, Brenda, has been coughing up blood. And Johnny Horton got bit by a snapping turtle and his mom says his hand is all swollen up. Then a few house calls in the afternoon, if you're still standing."

"Okay, thanks, Nadyne. Send Mrs. Dilly in when she arrives."

The doctor phoned Deputy Roberts when he got back to his office. The toad expressed concern about a shooting in his jurisdiction, but was not interested in mounting a search for Lucky Lucilla around Indian Pass. He told the doctor that he was far too busy with other matters and, besides, he was confident that, despite the doctor being shot, the colored boy that Chief Lane was holding was the murderer and not some "mysterious, lunatic wop," who no one could find.

Henry Dorman was a slight, young fellow, with sandy hair and deep-set hazel eyes. He was dressed in denim and walked with an exaggerated limp. The doctor rolled up his right pant leg and unwrapped the homemade bandage and immediately saw the trouble. The man had a hole, the size of a number-two pencil straight through the back of his right anterior calf muscle.

"How'd this happen?" the doctor inquired as he began the preparations for cleaning the wound.

"I was walking home from supper last night at the Gulf View Tavern," the man said. "And just as I was getting to the door, I heard a shot and then realized I was hit."

"Could you tell where the shot came from?"

"No, it was dark by then. I didn't see anybody."

"Did you report this to the police?"

"Yeah, I'm staying at Mrs. Lawson's Rooming House, so I used her phone to call them."

"Why didn't you call me?"

"Well, Mrs. Lawson cleaned it up really good with soap and hot water and slathered it in mercurochrome and it stopped bleeding right off, so I figured it could wait till morning."

"It looks like Mrs. Lawson did a good job. In fact, probably as good a job as I could have done, but I'll just repeat the work, if you don't mind, and give you a new bandage. And I think I've got a pair of crutches around here somewhere I can loan you, since you need to stay off that leg for a while."

"Okay, Doc," the man said, as the doctor began cleaning his wound.

"So why would someone want to shoot you?" the doctor asked.

"Well, I suspect it's because I work for the International Brotherhood of Pulp, Sulphite, and Paper Mill Workers. I was sent down here by the home office in Fort Edwards, New York, to help these fellows organize at the new mill that just opened here. This isn't the first incident here, you know. One man's already been killed and another injured since we've started to organize. These duPonts really play hard ball. We know that; we've gone up against them before. You know the story of what really happened to Alfred duPont, don't you?"

"No, can't say as I do."

"Well, duPont's original will was written in 1932, and it put most of his sixty-million-dollar estate into a trust for his wife Jessica, stipulating that she should receive all the income until she died. Then the trust income was to go to the Nemours Foundation, a charity to care for crippled children and the elderly in Delaware and Florida. Mrs. duPont and her brother, Ed Ball, were named executors and trustees. But, for some reason, just before he died in 1935, duPont wrote a second will that reduced his wife's income and her brother's authority and gave most of the estate to charity. Then, before this second will had time to become valid, duPont suddenly died in his home. And there're a lot of people out there who think that maybe his death wasn't of natural causes, that maybe his wife and her brother may have had something to do with it."

"Well, I don't know about that. But there's no doubt that people will go to some lengths to gain money and power; that's for sure. At any rate, I don't envy you your job, but I expect you're gonna live if you stay off this leg and away from the workers at that mill."

"Well, Doc, I reckon, with the crutches, I can stay off my leg, but not away from the mill workers. I've still got work to do with those men. Without a union, they'll never get a fair shake."

"Alright," the doctor said, "I understand, but I'm going to talk to our chief of police about what happened to you. His name's Lane, and if you have any more trouble, let him know. And one more thing . . ."

"Yes?" the union organizer said.

"Be careful."

Chapter 26

After he had finished his morning appointments, the doctor ate dinner at Dad's Café—fried chicken, rice and gravy, and green beans—and then drove over to Chief Lane's office. Fortunately the chief was in, hunched over his desk, ponderously pounding something out on an old Royal typewriter with his two index fingers.

"Excuse me, Chief," the doctor said, easing into one of the office's hard, straight-back, oak chairs, "but I wanted to stop by and report another injury of someone who was trying to organize a union out at the new mill. A fellow named Henry Dorman was in my office this morning with a bullet through his calf. Like these other two men, he said he suspected that it had something to do with him being a union organizer."

"Damn," the chief muttered, shaking his head. "The dispatcher mentioned that someone had called last night. I reported the Ridler death and Cartwright's attack to the federal marshal in Panama City, since union busting falls under the Wagner Act, but I haven't heard a thing back from him. I guess I better start doin' something myself."

"Nadyne's got all this Dorman's contact information, so you can just give her a call. He's staying over at Mrs. Lawson's. I told him that I was going to report it to you."

"Alright, I'm gonna have to have another talk with Michael Mitchell, the head man out there. He's got to know who's behind all this. We've got enough trouble with just the routine accidents at that damn mill, without having to deal with people shooting people. Anyway, what else, besides catching the man who's been assaulting these union fellows, can I do for you, Doc?"

"Well, I was wondering about your prisoner. How's he doing?"

"To be honest with you, Doc," the chief answered, "I don't like what's happening to him. He's not eating hardly anything, and I haven't heard him utter a word for several days now. All he does is lay there on that mattress and stare at the wall."

"Well," the doctor said, "your jail's not exactly the most pleasant place in the world. No offence."

"Oh, no offence taken," the chief laughed. "I'm well aware of that. We're never gonna be accused of coddling prisoners here in Port St. Joe."

"Is there anything we can do to help," the doctor asked, "short of releasing him, which I assume is not in the cards?"

"No, I'm afraid not, but I do have an idea. You may not know this, but besides the shabby conditions of our jail, our town also possesses some pretty shabby characters, some of which have taken it upon themselves to call in threats to our dispatcher about what's gonna happen to Mr. Robinson if we don't take action pretty fast. Things like 'If you don't hang that nigger now, we will' and such nonsense. Hell, with the trial comin' up in just a few weeks, you would think the fools could wait."

"Do you know who's making these calls?"

"Oh, I have a pretty good idea, and I'd just as soon toss 'em in the bay as look at 'em, but I don't have any proof, so . . ."

"So what's your idea?"

"Oh yeah," the chief said. "I was talkin' to Bob Huggins the other day, and we were thinkin' that maybe Reggie would be more comfortable and safer over in the county jail in Wewa. It's newer and a lot nicer than ours and they have more men than we do here, better security, so I think Reggie might be better off over there."

"Hmm," the doctor said, thinking that this was a lot easier than he had expected it would be, "might not be such a bad idea. The only downsides are that Jewel and Gabriel would have farther to go to visit him and some of the deputies over there might have been friends of the sheriff and would want to take matters into their own hands in getting back at Reggie."

"Well," the chief answered, "I'll guarantee you that the sheriff didn't have many friends among his deputies. In fact, I can assure you that they're pretty unanimous in their dislike for the man. As far as Wewa being further away from Reggie's friends, I reckon that's true, but it might be a small price to pay if we keep him from dying, either by his own hands or the hands of these yahoos who've been calling us."

"Well, if you put it that way."

"What I'm gonna do is take him over there tonight. I've already talked to Judge Denton about it, and he thinks it's okay. Deputy Roberts says they got plenty of room, so I wanna do it at night so no one will notice until he's over there safe and sound."

"What if Gator Mica and I were to follow along behind you, just to help you out if you need it?" the doctor suggested.

"Well, you're free to do what you like, but I'll be leaving here at around nine."

"Thanks, Chief, see you then."

Then the doctor stopped at Wilbur Wells' Texaco station and thanked the mechanic for fixing his old Ford so rapidly. The doctor had no car insurance, hardly anyone did during the Depression, so he tried to pay the man out of his own pocket, but Wells reminded the doctor that he had not been able to pay for the doctor's treatment of his mother's gout last year and that he would consider them even if the doctor would. The doctor definitely would, since he didn't have much cash and had already forgotten about Wilbur's mother and written off the debt long ago.

Then he drove by his house to get his shotgun that Gator had left with him when he had dropped him off the night before, as well as some shells from the upstairs closet. As he was putting the box of shells in his suit coat pocket, he thought he heard a car pull into the driveway in back, and then a minute later, he heard the creaky back porch screen door open, but not slam shut. It must be Jewel returning, he thought. "Jewel," he hollered, "is that you? Jewel?"

He had left the door from the back porch to the kitchen unlocked, but unfortunately it didn't creak like the outside door. The doctor listened for footsteps or any sound at all downstairs. Nothing. He stood there, holding his breath, with the shotgun in his hand. It was loaded. All he had to do was pump it and fire. Unless someone fired first. He could still hear nothing downstairs, but, of course, his hearing was so bad that there could've been a riot going on down there and he wouldn't have noticed it. So he pumped the shotgun, cradled it on his shoulder, and moved toward the stairs, one delicate step at a time. The staircase was dim even in the midday sun, but he eased himself down it, slowly, soundlessly, until he got to the kitchen. He peaked his head out of the stairwell and looked around. The kitchen was empty. He tiptoed through the kitchen and pushed the door to the back porch open. It was empty as well—except for a cardboard box of Satsuma oranges with a note of thanks from the possibly pregnant Mabel Dilly. They would know for sure in a couple of days when the doctor would kill the female rabbit whose ear he had injected Mrs. Dilly's urine into. If the rabbit had ovulated, Mabel could start knitting baby booties.

The doctor left Jewel a note on the kitchen counter letting her know that he would not be home for supper that night. Next, he began his house calls which today, as usual, consisted mostly of the elderly who

were too infirm to come to his office. During the Depression, many
younger people had moved from Port St. Joe to find work in larger cities,
leaving their parents behind to fend for themselves. The doctor thought
that maybe some of them would move back now that the new mill had
opened, but he hadn't seen them yet. It appeared that many of these
young people had just absconded, leaving their elders to languish alone,
poor and enfeebled, here in this bleak, bucolic backwater by the bay.

After he had visited his last patient of the day, Lottie Newman, who
was dying of tuberculosis, he set out to find Gator. Since Gator didn't
own a phone, the doctor drove out to Indian Pass to see if he was at home
in his little camp in the woods. He wasn't, so the doctor left another note,
telling Gator to meet him at the Indian Pass Raw Bar at seven. Then
he drove over to the Thirteen Mile Oyster House where Gator worked.
Despite its fishy function, the little dock and clapboard shack smelled
crisp and clean like sunshine and saltwater. According to Dewey Miller
who was packing oysters in a wooden box on the dock, Gator was still
out in a boat tonging oysters in Big Bayou. Off in the distance, across the
choppy waters of St. Vincent Sound, the doctor could see the little fleet
of four oyster boats, with their circular aft cabins and humped midship
hatches, bobbing out in Apalachicola Bay not far from the northern
shore of St. Vincent Island. The doctor told Dewey to ask Gator, when
he returned, to meet him at the Raw Bar at seven o'clock.

Then he drove back to Albert Cunningham's decrepit cabin on the
unmarked dirt road between Thirteen Mile Road and Indian Pass Road.
It was still light out, so the doctor was able to locate it this time without
too much trouble. Albert Cunningham looked a lot better than the last
time the doctor had seen him. His fever was gone, and he was able to sit
up and talk, even though his undershirt and bedclothes remained soiled
and filthy.

"You look better, Mr. Cunningham. How're you feeling?"

"Better, much better," Cunningham groaned. "I'll be back on my bike any day now."

"You takin' the medicine I gave you and eating okay?"

"Yep, thank you, Doc. Sorry I ain't got no money to pay you."

"That's okay. You rest and get better."

"All right."

"By the way, Mr. Cunningham, now that you're feeling better, I have a question for you. In your travels on your bicycle, have you ever run across a tall, curly-haired man in a white, panel truck?"

"Yep, I seen him."

"Do you know where he lives, by any chance? It's very important that I find him."

"No, I'm sorry, Doc," Cunningham answered, "but if you say it's important, I'll find him. I know these swamps like the back of my hand. And iffen he lives around here, I'll find him all right."

Chapter 27

According to the Hamm's beer clock behind the bar of the Indian Pass Raw Bar, it was 6:10 p.m. when the doctor settled down at the bar there to wait for Gator. He ordered a Spearman beer and surveyed the dozen or so men who had stopped by after work to loosen up a bit before heading home. He didn't recognize a soul, except for the proprietor, Sadie McIntire, who was at her usual position behind an ancient cash register near the front door. The Shelton Brothers' new hit, "Aura Lee," was playing on the juke box, and smoke was beginning to permeate the dim room. Four men in overalls at a corner table near the back door were in the midst of a noisy game of dominoes, the clickity-clack of the pieces clapping on the wooden tabletop.

The doctor loosened his tie and thought about poor Reggie still in jail for a crime he didn't commit. Once again he rolled over in his mind all the possibilities, trying to figure out if there was a better course of action that could lead to the exoneration of the bluesman. He thought again that maybe it was now time to give up this quixotic search for Lucky Lucilla and tell Chief Lane the entire truth. But he knew if he did, this would spawn a whole series of undesirable events that he would be sorry for.

But sitting there in that smoky and by now all-too-familiar

roadhouse, his side was beginning to hurt, his eyes were watering, and his spirit, ebbing. He had to wonder if it was all worth it, not only this quest for an elusive crazy man, but also this continuing debacle that his life had somehow become. Sally Martin had come along at the right time, when the doctor was frankly tiring of his existence, but now she was gone from his life forever. And the only other bright spot in his daily drudgery, Jewel Jackson, was about to abandon him as well. What was the point? Maybe it was time to just tell everyone the truth and then choose the final way out and cut short the suffering.

Sadie McIntire interrupted his rumination by sitting down on the bar stool next to him and blowing cigarette smoke in his face. "You look like you're pondering something heavy there, Doc," she said. "Ain't seen you for a while. To what do we owe the pleasure?"

"Just waiting for Gator Mica," he answered. "I'm supposed to meet him here at seven."

"Still lookin' for that man Lucky?"

"Yeah, I'm afraid so, without much luck so far. You sure you don't have any idea at all where he lives?"

"No, I told you before about all I know. Remember, I warned you to stay away from him though?"

"Yeah, I do remember that," the doctor answered, "but you didn't tell me why."

"Well," she said and paused, as if trying to decide how much to tell the doctor, "the man was not right in the head."

"Yeah?"

"He had this look in his eyes. A faraway look. Like he wasn't quite all here, if you know what I mean. One time, and I ain't gonna say no more, I heard a blood curdling howl out back, and I went out there to see what was goin' on. There was Lucky down on his knees in the parking lot, stabbing this little spotted dog over and over again with a pocket knife. The dog was way past dead by the time I got there. But he just kept stabbing him. Blood squirtin' all over the place. I screamed at him and asked him what he thought he was doin', and he said the dog had tried to bite him. Why, that dog was a stray that the cook fed, friendliest dog you'll ever meet, always waggin' its tail and lickin' yo hand. Wouldn't hurt a soul. But the strangest thing, you know what he was doin' while he was stabbing that poor animal over and over again?"

"What?"

"Why he was cryin', cryin' like a little baby boy."

True to her word, Sadie McIntire would say no more. She stubbed her cigarette out in a dirty ashtray on the bar and promptly returned to her post behind the cash register, shaking her head as she walked away. The doctor didn't know what to make of the story she had told him, but it sure didn't make him feel any better about pursuing this man Lucky Lucilla.

Gator finally arrived a half hour late, but they still had time to eat supper before meeting the chief at nine. They both started with raw oysters from Dr. Price's plant on Thirteen Mile Road—"milers" Gator called them—and then Gator had a big bowl of gumbo, while the doctor peeled and ate a plate of steamed shrimp that he doused in Ed's Red Hot Sauce. And then in an attempt to assuage his depression, the doctor ignored his diet and joined Gator in imbibing in a slice of key lime pie and a cup of coffee for dessert. The Raw Bar's menu was not extensive, but the limited choices were all good.

They drove in separate cars the ten miles into Port St. Joe, so the doctor would not have to drive Gator home later that night. Chief Lane was waiting for them in his office when they arrived there a little before nine o'clock, a double barrel shotgun at the ready, resting on a pile of papers on the top of his desk.

"I'll go get the prisoner, if y'all wanna wait here," he said, pulling a ring of keys from the nail behind him on the wall. "But before I do—and I hope it's unnecessary—raise your right hands. I hereby deputize you two as authorized patrol men of our fair city of Port St. Joe, Florida—but only for the night and at no pay. Sorry I can't afford to pay you nothing."

Gator and the doctor smiled at each other. This little ceremony seemed to strike both of them as funny, but they didn't laugh, because Chief Lane as usual looked as serious as a cemetery.

But not as serious as Reggie Robinson. The chief and Gabriel were right. Reggie did not look well at all. He was small to begin with, but he looked more like a despondent child than a bluesman, as the chief led him handcuffed to the back seat of his patrol car. The doctor and Gator both said hello as he walked by them, but he only nodded in return. His natty blue pin-striped suit was rumpled and his hair was a nappy mess. He looked like he was about ready to cry, which made the doctor sad and exasperated at his inability to help him.

It's a straight fifteen mile shot north from Port St. Joe to Wewahitchka, the road only jutting slightly at the bridge over the Intercoastal Waterway just south of White City. The doctor drove his old Ford several car lengths behind the chief with Gator beside him in the front seat. It was a clear night, with a half moon and stars aplenty shining brightly. The air was warm enough that they needed to keep the windows open. There wasn't much traffic at this hour of the night going in either direction, so the chief was driving fast.

It was about a mile or so beyond the bridge and the tiny village of White City that they saw the lights ahead on the highway where no lights should have been. The chief slowed and came to a stop, and the doctor pulled in behind him. There, blocking the narrow two-lane road was a line of eight men dressed in white sheets and hoods, each with a lit torch in one hand and a shotgun in the other. Along both sides of the road were parked their pick-up trucks, listing awkwardly in the steep, banked ditches.

As the chief jumped out of his car, Gator and the doctor opened their doors on each side of the doctor's car and crouched behind them like shields as they poked their guns through the open windows.

With the patrol car's headlights lighting his way, the chief stomped like an angry drill sergeant to the middle of the road, not more than ten feet away from the line of costumed men, threw his Panama hat to the pavement, and screamed, "What on God's green earth are you doing here? This is a public highway, you fools. You can't block it. What if a loaded logging truck roared through here? You'd all be dead. Jesus Christ! This ain't fuckin' Georgia, you dumb crackers. You don't think I don't recognize your rattletrap trucks parked over there. And your scuffed snakeskin boots, Marvin Mills. Oh yeah, there's Lance Herman's Dodge right there. Lance, does your ol' lady know you're out here? She'll bust your butt when she finds out. You'll be out back in the doghouse with that useless hound dog of yours for a year.

"And you, Earl Farmer, when are you ever gonna fix that back fender on that old International? Where does your mama think you are tonight? She's gonna tan your hide, sure as shootin'. You won't be able to sit on your fat ass for a month.

"And Oliver Muller, that's your GMC flatbed right there. I can't wait to tell Reverend Babcock what you're doing. You think you've heard holy hell, fire, and brimstone sermons about your drinkin', you ain't heard nothing yet.

"I'm sick to death of the lot of you out here in those ridiculous outfits. Go home and put them back on the beds where they belong, where y'all belong, before I tell Gator to start takin' target practice on you. Y'all be easy to hit in all that white. Ready, Gator?"

"Ready, Chief," Gator shouted, his shotgun aimed at the middle of the line of men.

The men, at first, stood frozen. None had anticipated the chief's wrath it appeared and none seemed to know exactly what to do about it, standing there in the road with their heads covered and their hands filled with smoking torches and heavy guns. Finally, one man dropped his torch to the pavement and raised his shotgun. "We ain't got no truck with you, Chief," he said. "Just hand over yo' prisoner and we'll be on our way."

"You'll damn well better be on your way right now," Chief Lane commanded. "Gator!"

Gator instantly pumped his shotgun and aimed directly at the man.

"Now, move it," the chief shouted. "I see any one of you again in those silly bed sheets, I'm gonna run you in and throw away the goddamn key. Go!"

The man lowered his gun and the rest, one by one, followed him, shuffling slowly to their parked trucks. "Stupid peckerwoods," the chief muttered.

As they extinguished their torches and started their truck engines, the chief picked up his Panama hat, dusted it off, carefully reshaped it, placed it back on his head, and returned to his patrol car. Gator and the doctor looked at each other and chuckled. "Damn, who knew the chief had it in him," Gator said.

"Who knew," the doctor said.

Chapter 28

Apparently no one had reported to Jewel what had happened the night before on Highway 71 between Port St. Joe and Wewahitchka, so the doctor simply told her that he had talked to Chief Lane and that Reggie was now safely in the county jail. Jewel served the doctor a breakfast of scrambled eggs and cheese grits and poured them both a cup of black coffee and sat down again with the doctor at the kitchen table.

"That's good," Jewel said. "I hope he feels better over there. I've got the word out about this Lucky man bein' somewhere out there around Indian Pass, but I don't have high hopes. There ain't a lot of colored folks who live way out there. Not a lot of any folks, for that matter. Just mosquitoes and gators and lots of swamp."

"What about Gabriel?" the doctor asked, afraid to hear the answer. "What's he up to?"

"He's decided to take your advice, Doc, and head on up there to New York City, so he don't lose his job. Hopefully, they'll let him perform without Reggie. He said rehearsals was to last for the next few weeks and then the first live show was to be broadcast on July ninth. They're gonna give him a few days off around the July fourth weekend, so he plans to find a place to stay while he's up there rehearsin' and then come and get me and Marcus to take back with him before the first show. But I told him whether me and Marcus goes depends on what happens to Reggie. I ain't gonna leave that poor boy in jail all by hisself. All his people are over in Eatonville, so he ain't got nobody but me here to visit him and make sure he's still alive."

"I see," the doctor said. "Well, if we don't find Lucky, then Bob Huggins says Reggie goes to trial on June twenty-eighth. I don't expect it'll last too long, so we should know by the time Gabriel returns what's gonna happen to him."

"What do you think, Doc? Will they 'lectrocute him?

"Good question. Bob says they have no hard evidence against Reggie—it's all circumstantial—but, as Reggie pointed out, he's colored and that doesn't bode well, especially in this part of the country. Judge Denton will be presiding, and he's up for re-election in November, so he won't want to look soft on crime, or on colored folks, for that matter. Bob's a good lawyer, but there's never been a Negro put on a jury in Gulf County in the history of Gulf County, so he'll have to convince twelve white jurors that there's not enough evidence to convict him."

"I don't like it," Jewel said. "Not atall."

"Me either. It doesn't look good."

"Well, thanks anyway, for you and Gator helpin' out the chief last night. Looks like you two managed to squeak out of another one."

"But, how . . . ?"

"Makes no never mind, Doc," Jewel said. "But, you must know by now that I'm always watchin' out for y'all. So, just so y'all know, assuming me and Marcus do go with Gabriel, I'm gonna start lookin' for a replacement for me, so there'll be someone to keep lookin' after you when I'm gone."

The doctor had not yet contemplated this. He couldn't imagine a life without Jewel and had therefore pretty much ignored the possibility. But now it looked like he was going to have to face the inevitable, but he sure didn't want to, not this morning, not tomorrow morning, not ever.

"Jewel," he said, wiping his mouth and throwing his napkin down on the table, "I'm not gonna deal with that right now. If you want to do that, it's up to you, but I'm just not gonna deal with it."

With that, he grabbed his black bag and stalked out the back door. He didn't purposely slam the screen door behind him, but it did somehow bang emphatically shut as he descended the stairs, like an exclamation point on their brief conversation. He didn't care. He shouldn't want Jewel to feel bad about leaving him, but he did.

Nadyne laid out the day for the doctor, and then he repaired to his office to await his first patient. He knew he was being childish by being angry with Jewel. He had previously given her his blessings for the move, after all. And she certainly deserved to be happy by being with man she loved and Marcus's father. The truth was, the doctor realized, he was jealous. It wasn't just that he'd miss her cooking and cleaning, although he would, but more than that he would miss her company and companionship. Thinking about it now, he understood that he had been taking for granted for the last three years a relationship that had developed into something very much like a marriage, without the sex. There was an old joke about there not being any sex in marriage anyway, but he couldn't remember it. And now Jewel was seeking a "divorce" to be with another man, and the doctor would, for the first time in a very long time, be alone. All alone.

After he had finished his morning appointments and taken his midday dose of morphine, Nadyne tapped on his door.

"Come on in," the doctor said, stashing the morphine bottle in the back of the top, left-hand desk drawer.

"Doctor," Nadyne said as she stuck her head in the doorway, "Albert Cunningham just arrived on his bicycle and says he would like to see you."

"Send him in."

Albert Cunningham was still dirty and smelly in his tattered overalls and stained undershirt, but his skin color had returned, and he looked alert and healthy, although a bit disconcerted in the sterile white confines of the doctor's cramped office.

"Please sit down, Mr. Cunningham. How are you feeling?"

"Much better," he answered. "As soon as I can, I'll pay you. I find many treasures along the side of the road. Is there anything from there that you might want?"

"Well, not that I can think of, off hand, but if I lose a hubcap or muffler or anything like that, I'll let you know."

"Okay," Albert Cunningham said, extending his right hand across the desk to the doctor, "it's a deal. You tell me what you want, and I'll find it, just like I found that white panel truck you been lookin' for, that is if it's got a busted headlight."

The doctor recalled the rainy night on the road to Wewahitchka when he had shot the headlight out of what he thought was Lucky Lucilla's white panel truck. "Where?" the doctor asked. "Where is it?"

"In a barn, an old abandoned barn not more than a couple of miles from my place."

"Did you see any sign of the man who owns it, the tall, curly-haired man?"

"No," Cunningham said, "but I'll keep lookin' if you want me to."

"No, that won't be necessary, Mr. Cunningham. This man may be dangerous, so I'm gonna have the police help me find him. Now tell me exactly where you found his truck, okay?"

"Sure, okay, it's down the second dirt road past the road I'm on, right off of Sand Bar Road, toward the bay. You gotta look really hard off to yo' left about a half mile down, cause it's all covered in vines and such."

"Thank you, Mr. Cunningham," the doctor said. "Thank you so much."

"Sure, Doc, just let me know what you lookin' for," Cunningham said, as he stood and smiled and shook the doctor's hand once again, "I'll find it, sure as shootin'."

As soon as the man was gone, the doctor quickly phoned Chief Lane and told him what Cunningham had reported. "I know Indian Pass isn't in your jurisdiction, Chief," the doctor said, "but the last time I called Deputy Roberts about this, he brushed me off. I really think we have a chance of catching this man Lucky now that we've located his truck if we mount a coordinated search. If you could use your influence on him, I'd be much obliged."

"Well, I'll give him a call and do what I can, but in the end it's up to him."

"I know, Chief, but I really don't want to go after him by myself. The last time Gator and I tried that, we about got ourselves killed. To be honest with you, I would feel better if you would help us find him even if it's not in your jurisdiction. I don't want to be presumptuous here, but if you offered to help Roberts and his men, maybe he would agree."

"I'll talk to him and get back to you," the chief said. "Oh, by the way, thanks to you and Gator for helping me out last night. I guess I do owe you one."

"Oh, I don't know about that, Chief. I have a feeling that you would have handled it pretty well without us."

"Maybe."

The doctor then phoned Jewel and asked her if she could stay around that evening so he could discuss all this with her. He next ate dinner at the Black Cat Café—pork loin, mashed potatoes, and creamed corn— and then rushed through his afternoon house calls so he could get home to Jewel. When he had returned to his office, Nadyne said that Chief Lane had phoned and asked him to call back when he returned.

"Okay, here's the story," the chief said when Edna had connected them. "Mel Roberts and two of his deputies will join you and me on a search of the area where Cunningham found the panel truck. We'll meet at one o'clock tomorrow afternoon at the Indian Pass Raw Bar, and you can lead us to the barn where the truck is. Neither Roberts or I know that area very well, so we'll need your help. If we could find Cunningham that might help too. Gator Mica. Anyone who knows their way around out there. Because we're gonna divide up. You and me will stake out the barn where the truck is. The deputy and his two men will begin searching in their three cars. The idea being, if this man Lucky sees them looking for him, he'll most likely make a break for his truck, at which point we'll nab him."

"Okay, Chief, sounds like a plan. Thanks for dealing with Roberts. The only problem I see is that there's just a lot of dense marsh, swampland, and forest out there for this guy to hide in. I just hope the five of us can root him out, if he is, in fact, there."

"Well, you've convinced Roberts and me it's worth wasting an afternoon on, so that's about the best we can do, I think."

"See you at one."

Jewel and Marcus were waiting for the doctor on his screened-in back porch. Marcus was reading a book, and Jewel was snapping pole beans into a large, porcelain bowl. "Marcus, go set the table," Jewel ordered when the doctor had sat down next to her in one of the white wicker chairs. Then the doctor told her all about his conversations with Albert Cunningham and Chief Lane.

"Well, that sounds pretty encouraging, don't you think? At least we got a plan now to capture the nut," she said when the doctor had finished.

"Yeah, I think it's the best we can hope for under the circumstances. They're expending considerable manpower to help a Negro, but I'm still not sure it's enough. There's just so much wilderness out there, and I bet this Lucky is more familiar with it than we are. I can see him slipping away from us pretty easily, if in fact he's really out there. But I don't know what else to do. As my mother used to say, 'One must do everything one can and then say 'God have mercy!' "

"Well," Jewel replied. "I think you done pretty damn good, Doc. Let me see if I can round up Gator and Albert Cunningham and anyone else who might know the area in the morning. I'll jump on it like a duck on a June bug. Meanwhile, I got a rabbit that Albert Cunningham brought by roastin' in the oven and some biscuits to go with these here pole beans. Sound good?"

"Sounds mighty good," the doctor said, although he was thinking about where Albert Cunningham found most of his gifts and decided he might dine sparingly on the rabbit.

Chapter 29

The doctor could not understand why, in the middle of the day, the parking lot of the Indian Pass Raw Bar was filled when he arrived there at one o'clock the next day. There were even cars parked in the ditches on both sides of Sand Bar Road near the roadhouse. Leaning on fenders, lounging on running boards, sitting in the front car seats with doors open, and huddled in small groups were at least a hundred Negro men and women. Some were eating sandwiches wrapped in waxed paper, fried chicken in greasy napkins, or pickled pigs' feet from large, unmarked jars. Others were smoking cigarettes or drinking from jars enclosed in brown paper bags.

The doctor parked in a ditch about a quarter mile from the Raw Bar and started hiking towards it. The people nodded and said hello as he passed. Some he knew by name, others looked vaguely familiar, and a few he was sure he had never seen before in his life. He found Jewel near the front door of the roadhouse, looking pretty as usual in a freshly starched white summer dress. Next to her stood Gabriel White in his gray Fedora, bib overalls and starched white shirt. And there too were the less nattily-attired Gator Mica and Albert Cunningham, standing next to his rusty bicycle.

"Jewel," the doctor said, "do you mind telling me exactly what the hell is going on here. It looks like an A.M.E. church picnic."

"Well, not exactly," she answered. "You said we had a lot of land to cover, so I thought we might need some help."

"Yes, but . . ."

"Don't worry, partner," Gator interrupted. "Albert and me will tell 'em where to look. Between the two of us we know every abandoned shed, shack, and shanty around this here part of the country. We'll find the son of a bitch, don't you worry."

"Gabriel," the doctor said. "I thought you were on your way to New York City."

"Well, not quite yet. I thought I would delay it one more day. See what I could do to help out here."

"Has anybody seen Chief Lane or Deputy Roberts?"

No one answered, but in a few minutes, Chief Lane pulled up in his black and white Port St. Joe Police squad car and parked it in the middle of Sadie McIntire's front yard. The old lady who owned and operated the Indian Pass Raw Bar lived alone here next door in a square, white cottage surrounded by a thick patch of coralbean. The chief too knew most of the people in the crowd who pointed him toward the doctor at the roadhouse door. "Rounded up some help, I see," he said to the doctor.

"Yes, it appears so," the doctor said. "It looks like Jewel may have gotten a little carried away."

"Well, we'll see about that. Where's Roberts?"

And then, as if on cue, the three black Gulf County patrol cars rolled up and parked next to the chief's car, at which point Sadie McIntire, dressed in a faded blue house coat, her gray hair in a tangled mess, a cigarette dangling from her lips, opened her front door and marched over to the toad and demanded an explanation. The deputy shook his head, ignoring her, and he and his two companions were directed by the people in the crowd to the doctor and Chief Lane at the front door. "Okay," he huffed, as he stepped onto the porch, his belly bursting out in front of him, "what the hell is going on here?"

"Apparently my housekeeper, Miss Jackson—here she is—decided we needed some help."

"I hope it's not too much. I just made a couple of telephone calls. I wasn't expectin' all this," Jewel said sweetly, raising her arm to take in the crowd.

"I'll be damn," the toad said to no one in particular. "Whatta we do now?"

"I believe my friend, Gator Mica, who lives near here, has a plan," the doctor said. "Gator, come over here, willya, and bring Mr. Cunningham with you. This is Gator Mica, who resides on the other side of that hammock over there, and this other gentleman is Albert Cunningham, who lives down the road a piece and knows this area well enough to locate a missing man's panel truck within a matter of hours. They'll tell us where to look."

The toad and his deputies looked at Gator and Cunningham, who were both dressed in their usual dirty bib overalls that may have been washed sometime in the past year, may have, and dingy, once-white undershirts. Gator wore an old straw cowboy hat that had more holes in it than a Tarpon Springs sponge, and Cunningham's matted black hair hung to his shoulders in unruly, dandruff-flecked locks. "These are the men who are going to lead our search?" you could almost hear the deputies thinking.

"Okay," Chief Lane said, "Let's hear what you have to say."

"Gator," the doctor prompted, "he's talking to you."

"Uh, okay," Gator stammered, not being used to addressing this many people, particularly not uniformed, police-type people. "Let's put a couple of men at Lucky's panel truck. The idea is, as I understand it from Jewel, is for the rest of us to flush him out so that he runs to his truck to escape. Then we grab him or shoot him or something."

"I'll take the doctor and Mr. Cunningham in my car," Chief Lane volunteered.

"Then everybody else," Gator continued, "will follow me behind my truck. I will point down the roads where I want each car to go. Each car should drive down the road and search every shack, cabin, barn, shed they find. They're all s'posed to be abandoned so they shouldn't find any people. But if they do, they should bring 'em back here for the sheriff, the deputy, to question. If they resist, then get the hell out of there and come back and get a deputy. With all these people, we should be able to cover a lot of land quickly."

"Let's put Deputy Roberts here at the Raw Bar to coordinate activities," Chief Lane suggested. "If someone finds someone out there, bring 'em back to him, like Gator says. If they won't come back with you, then come and get Mr. Roberts. The other two deputies can follow me. Mr. Cunningham will point out roads where there are buildings near the barn where they can search. These are the most likely spots, near the barn, that he might be, so I want you men with guns searching them."

"One more thing," the doctor said. "This is not a game. Everybody must be warned to be careful. This man is armed and dangerous." The doctor had always wanted to say that.

"Who's telling all these people this stuff?" Jewel asked.

"It should be Deputy Roberts," Chief Lane said. "This is his jurisdiction, and he should be in charge. Mr. Roberts."

Deputy Roberts suddenly jerked to attention and instructed one of his men to bring him a bull horn from his squad car, and then he stood at the edge the Raw Bar's front porch and told everyone what to do. As the toad's instructions echoed across the parking lot and Sand Bar Road—"Remember, this ain't a game. So be careful. This man is armed and dangerous . . ."—the doctor just hoped that Lucky Lucilla wasn't so close that he could hear every word the toad was bellowing, which at this point wouldn't surprise him one bit.

Everyone headed for their cars, and Sadie McIntire, still in her house coat, walked across her front lawn and stopped the doctor as he was returning from his car with his shotgun under his arm. "Be careful," she said. "I just called some folks who work for us and asked them to come in early. We normally don't open till five, but we'll try to open earlier today for those of you who's hungry."

"All of us?" the doctor asked.

"Yes, all of y'all"

"Even the colored folks?"

"Yep, even the colored folks," the old lady replied, as she wrapped her old house coat tighter around her ample waist, tossed her cigarette on the ground, and hurried back to her house.

The doctor sat in the front seat next to Chief Lane and Albert Cunningham sat in the back. As they were backing out of Sadie McIntire's front yard, a new black Plymouth pickup truck pulled up next to them. Behind its wheel sat Jed Washington, his right hand on the steering wheel and the other still in a sling. "Good afternoon," he yelled. "Welcome to Indian Pass."

"Thank you, Mr. Washington," the doctor shouted back. "What are you doing here?"

"Gator told me what was going on. I just drove up from the boat launch—we keep this truck over here on the mainland—to let you know that I'll be patrolling Indian Pass in our Chris Craft. If this man tries to escape by sea, I'll get him."

"Thanks, Mr. Washington," the doctor said. "I never thought about that. Why don't you join us later at the Indian Pass Raw Bar. The owner's gonna open it for us."

"For us?" Washington asked.

"Yes," the doctor answered, "for all of us."

"Well, I'll be," he muttered, as he turned the truck around and drove back toward the pass.

The doctor asked the chief to stop at Jewel's car, and he told her that the Raw Bar would be open to them all later this afternoon and asked her to spread the word. Then Cunningham directed the chief to the old barn. Just as Cunningham had reported, the barn was about half a mile down a narrow dirt road off of Sand Bar Road, not more than a couple of miles from the Raw Bar. At first, the doctor could not even tell a barn was there; it was completely covered by a thick, tangled mass of green vines: grape, passion flower, poison ivy, Virginia creeper, and greenbrier. "How on earth did you find this place?" the doctor asked Cunningham.

"I used to work in this barn," he said, "many years ago. Before the Depression, before duPont. To you it looks like a vine-covered hammock, but to me it looks like home."

"What did you do in there?" the doctor asked.

"Bit of everything, mostly store farm equipment for growing sugar cane, some rice, watermelon . . ."

They slid the barn's big, weathered door open, and, sure enough, there it stood: the worn, white panel truck that was presumably owned by Lucky Lucilla, dirty and dented, facing toward the door, with its shattered headlight that the doctor had shot out, hanging limply from its right front fender by a few thin black wires. The chief pulled out his pistol as the door opened and the sunlight shone in. The interior was damp and dark. They searched inside and under the truck, but there were no clues, only a bald spare tire and an old jack in the back of the truck. The single-room barn too was nearly empty: a rotting bale of hay in one corner, a rusted shovel with a broken handle against the wall, a beat-up, old circular hay rake on the back wall.

There was only the one door in the barn, so they closed it, leaving it like they had found it, and drove back up the road to a grove of scrub oak, where they could hide the squad car, out of sight from the barn and the road. Then they hiked back to the barn and found a high palmetto thicket on a little hammock that they could hide behind. From there they could see the barn's door and anyone approaching on the road or across a flat, fallow field, now grown over with marsh grass. The men rolled down their sleeves and buttoned up against the mosquitoes the best they could. The doctor had thought to bring along a bottle of DMP which he passed around. He hoped their wait would not be long, because the DMP was only slightly effective and the usual heat and humidity was oppressive and getting more so as the afternoon progressed.

Albert Cunningham had apparently reached his communication limits and sat silently. The chief, usually talkative, slapped at the mosquitoes with his Panama hat without speaking. The doctor didn't want Lucky Lucilla to hear anything if and when he approached, so he too was quiet. The mosquitoes and flies buzzing about their faces, the cry of a gull above, the rustle of the salt marsh in the sea breeze were the only sounds they heard, as they sat waiting.

Chapter 30

The doctor was tired of lamenting the loss of Sally Martin, tired of being angry with Jewel for leaving him, tired of the pain in his side, and tired of swatting the mosquitoes that kept him from getting a decent nap. He had decided that they were never going to find Lucky Lucilla, so he might as well get some sleep.

Therefore, he thought he must be dreaming when he saw him: tall, lean, and curly-haired, sprinting through the fallow field toward the barn, as fleet as a frightened deer, the elusive Anthony Lorenzo "Lucky" Lucilla. The doctor raised his shotgun and saw out of the corner of his right eye that the chief was already drawing a bead on him with his pistol.

"Hold it!" Chief Lane shouted. But the man continued, now at the barn door, trying to slide it open. "Stop! Don't move or we'll shoot!" the chief warned again, but the man now had the door all the way open.

They fired almost in unison just as the man started into the barn. He dropped immediately, and the three of them rushed toward him, not more than twenty yards away. They fought their way through the brambles, the doctor with his shotgun in one hand and his black bag in the other, and found the young man slumped there against the side of the barn, unconscious, bleeding profusely from the upper chest, just under his chin, the front of his shirt now wet and red in the late afternoon sun.

Chief Lane pushed the doctor away and patted the man down, checking for weapons. When he was satisfied that there were none, he said, "He's all yours, Doc. He's not armed."

The doctor ripped off Lucilla's bloody shirt and felt his heart. It was still beating, pumping blood fiercely onto his thin chest from an uneven pattern of buckshot wounds that had been delivered by the doctor's shotgun. The doctor gave his entire body a cursive, visual search and then saw the larger, bleeding hole farther down on his chest where the chief's bullet had entered. There was no exit wound in his back, so the bullet must still be in there somewhere. The doctor began cleaning, first the bullet hole, then the buckshot tears from the shoulders down, with alcohol, mercurochrome, and big wads of gauze, as the chief stood watching with his pistol aimed at Lucilla's head and Cunningham, standing behind the chief, staring in disbelief.

As the doctor was raising him up to wrap a bandage around his torso, his patient's torpid eyes opened and looked into the doctor's. There was indeed something eerie and vacant in those eyes, just as Dr. Price and Sadie McIntire had reported. Or it might have been just the shock of being shot and the resulting loss of blood. The doctor kept working, wrapping the bandage tightly to stop the bleeding. "How are you feeling?" the doctor asked him.

"Not too good," Lucilla panted, his voice leaden and remote.

When the doctor had finished his bandaging and propped the bleeding man against the side of the barn, he stood up and pulled the chief aside. "Chief," he whispered, "I think now would be a good time to ask this man any questions you have. He's lost a lot of blood and will likely pass out again soon. But make it quick, because we need to get him to the hospital in Panama City as fast as we can. I believe that he'll be okay now that I've slowed the bleeding, but I can't be sure. We need to get that buckshot and bullet out and make sure there isn't too much internal damage. If there is, this may be your last chance to question him."

"Okay," Chief Lane said. "Hold this gun on him while I talk to him. It's cocked, loaded, and ready to go. All you have to do is pull the trigger."

The chief knelt down next to the man. "Can you tell me your name?" he asked. The man looked up at him, decidedly confused and groggy.

"Lucilla," he finally muttered.

"Look," the chief continued, "we need to get you to a hospital if you're gonna live, but I'm not radioing for an ambulance until you answer a couple of questions, okay?"

Lucilla peered at the chief with those lost, inscrutable eyes as if the policeman were an anomalous, alien apparition. Finally, Chief Lane said, "Look, Lucilla, you either answer my questions or you bleed to death. I don't care which. I've got all night. The doctor here wants to save your life, but I don't particularly care, so just let me know when you're ready."

Their prisoner, the man who had apparently wreaked so much death and havoc during the past few weeks, now looked very young and vulnerable slumped there against the rough boards and tangled vines on the side of the barn. He was dazed, his breathing labored, and his eyes, glazed and unfocused.

"Look," Chief Lane tried again, "if you cooperate and answer my questions, I'll see that you get a fair shake. I'll tell the court that you cooperated and don't deserve the electric chair. But if you don't answer me, I'm just gonna let you lie here and bleed to death. It's your choice."

Lucilla looked down at the blood darkening the bandages on his chest. "Okay," he muttered.

"Did you kill Earl Martin? Martin, the assistant lighthouse keeper?

Lucilla did not respond. His eyes closed and his chin dropped limp against his bandaged chest.

"Lucilla!" Chief Lane barked.

Lucilla slightly opened his eyes and squinted up at the chief, who was now leaning within inches of his prisoner's ear. "Martin. Did you kill him?"

"Uh-huh."

"Why?"

"I was hired."

"By who?"

"The sheriff."

"The sheriff? Sheriff Batson? Are you sure? But why?

"Donno."

"What about the sheriff, did you kill him too?"

"Yeah, I did."

"But why?"

"I was hired."

"But by who?"

"Mitchell."

"Mitchell? Mitchell who?"

"Mitchell at the mill."

"You mean Mike Mitchell, the head man at the St. Joe Paper Mill?"

"Uh-huh."

"But why?"

"The sheriff was trying to collect evidence that the mill was poisoning fish in the bay."

"But how did Mitchell find you?"

Lucilla slumped over again, his body contorting at an odd angle against the barn. A strange sound, a mixture of coughing, crying, and cackling, came, with a thin stream of blood, from his mouth.

"Mitchell," the chief demanded. "Why did he hire *you?*"

"Well," Lucilla uttered with a creepy snicker, "the sheriff recommended me to him to go after some union organizers. . . ."

"So you're responsible for all these assaults on those union men out there?"

"Well, actually, Mitchell is," Lucilla corrected. "He wanted to make an example of that man in the vat. Figured if he got rid of him, that would put an end to all that union talk, but . . ."

"What about Winn, Harvey Winn, the head lighthouse keeper, did you kill him too?"

"No, not me."

"And the doctor here. You're the one who's been trying to kill him."

"Well, nothing personal, Doctor. It's just that you wouldn't give up."

"Well, I'll be damn," Chief Lane said, as Lucilla closed his eyes and crumbled into an unconscious ball. "I'll be goddamned."

"I think you better radio for that ambulance now," the doctor suggested, "if it's not too late."

"Okay," the chief said. "Hold my gun on him till I get back. If he tries anything funny, shoot him. I'm gonna hike back to my car. I'll radio for an ambulance and radio the dispatcher to notify everyone else, Roberts and his men and Judge Denton, that we've got our man and they can release Reggie Robinson."

Albert Cunningham was looking a bit pale now, so he took the opportunity to walk back to the car with the chief, so he wouldn't have to see any more blood, the doctor guessed. The doctor had a bottle of water in his black bag and he offered it to Lucilla. He opened his eyes, took the bottle, and, between sharp wheezes, gulped down most of it.

"Mr. Lucilla," the doctor said, as he knelt back down beside him, "I know this may not be the best time, but I've got a couple of more questions."

"Yeah?"

"Why the note to Sally Martin, demanding two thousand dollars?"

"Can you keep a secret?"

"Sure."

"Because I'm not telling anybody about Sally's involvement in this, so you need to continue keeping your mouth shut too, okay?"

"Okay."

"Well, that letter. That was for your benefit, to make you believe Martin had really arranged his own death, not her or the sheriff."

"And the sheriff's head?"

Lucilla coughed up more blood that dribbled unevenly down his chin. "Do you know the story of Salome?" he finally asked.

"Yes, vaguely. Wasn't she the one who did the dance of the seven veils?"

"Uh-hm, yeah, a real beauty, that one, a charmer. She charmed her stepfather with her dancing so much that he offered to give her any gift she wanted. And do you remember what she asked for?"

"Yes," the doctor whispered.

"That's right, Doctor, a head. The head of John the Baptist, who her stepfather was holding in prison."

"And that's what she got, as I recall. But . . . I still don't follow?"

"You see," Lucilla murmured, "Sally saw herself as Salome, probably still does, I wouldn't be surprised. She thought she could use her feminine wiles to get whatever she wanted. Anyway, I asked her after I killed her husband, if there was anything else I could do for her. At first she said no, but, as time went on, she said yes, and then told me the story of Salome."

"And you granted her request for a gift, right?"

"Yes, a gift. She wanted the sheriff's head."

"So you delivered it?"

"I did, and she was very happy, but she wanted more."

"More?"

"Yeah, to implicate you in the sheriff's death. She thought you knew too much."

"So she gave me his head?"

"Yeah, she told me to deliver it to you and make an anonymous phone call to Chief Lane."

"Which you did?"

"I love her."

"So what did Chief Lane say when you called?"

"He laughed."

"Laughed?"

"Yeah, had a really good laugh about it. I just hung up and that's the last I heard of it."

Lucilla then groaned an odd snort and fainted again, his frail body bleeding silently into the sand. The doctor stared at him, lying there helplessly before him, his bandaged chest heaving unevenly. So this was the end, the end of Lucky Lucilla's strange reign of terror on their previously sleepy little village by the bay.

But before the doctor had a chance to digest all this, the chief was back with Albert Cunningham. "Still out cold?" the chief asked, pointing to their prisoner.

"Yeah, still passed out," the doctor answered, peering at his assailant, collapsed on the ground before them.

"Well, I radioed our dispatcher and had her patch me through to Judge Denton. He wasn't too keen on releasing your friend Reggie, but I told him, with Bob Huggins as his lawyer, he might be in more trouble if he continued to hold him—false arrest, false imprisonment, all that— than he would be if we just quietly let him go. Not good publicity in an election year. I advised him that the sooner we arrested the right guy, even if he was white, the better off we'd all be. I told him we'd all be heroes for bringing in the man who not only killed the sheriff, but also the assistant lighthouse keeper, as well as assaulting all those union people. He said he'd radio Roberts and tell him to release Robinson. But, just between you and me, let's not waste any time here. I'll officially arrest Lucilla, but I need you to get this colored boy out of town as fast as you can, just in case some of our local rednecks don't entirely agree with the judge."

"Okay."

They waited there in the gathering darkness for the ambulance, the chief standing over Lucky Lucilla with his pistol at the ready, the doctor and Albert Cunningham sitting in the sand, next to the fallen killer, with their backs against the side of the barn.

"Well," the chief said, "it looks like you were right all along, Doc. This is the man who's been terrorizing us for the last couple of months. It all seems to make sense now, except I don't understand why the sheriff would hire him in the first place to kill the assistant lighthouse keeper."

"Beats me," the doctor said.

"And what about Harvey Winn? How did he end up in the bay?"

"Brakes," the doctor answered.

"Brakes?"

"The brakes were bad on his car."

"Oh," the chief replied, apparently satisfied.

When the ambulance finally arrived, they rolled Lucky Lucilla onto a stretcher and raised it into the back of the ambulance and then the chief hopped in with him. "I'm not taking any chances," he said with his gun aimed at Lucilla. "I'm arresting this man and goin' all the way to Panama City, and when I get there I'm gonna make sure he's under police watch twenty-four hours a day until we send him to the electric chair or back to the insane asylum. Doctor, please drive Mr. Cunningham back to the Indian Pass Raw Bar in my car, and then see that he gets home safely. And thanks for your help, sir. You can leave my car at the Raw Bar. Give the keys to Sadie McIntire and I'll pick it up when I can. Goodnight, gentlemen." And with that he tossed the car keys to the doctor, slammed the ambulance's door shut, and the doctor and Albert Cunningham watched the red and white van roar off into the night, siren wailing.

Chapter 31

The doctor could hear the commotion from the Indian Pass Raw Bar before he could see it. When he did see it, the parking lot was again packed, so, taking a cue from Chief Lane, he parked his cruiser on Sadie McIntire's front lawn, took his shotgun and put it under the seat of his own car, and walked with Albert Cunningham to the roadhouse. When they entered the front door, they were met with a thunderous roar. The place was packed with the impromptu search party, except for the toad and his two men, who, according to Gator, were already headed back to Wewa to release Reggie Robinson. Gabriel White was following behind in his bright red Cadillac to bring Reggie back. And Jewel was holding court in a back corner table, explaining to everyone around it how they had tracked down the real murderer.

As Fats Waller pounded out "The Joint Is Jumpin' " on the juke box, the doctor made his way through the back-slapping, beer-drinking crowd to Sadie McIntire, puffing on a cigarette behind her old cash register. "Here're the keys to Chief Lane's patrol car," he shouted above the din of the crowd. "He'll be back later to pick it up."

As the old woman took the keys, the doctor eased closer and asked, "By the way, Mrs. McIntire, I have a question for you."

"Yeah?"

"Why'd you invite all these folks in here tonight?"

"You know, Doc, I'm not sure. I've worked with Negroes most every day of my long life. They raised me from a little baby. They've cooked my food. They've cleaned my house. They've raised my kids for me. And these folks, well, they looked hungry and thirsty this afternoon. The least I could do is help them out a little after all they done for me. Not to mention y'all catchin' that eye-talian nut Lucilla, so's I don't have to worry no more about him."

"Thanks, Mrs. McIntire, I'm sure it's appreciated."

The doctor wanted Sadie McIntire's motives to be as she claimed, but he could not help thinking that this new found magnanimity might have more to do with the evident opportunity for her to pad her profits for the night than any sudden surge of sympathy. Whatever the case, the crowd seemed to be having fun and Sadie McIntire, regardless of her motives, was proving to be a gracious hostess to a group who heretofore had been banned completely from her rural roadhouse.

Gator and Jed Washington were sitting at the bar, but a pretty, blond waitress, dressed in a tight, low-cut blue dress cleared a table near the back wall for them and the doctor and Albert Cunningham. They ordered food and drinks from the flirty waitress who seemed to enjoy their attention. After Gator had complimented her on her freckles—"A face without freckles is like a night without stars"—she said, "Y'all the funnest bunch of people we've ever had in here."

The doctor had to agree, at least from his limited experience. This was a lot more fun than sitting around with a bunch of boring old white men drinking beer and getting drunk. Soon their table top was filled with large tin trays of oysters and bottles of beer. The doctor, Gator, and Washington reminisced about their recent adventures on St. Vincent Island, which were a lot more entertaining in retrospect than they were in reality, while Albert Cunningham sat quietly eating and drinking. Every once in a while, the doctor noticed that a white face would appear at the front door and then quickly disappear into the night.

At around nine o'clock, Gabriel and Reggie showed up. They received a hearty round of applause and all the free beer they could drink. They slowly made their way through the noisy crowd to the doctor's table. Reggie still looked thin, wrinkled, and bedraggled, but besides his dirty pin-striped suit, he also wore a wide, toothy grin and a relieved look on his ashen face. "Thank you, Doctor," he said. "Thanks for everything."

"You're very much welcome, Reggie. I'm sorry it took so long, but thanks to Mr. Cunningham here, we were able to pull it off. Of course, we had a lot of help. Gator here for one, and Jed Washington too, and Jewel and Gabriel, and of course all these other people here. They all helped."

"Thank y'all," Reggie said.

And then, after Reggie and Gabriel had eaten supper and accepted several rounds of free drinks, Jewel and some of her friends coaxed them into fetching their instruments from the trunk of Gabriel's car. Their cute waitress and Gator found some empty oyster crates in the back of the building, and they set up a backshift bandstand on the back wall. When the juke box was unplugged, the duo sat on a couple of bar stools on the narrow platform and launched into a well-rehearsed set of straight ahead blues. There was no nod to pop music tonight with this crowd; they were playing the blues and nothing but the blues.

And as the music grew louder and faster and more intense, people pushed some tables to the wall and began to dance. Gator broke out a box of Partagas cigars and passed them around. The doctor could not remember the last time he had been to a dance, probably somewhere with Annie way back when, and he sure didn't remember the wild gyrations of these couples, who were doing something erotic and exotic called the jitterbug that he thoroughly enjoyed watching.

It didn't take long before some of the single ladies led everyone at the doctor's table out to the crowded dance floor for a spin. None of the four were any good, except for Cunningham who seemed to possess more rhythmic sense than all the others combined, but they all had fun.

Gabriel and Reggie were much louder and animated than they ever were on the doctor's back porch, and he could now understand why they were so popular. They shifted seamlessly without stopping from one song to the next and kept the strong beat going so that people would continue to dance to songs like "Boogie Woogie Guitar," "Good-Time Papa," "Hold Me Baby," "They're Red Hot," and "Drunken Hearted Man." At some point, Reggie put down his guitar, produced a pair of drumsticks and an empty five-gallon lard can and began beating its bottom in an increasingly raging rhythm. He also connected a funny-looking, wire contraption around his neck that held a harmonica and allowed him to play it without using his hands. Gabriel had to really wail to be heard above Reggie's beat and the partying of the crowd. He strummed his guitar so violently on one song that he broke a string, but he just kept right on playing.

Finally, after they had about worn themselves, and the dancers, out, they sang a slow blues called "Cold Love" and took a break. It was past midnight by now and the doctor was tired and more than a little drunk. He said goodnight to Gabriel and Reggie and wished them good luck in the big city. He shook Jed Washington's hand and asked him to pay his respects to Dr. Price. He shook awake Gator, who had passed out face down on the table, fed him a cup of coffee, and asked him to put Albert Cunningham's bicycle in the back of his truck and take it and its owner home. Then, feeling tired and sentimental and emboldened by all the beer, he found Jewel and gave her a big hug and a kiss on the cheek goodnight, and drove home.

Chapter 32

The doctor awoke from a bizarre dream in which his third wife Jenny had replaced Jewel as his housekeeper. In the dream, she was just as beautiful and temperamental as she was in real life. He was arguing with her about his morphine habit when he was awakened and relieved by the sound of Jewel, he hoped, downstairs in the kitchen. The doctor looked at the clock and was surprised and pleased to hear her at her usual time preparing breakfast. He reached for the small brown bottle on his bedside table and poured the morphine into the waiting glass of water. He would never get used to its bitterness, but it was a small price to pay for the pleasant, numbing, familiar feeling of lightness that he had now come to depend on so much each day.

The doctor had tried to hide his addiction from Jenny, but she had caught him sipping the drug one night before he went to bed. They had had a terrible row. She had accused him of keeping secrets and being irresponsible in his dependency. He had apologized for his secrecy, but explained that he was only trying to protect her and simply needed to salve the arthritic and old-age aches that had grown so painful over the years. Then, at her insistence, he had tried to stop, but found that he could not. He loved her, but the truth was he loved the drug more, and she knew it.

"What are you doing here so early?" the doctor asked Jewel as he sat down at the kitchen table. She looked as radiant as ever, he thought, despite the late night and lack of sleep.

"Fixin' you breakfast, as usual," she said. "Here, enjoy it. The porch was packed this mornin'. We got food enough to last us a week. Look at this here melon, sweet and juicy. And this fatback bacon, Lord! These eggs so fresh they was warm to the touch when I picked them up off the porch, and so big, I swear, it'd take only four to make a dozen."

"Hmm, looks awfully good. Hope it cures a hangover."

"Can't hurt, but, at any rate, there's an aspirin there next to your plate, as well as a big glass of orange juice and a cup of black coffee."

"Thanks, Jewel. What did I miss after I left last night?"

"Oh, not much. Everybody was pretty tired after dancin' around all night like they was a chicken on a hot stove, so most everybody went home not too long after you left. Reggie was just completely worn out. If he hadn't been so tired and it hadn't been a week night, they'd still be partyin' though."

"How about Gabriel and Reggie? Did they take off yet?"

"Yep, I fed 'em breakfast, packed 'em a lunch, and sent 'em on their way already this morning."

"Good, I'm glad we got Reggie out of jail and out of town before somebody began having second thoughts."

"Yeah, me too. I'm gonna miss 'em, but it's for the best. But tell me, Doc, I'm dyin' to hear what all Lucky Lucilla told y'all. I didn't git a chance to ask you last night, and all the deputy said was that he had confessed and that Reggie could go free."

"Well, he told the chief what he had done, but he blamed it on the sheriff and Mitchell. Said the sheriff had hired him to kill Martin, the assistant lighthouse keeper, and that Mitchell, the big boss at the new paper mill, had hired him to scare off the union organizers and to kill the sheriff, who was trying to prove they were polluting the bay. Never said a word about who was really responsible."

"Who?"

"Well, after the chief had left to radio everyone, then Lucilla told me the truth, that Sally Martin had hired him to kill both her husband and the sheriff. Asked me to keep it a secret. He said he loved Sally."

"But why?"

"Why did he love her?"

"No," Jewel said, "why did Sally have this nut kill her husband and the sheriff?"

"Money, of course. It's always money, or sex, isn't it? This time some of both. Sally upped her husband's insurance amount and conspired with the sheriff, who she'd been shacking up with behind her husband's back, to kill her husband. The sheriff hired Lucky Lucilla to do it and he did."

"But what about the sheriff? Why'd Sally have Lucilla kill him?"

"Money and sex. She didn't want to share the insurance money with the sheriff, especially after she had found out that the sheriff had been beating up on some of our local ladies of the night and was starting to get rough with her."

"Damn," Jewel said, shaking her head. "Whatta we do now?"

"I don't know, Jewel. All I know at this point is that my head hurts, my side hurts, my whole body hurts, and something else inside me hurts. But by now, I'm sort of numb to it all. It seems like a bad dream. If I didn't know better, I'd think it was dementia comin' on, some weird, old-age hallucination."

"Every time you think that, Doc, reach down and feel that hole in your side."

The next Saturday morning the doctor was listening to the radio news of Hitler's recent visit to Rome to meet with Mussolini and his May twenty-eighth conference at the Reichs Chancellery where he had declared his decision to destroy Czechoslovakia by military force. This did not sound good at all. Hitler was obviously a megalomaniac who was determined to take over Europe, and the doctor was afraid he just might pull it off. He turned off the radio in disgust and had just picked up Hemingway's *To Have and Have Not* when Gator's truck slid to a slow stop on the doctor's crushed shell driveway in back.

"How 'bout we do a little fishin' today?" Gator asked, as he bounded up the porch stairs. "It's a beautiful day and I'm bettin' they'll be bitin' out in Depot Creek. Whatta you say?"

It *was* a beautiful day; the doctor could not deny it. And although he was looking forward to a quiet weekend at home and had sworn off fishing with Gator Mica for a while, he just couldn't pass up Gator's offer, not so much for the fishing, but just to get out of town for a while and put some distance between the events of the past few weeks and what little he had to look forward to in the weeks ahead.

So the two drove southeast out of Port St. Joe on Constitution Avenue in Gator's old truck. When Constitution Avenue had changed into Highway 98, about four miles from Port St. Joe, Gator turned off on a dirt road just before a wooden bridge over Depot Creek. At the end of the road, Gator turned the truck around and backed it to the creek's edge. Then the two wrestled the skiff from the back of Gator's truck into the creek. Gator pulled his truck into a pine grove, while the doctor held the floating boat by a hemp rope. The doctor took his usual seat in the bow, as Gator pushed them off and jumped onto his perch in the stern. The recently refurbished hothead sputtered to life on Gator's first pull and they were off down the wide stream which meandered east and then north and then east again, eventually emptying into Lake Wimico, aside which sat the Lake Wimico Cabins, where Sally and Sheriff Batson had done what Sally and the doctor had only once experienced. He remembered that night and blocked as well as he could the vision in his head of Sally and the sheriff in each other's arms.

When Gator spotted a pool to his liking, he guided the boat in, dropped anchor, and they fished. As usual, Gator had brought along the three five-gallon lard buckets. They baited their hooks with crickets from one of the buckets, and then Gator passed out bologna sandwiches and bottles of Spearman beer from the other two. Gator pointed out a napping black alligator as long as their boat on the shore, as a red-shouldered hawk circled high above. The shoreline was sandy and steep at this bend in the creek and covered on its high bank with scrub oak, slash pine, palmetto, and a forbidding tangle of wild vines.

"So, partner," Gator said, as they waited for a bite, "glad this whole business with Lucky Lucilla is over?"

"I guess so."

"What's the problem?"

"Well," the doctor explained. "Reggie is free and that's good. And Lucilla has confessed and that's good too. But when he confessed to Chief Lane, he didn't tell him the truth about who had hired him to kill them. He blamed the keeper's death on the sheriff and the sheriff's death on the head man at the new mill, Mitchell. Said the sheriff had hired him to kill Sally's husband and Mitchell had hired him to kill the sheriff because the sheriff was trying to collect evidence that the mill was polluting the bay."

"So who really did hire him?"

So the doctor explained the whole conspiracy just as he had to Jewel a few days before.

"No shit," Gator exclaimed. "And you ain't told nobody?"

"Right, the only ones who know are you, me, Jewel, and, of course, Lucky Lucilla."

"So whatta we gonna do?

"Beats me," the doctor said.

They continued upstream, stopping wherever Gator thought looked promising. They watched the red-shouldered hawk still gliding high above them. When Gator dropped anchor in a quiet backwater, they saw a pair of river otters slide down the muddy bank and play in a shallow pool. Gator reached for his rifle, but the doctor shook his head. "Let 'em play," he said.

Before the afternoon was over, between them, they had caught two largemouth bass, three bluegill, and one big bullhead. They saved enough for supper and threw the rest back. Then, as the afternoon clouds gathered in the west, they headed back to the doctor's house to clean and cook their catch.

Chapter 33

The hole in his side curtailed his walking to work, at least for a while, so on Monday morning the doctor was back to driving there in his old Ford sedan. Nadyne reviewed the day's schedule with him when he arrived, but stopped when she got to the house calls. She looked up over her wire-rimmed glasses at the doctor. "Uh, this one I don't know about," she said. "A few minutes ago, Sally Martin called and asked if you could stop by to see her. I asked her what was the matter, but all she would say was that she was sick. So I don't know how you want to handle that. I told her I would phone her back after I talked to you."

"What time did you say we were finished with this morning's appointments?"

"Around eleven-thirty, barring no emergencies."

"Call Mrs. Martin and tell her I'll be there at noon. Then I'll do the rest of the house calls afterwards."

"Are you sure, Doc?" Nadyne asked. "If you don't want to face her again, I can handle it."

The doctor thought for a moment. He had never really discussed Sally Martin with Nadyne, but Nadyne seemed to be showing a discerning sensitivity here. It didn't really matter, but there was no way he was going to pass up another chance to talk to the widow. "No, I'll do it, but thanks," he said.

Before he started seeing patients, Bob Huggins called and congratulated the doctor on Lucky Lucilla's capture. "I have to hand it to you, Doc," he said. "I didn't think you had a chance in hell of catching this man, but you not only caught him, but, according to Chief Lane, you got a confession out of him as well."

"Well, it was more the chief's doing than mine."

"Yeah, but you're the one who stuck with it, goin' after this lunatic when no one else wanted to be bothered."

"Tell me, Bob, now that Reggie's free, what were his real chances if he had gone to trial?"

"Not too good, Doc. Not too good at all. The fact that the sheriff admitted to you and Gator that he had dumped a body in Lighthouse Bayou may have helped, but probably not enough. The jury would likely believe the sheriff's version of the story even though he's dead. In the end, Reggie's a colored man who had a dispute with a white person of authority, and then that person was murdered. You tell me what a white jury's gonna do. I probably would have gone for some sort of plea bargain to keep him from going to the electric chair, but with this being an election year . . . I don't know."

"I guess we never will, thank goodness," the doctor said. "So write me up a bill and send it over. I can't afford to pay you right now, but maybe we can work out some sort of payment plan."

"Well, maybe sooner than you think. My wife's missed her last two periods and is gettin' thick around the middle, so I suspect she's expectin' again."

"Have her come by the office and we'll find out. And thanks, Bob, for everything."

After the doctor had cleaned and bandaged the bite on H.D.

Kneeland's arm, delivered by his wife in some sort of senseless dispute, the doctor drove over to Sixth Street to see Sally Martin. Her new home was an unremarkable white, two-story bungalow, with blue trim and a big, blooming magnolia tree in the front yard. She answered the door soon after the first knock and stood there before him more striking than ever in a form-fitting eyelet dress. "Come in," she said, as she opened the screen door for him. She smelled like ivory soap and tupelo honey. "Thank you for coming. Let's sit in the kitchen and have a cup of tea, if you don't mind. The kids are all at school, and I called in sick this morning."

"Are you sick?" the doctor asked.

"No," she said, "not really, but I've been worried sorta sick ever since I heard what happened last Thursday out at Indian Pass and I wanted to talk to you about it."

"Okay," he said, as Sally filled a tin teakettle with water from the sink's spigot, "what would you like to know?"

"What did Lucky tell y'all?"

"You mean, did he implicate you?"

"Yes."

"Well," the doctor said, "he didn't mention you at all to Chief Lane. He blamed it all on the sheriff and Mike Mitchell at the mill. But, when I was alone with him, he told me the truth."

"And so?" she asked, sitting down to face him, her green eyes beginning to tear.

"And so what? Am I going to tell the chief what really happened? How you arranged for the murder of your husband and the sheriff and the delivery of his head to me?"

"Yes," she whimpered.

The doctor looked at her, weeping with her head in her hands, and oh how he wanted to comfort her.

"No, Sally," he finally said, "I'm not. I'm going to finish my house calls and go home." He stood up and admired her beauty for the last time, as she wept softly over her teacup. "Good-bye," he said and left.

"Van, wait . . ." he heard her cry.

But he just kept right on going.

Chapter 34

The pleasant spring turned into the hot, humid, oppressive summer all too familiar to the inhabitants of the little village of Port St. Joe on the forgotten coast of Florida. The doctor kept more and more to himself. He finished *To Have and Have Not,* which he thought was crudely cobbled together but captured dramatically the desperation delivered by this awful Depression. He saw a bit of Harry Morgan in himself and in many of the patients he saw every day. Sometimes hard circumstances forced hard choices. He listened to the radio that reported that Hitler's army had rounded up, beat, and jailed the Roma and Sinti gypsies throughout Germany. And he got most of his local news from Jewel and Chief Lane who kept him informed about all the legal ramifications of their capture of Lucky Lucilla.

Lucilla's injuries had been worse than the doctor expected. Apparently, according to the chief, because they were at such close range when they had fired, the buckshot from the doctor's gun had caused considerable internal damage to their prisoner. The bullet from the chief's .22-250 Remington pistol had punctured Lucilla's left lung and lodged in his spleen. Several operations were required to repair all the damage, so Lucilla remained in his room in the Panama City Hospital under around-the-clock police guard.

Chief Lane had interviewed him in the hospital and said that Lucky's story remained consistent with the confession he had made when they had captured him at the old barn. The prisoner had also told the chief where he had been living: at an abandoned beach house, on St. Vincent Sound, that had once been owned by Sheriff Batson's father before being acquired by Alfred DuPont in 1933. Apparently, the sheriff had told Lucky about the house and allowed him to live there without the duPont's knowledge for the past few years.

The chief had also asked Lucilla about the sheriff's missing head. Lucky had told him that he had lopped it off on a whim, when he had spotted the big circular saw at the mill near where he had cold-cocked the sheriff with a crowbar. According to what Lucky told the chief, he had dragged the unconscious sheriff to the saw, wedged him into the infeed table on it, powered the motor up, and then severed his head, which he had then tossed off the bridge into the mill's canal on his way home. The chief allowed that he had received an anonymous phone call the day after the murder in which the caller had claimed that the doctor was in possession of the head. Chief Lane said he had just laughed it off, because he knew that if the doctor had found the head he would have immediately informed the chief. The doctor, when he heard this from the chief over a cup of coffee at the Black Cat Café, had just smiled and shook his head.

Now that Lucky seemed to be locked away, the doctor finally felt safe enough that he moved his shotgun from under the front seat of his car back to his bedroom closet, but he kept it loaded, just in case.

Chief Lane had not waited for the federal marshal to arrest Michael Madison Mitchell, the head man at the St. Joe Paper Company who looked like W.C. Fields. The chief had gone to the mill and arrested him the day after Lucilla's capture. He was charged with the murders of Sheriff Batson, Robert Ridler, the man who had died in the cooking vat, and the attempted murders of the union organizers Pete Cartwright, the man who had been pushed onto a shredder, and Henry Dorman, the man who had been shot in the leg. According to the chief, the feds would also be charging him with union busting activities under the National Labor Relations Act of 1935. Mitchell had vehemently denied all the allegations, especially the one accusing him of murdering the sheriff, and proclaimed Lucky Lucilla a crazy man whom no one should believe. Mitchell awaited trial in the city jail where Reggie had recently resided, but his lawyer, Bob Huggins, as it turned out, was still trying to persuade Judge Denton to set bail or at least have Mitchell moved to the county jail in Wewa.

Meanwhile, a new manager took over at the St. Joe Paper Company as it continued to flourish, despite the fact that most of its non-management workers had now joined the newest chapter of the International Brotherhood of Pulp, Sulfite, and Paper Mill Workers.

Jewel found out from her friend, Cecil Burnett, who was the janitor at the Indian Pass Raw Bar, that Sadie McIntire had hired Albert Cunningham to enlarge and maintain her vegetable garden, whose produce she planned to use to expand the roadhouse's limited menu. Jewel said that Lonnie Duncan, a colored man, who had been at the party after Lucilla's capture, had tried to buy a beer there a few days ago, but was turned away.

Upon the death of Harvey Winn, the former head lighthouse keeper, the Civilian Conservation Corp in Highlands County sent his eldest son, Preston, back home to see to the family. According to the *Star*, the Lighthouse Service had just named him the new assistant lighthouse keeper, replacing the murdered Earl Martin, since he knew more about the job than anyone else, having assisted his father there for most of the last five years. But since the Winn boy was only eighteen years old, the Service named Johnny Jones, who was thirty-seven and had helped out at the lighthouse over the years, the new head lighthouse keeper, replacing Harvey Winn.

Sunday, June nineteenth, was Father's Day. The doctor had no children. For some reason no doctor could diagnose, he was sterile, unlike Mabel and Charlie Dilly and Bob and Lizzie Huggins who, since the deaths of two ovulating rabbits, were expecting their new babies in the fall. But he did think about his own father, who had been run over by a streetcar near Watertown Square in 1924. The police had ruled it an accident, but the doctor suspected suicide. In his later years, his father had become so depressed that he had seldom left his room. Finally, one day he had emerged to buy his wife a pack of cigarettes at the corner store and had never returned. The doctor's mother had died from lung cancer two years later.

His father had been a quiet man, probably suffering from depression most of his life, now that the doctor thought about it. When he did talk, he spoke with a thick Armenian accent. He had worked as a janitor at the Perkins School for the Blind in Watertown, Massachusetts, while his wife had stayed home to take care of Van and his two younger sisters, Sona and Lora. Sona now lived with her husband, a school teacher, and three children in Newburyport, Massachusetts. Lora was a single nurse in Providence, Rhode Island. He rarely spoke to them. When he was a child his family had little money and their parents fought about it. The doctor was glad to grow up and move on. He wondered about his father bringing his family to America. What was he expecting? Surely not the cold and snow of New England, the menial, dead-end job, the constant arguing, the growing depression. Was the doctor any better off than his father, he wondered. Alone down here in this struggling village where the suffering, his own included, never seemed to cease.

The new Port Theater, across Reid Avenue from the doctor's office, finally opened on June twentieth with "The Gold Diggers of Paris," starring Rudy Valle and Rosemary Lane. The theatre was being advertised in the *Star* as the most modern in north Florida. Admission for white folks on the main floor was ten cents for seats in the back rows and twenty-five cents for seats closer to the screen, and for the colored audience in the balcony, ten cents for the highest seats and fifteen cents for the lower ones. A free dance, featuring Bill Farmer and his orchestra all the way from Dothan, was held, for whites only, in the lobby of the Port Inn to celebrate the occasion.

Jewel, too, like the doctor, grew more morose as the summer solstice passed, but the next day, June twenty-second, she was more animated than she had been in a long time. "What's going on with you, today?" the doctor asked as he sat down at the kitchen table for breakfast. "I haven't heard you humming like that for quite a while."

"Big fight tonight," she said. "Ain't you heard? Joe Louis gonna fight this fascist Max Schmeling again. Gabriel called and said he and Reggie tried to get tickets, but the whole Yankee Stadium is done sold out."

"Schmeling knocked him out the last time they fought a couple of years ago, you know. You think Louis has a chance?

"Just you wait and see," Jewel smiled.

"So are you going to listen to it on the radio?" the doctor asked.

"Oh yeah. Mama don't like boxing, but Marcus and me wouldn't miss it for the world."

"Well, you're welcome to listen to it here if you like. I plan on listening. I'm not a big boxing fan myself, but this should be something else. Did you hear what Roosevelt said to Louis when he had him to the White House last week?"

"Yeah, he said, 'Joe, we need those muscles for Democracy.'"

"That's right," the doctor said. "Don't know how Joe Louis's muscles are gonna save Democracy, but it sounded good."

"Well, at least there was a colored man in the White House that wasn't a servant. That's somethin' that'll never happen again, that's for sure. And thanks for the invitation, Doc. You know, I think we'll take you up on that. That way we won't upset mama, and we can scream and yell all we want, if y'all don't mind."

So Jewel cooked a big dinner of pot roast, collard greens, and scalloped potatoes. The doctor had some of Gator's moonshine left over from his last visit, so he brought it out and poured Jewel and him each a glassful. They sat on the back porch while Marcus cleaned up until eight o'clock when they all went inside and gathered around the big Philco radio in the doctor's parlor.

"Fifteen rounds for the World's Heavyweight Championship!" the ring announcer bellowed. "Weighing one hundred and ninety-three, wearing purple trunks, outstanding contender for heavyweight honors, the former heavyweight title holder, Max Schmeling . . ."

It didn't take long.

"A lightning to the head," the radio announcer barked. "A left to the jaw, a right to the head, and Donovan is watching carefully. Louis measures him. Right to the body, a left hook to the jaw. And Schmeling is down. The count is five, five, six, seven, eight, the men are in the ring, the fight is over on a technical knockout. Max Schmeling is beaten in one round!"

"Well, tie me to a pig and roll me in mud," Jewel exclaimed. "I'll be dang if he done done it!" They could hear the screaming and chaos at ringside, as the ring announcer came on again and pronounced, "The time . . . two minutes, four seconds, first round. Referee stops it. The winner and still champion . . . Joe Louis!"

The doctor took Jewel in his arms and Marcus hugged their legs as they literally jumped for joy. Then they heard guns being fired in the air in North Port St. Joe as the celebration began all across America. After they had eaten Jewel's peach cobbler and finished the moonshine, the radio announcer said, "In the dressing room after the fight, Louis was as jubilant as it is possible for him to be."

"I waited two years for the revenge and now I got it," the champion said.

The following week Jewel brought in the young woman she had selected to replace her as the doctor's housekeeper and her mother's companion. Her name was Vivian; she was Jewel's cousin, somehow removed. She was a thin, reedlike thing—according to Jewel, "as fat as a darnin' needle; why she could stand under a clothesline in the rain and never git wet." The girl seldom spoke and seldom made eye contact. She was much younger than Jewel, just out of high school and as shy as Jewel was outgoing. About all the doctor could get out of her was an occasional "Yes, sir." But if Jewel thought she was okay, the doctor wasn't going to argue. He didn't have the energy or the inclination to find anyone else.

Chapter 35

As Port St. Joe prepared for a big Fourth of July celebration, with plans, according to the *Star*, for a baseball game (Port St. Joe's town team versus Blountown's), a downtown parade, a beauty contest, a fashion show at the new Port Theater, and a spectacular pyrotechnic display from the Port Inn Pier, Jewel invited Gator over on the Friday night before the three-day weekend—the weekend when Gabriel was supposed to return to Port St. Joe to pick up Jewel and Marcus and take them to New York City. Neither the doctor nor Jewel had seen the big Indian for a while, so it so was good to hear his old truck skid to a stop in the shell driveway out back. As usual, he gave Jewel and Marcus each a grand hug and plopped a burlap sack full of food on the kitchen counter. "I told Jewel not to buy nothin' and not to fix nothin'. You and me, partner, we're cookin' and cleanin' up for Jewel and Marcus tonight. It'll be our goin' away present to 'em."

"What do you have in there?" Marcus asked, eyeing the big burlap bag.

"I'll show you, and then you can go pick out one of the doctor's records to put on his new phonograph, if he don't mind. Let's see what we got here," Gator said, as he began unpacking the bag. "Corn on the cob—might need a little help from you, Marcus, shuckin' it—a ham hock to go with these here green beans fresh from my garden, and four big venison steaks from a deer I shot the other day. Oh, and look what Jed Washington's wife cooked up for the special occasion: a nice, big, banana cream pie."

"Wow," Jewel said. "Some feast! Sure you don't want some help?"

"Nope," Gator answered. "It ain't gonna taste as good as if you cooked it, and it ain't gonna be nothin' fancy, but we'll do our best. Right, partner?"

"Right, what do you want me to do?"

"Pour everybody a drink, first off," Gator said, pulling a Kerr-Mason quart jar of clear liquid from his bag. "Can't cook without a drink."

Marcus put on Ella Fitzgerald's "A Tisket A Tasket," with Chick Webb's big band blasting away behind her. Jewel had to tell Gator where to find the pots and pans that he required, but otherwise she sat back, smiling, at the kitchen table and watched as Gator filled two big pots with water and the doctor snapped the fresh string beans and Marcus shucked the corn. When the first pot came to a boil, he added the ham hock and snapped green beans. Then he melted some butter in the two big cast-iron skillets he had placed on the front two burners of the stove and tossed in the venison steaks, liberally seasoning them with salt and pepper. Since they were thick, he gave them about ten minutes on each side. When he flipped them, he added the corn to the second boiling pot, and they all set the table. The doctor retrieved some more butter from the ice box and placed the salt and peppers shakers on the table, and they were ready to eat. It was simple, but good.

As they were finishing, Gator told everyone he had an announcement. "I'm moving to St. Vincent Island," he said. "Jed Washington got that assistantship at Florida A&M, and I'm takin' over for him. Movin' into his house. I got the oyster business goin' good, but I'll keep an eye on it while I'm doin' what Jed was doin'—keepin' track of all the livestock out there."

"What about the school teaching?" the doctor asked. "You gonna do that too?"

"Well, if I did, those kids wouldn't learn much, that's for sure. No, Jed's two kids are goin' with him, of course. Three others belonged to the white family that quit awhile after we started oyster fishin'. Dr. Price hired another couple to keep his garden, but they ain't got no kids. And the other three, Tom Black's kids, they're old enough they should be goin' to regular school in town anyway, come fall."

"That sounds great, Gator," the doctor said. "You're like Dr. Price's new right-hand man. You deserve it. Since our adventure there, you know more about that island than about anybody else except Washington and Dr. Price himself, but still . . . well, I just hope you don't get so busy that we can't go fishing now and again."

"I'll never git that busy. I'll guarantee you that. But, to tell y'all the truth, it was gittin' kinda lonely out there in my little shack on Indian Pass without nobody else around. This'll be different anyway. I'm lookin' forward to it."

After dinner, Gator and the doctor cleared the table and washed the dishes. Then the doctor asked Gator to help him move the burnt cross that still lay awkwardly across his front porch. Its charred remains were black and heavy. With some effort, they dragged it to the backyard and leaned it up against the side of the shed. Maybe the doctor would chop it up for firewood someday.

Gator and the doctor returned to the kitchen and found Jewel wiping off the counter that they thought they had already cleaned. They left Marcus inside to play more records, as they went out to the back porch to sip the remaining moonshine and smoke the Partagas cigars that Gator had brought.

With Larry Clinton's band and Bea Wain's "My Reverie" wafting from the record player inside, Jewel joined them, settling into the wicker chair next to the doctor. "Well," she sighed, "it's been quite a spring. People gettin' murdered left and right, Doc fallin' in love and almost gettin' killed, Gator goin' to work for Dr. Price, and Gabriel, me, and Marcus goin' all the way to New York City."

"We're gonna miss you, Jewel," Gator said.

"Yes," the doctor added, "we're gonna miss you a lot."

They sat quietly for a while listening to Robert Johnson sing "Love in Vain" on the record player inside, the cicadas calling outside, and a dog barking somewhere in the distance.

"You know," the doctor finally said when the record was over, "I've been wanting to tell y'all something. I want you to know that you don't have to keep quiet about Sally Martin killing her husband and the sheriff, if you don't want to. I've kept my mouth shut so far, but y'all don't have to. You should do what you think is right."

"So why is that?" Jewel asked. "That you haven't reported her to the chief or somebody? You still stuck on the widow?"

"Well, maybe a little. But once I thought it through when Chief Lane arrested Reggie, I figured it was the only way."

"So you knew that Sally was responsible way back then, before Lucky's confession?" Jewel said.

"Yeah, I figured it out the night you told me about her seeing the sheriff out at the Wimico Lake Cabins. I confronted her that night and she confessed to it all."

"So you knew all along?" Gator asked the doctor.

"Yeah, except I didn't know who had actually killed the sheriff. Sally told me that the sheriff had hired Lucky Lucilla to kill her husband, but she didn't tell me who actually sawed the sheriff's head off. I assumed it wasn't her, and I suspected Lucilla, but I thought he was dead, because of what the sheriff had told Gator and me, but when I found out that they had fished a woman out of the bay, instead of Lucilla, I really began to wonder."

"But why?"

"Sally told me that her husband had gambled them way into debt. That he spent every night out at the Indian Pass Raw Bar drinking and gambling. Then she had started seeing the sheriff when her husband was out carousing, and they—Sally and the sheriff—had decided to up the value of her husband's insurance policy and hire Lucky Lucilla to kill him. Then Sally found out that the sheriff was beating up on some prostitutes, and when he started pushing her around she decided to keep all of the insurance money for herself."

"No," Jewel said, "why didn't you tell nobody?"

"Oh, well, at first, because I was so shocked and upset by it all, I didn't know what to do. So I just did nothing. Then Reggie was arrested and I tried to settle down and figure out rationally what was the best thing to do. I figured if I told the authorities that Sally had been responsible for both murders, they would naturally confront her. And, of course, she would lie and say she had nothing to do with either murder and that she didn't know any Lucky Lucilla. There was no real evidence to suggest otherwise. And I also figured that the sheriff had told Sally about Gator's little secret and my little secret and that she would likely tell everyone, if I tried to implicate her. And poor Reggie would still go to the electric chair."

"What little secrets?" Jewel asked.

The doctor and Gator just looked at each other and smiled.

"You ain't gonna tell me are you?" Jewel said. "I hate you guys."

"It doesn't really matter now. I just wanted y'all to know that you can do what you want."

"Look, Doc," Jewel said, "y'all can have your little secrets, but it don't take a lot of cogitating for me. Nothin's to be gained by telling Sally's secrets. Those two bastards, her husband and the sheriff, got what they deserved. Let the widow and her kids enjoy the insurance money. She just done what she had to do."

"Well, now that Reggie's free," Gator said, "nobody's got hurt by the whole business, except for the man at the mill, Mitchell, and he's guilty of goin' after all those union folks anyway, so he deserves whatever he gets. And now that Lucky's been caught, maybe no one else'll try killin' you, partner. So I'm happy with the way things turned out."

"Well," the doctor said. "Sometimes, I'm not so sure."

Later, when the moonshine was gone and everyone was tired and ready for bed, they went inside to check on Marcus. Gator found him asleep on the floor in front of the record player, the turntable rotating quietly, its needle gently nudging the platter post. As the doctor turned off the Gramophone, Gator picked up Marcus and carefully carried him over the back lawn to Jewel's car. The doctor and Jewel followed him. The doctor shook hands with Gator and congratulated him again on his new job on St. Vincent Island. He hugged Jewel goodbye and told her to be careful in New York City.

* * *

Then the doctor returned to his house. He locked the back door behind him and dragged himself upstairs. He went to his bedroom closet and pulled out the shotgun. It was heavy and solid in his hands. He broke it open. There were two new shells in its chambers. He closed the dual barrels and set it on the bed next to him. Wood and steel, solid and elemental. All he had to do was pump it, aim it, and fire.

But then he heard the creaky screen door on the back porch open and quick footsteps to the inside door and its opening. He was sure he had locked it, and only he and Jewel had keys. He reached for the shotgun.

"Doc," she said. "Where are you?"

"Upstairs," the doctor answered.

"Can you come down?"

"Sure."

The doctor left the shotgun on his bed and descended the stairs to find Jewel leaning against the kitchen sink. When she saw him, she extended her arms to him and he came to her. They embraced. Her hair smelled faintly of soap and lye. He felt tired and a little tipsy from all the moonshine. She felt warm and soft and snug against him. "I'm gonna miss you," he said.

"I know. I'm gonna miss you too, but we'll be back to see mama . . . and you."

"I know."

"And Vivian, she's gonna take good care of you."

"I know, but I still don't want you to go." He didn't know how to say it, but now that she was in his arms he wanted to tell her something else before she was gone, before it was too late. "I . . . I . . . I love you, Jewel," he finally summoned. "I think you know that by now."

"I do," Jewel sighed. "I've known it for a long time, maybe even longer than you, Doc. And, well . . . dammit . . . I . . . I love you too. Another time, another place, I guess . . . who knows."

"Who knows," the doctor said, holding her tight against the ensuing night.

Here are some other books from Pineapple Press on related topics. For a complete catalog, write to Pineapple Press, P.O. Box 3889, Sarasota, Florida 34230-3889, or call (800) 746-3275. Or visit our website at www.pineapplepress.com.

Secrets of San Blas by Charles Farley. Most towns have their secrets. In the 1930s, Port St. Joe on the Gulf in Florida's Panhandle has more than its share. Old Doc Berber, the town's only general practitioner, thought he knew all of the secrets, but a grisly murder out at the Cape San Blas Lighthouse drags him into a series of intrigues that even he can't diagnose.

Conflict of Interest by Terry Lewis. Trial lawyer Ted Stevens fights his own battles, including his alcoholism and his pending divorce, as he fights for his client in a murder case. But it's the other suspect in the case who causes the conflict of interest. Ted must choose between concealing evidence that would be helpful to his client and revealing it, thereby becoming a suspect himself.

Privileged Information by Terry Lewis. Ted Stevens' partner, Paul Morganstein, is defending his late brother's best friend on a murder charge when he obtains privileged information leading him to conclude that his client committed another murder thirty years earlier. The victim? Paul's brother. Faced with numerous difficulties, Paul must decide if he will divulge privileged information.

Doctored Evidence by Michael Biehl. A medical device fails and the patient dies on the operating table. Was it an accident—or murder? Smart and courageous hospital attorney Karen Hayes must find out: Her job and her life depend on it.

Lawyered to Death by Michael Biehl. Hospital attorney Karen Hayes is called to defend the hospital CEO against a claim of sexual harassment but soon finds she must also defend him against a murder charge. The trail of clues leads her into a further fight for her own life and that of her infant son.

Nursing a Grudge by Michael Biehl. An elderly nursing home resident, who was once an Olympic champion swimmer with a murky background in the German army, drowns in a lake behind the home. Does anyone know how it happened? Does anyone care? Hospital attorney Karen Hayes battles bureaucracy, listens to the geriatric residents ignored by the authorities, and risks her own life to find the truth.

Seven Mile Bridge by Michael Biehl. Florida Keys dive shop owner Jonathan Bruckner returns home to Wisconsin after his mother's death, searching for clues to his father's death years before. He is stunned by what he discovers about his father's life and comes to know his parents in a way he never did as a child. Mostly, he's surprised by what he learns about himself. Fluidly moving between past and present, between hope and despair, *Seven Mile Bridge* is a story about one man's obsession for the truth and how much can depend on finding it.

Death in Bloodhound Red by Virginia Lanier. Jo Beth Sidden is a Georgia peach with an iron pit. She raises and trains bloodhounds for search-and-rescue missions in the Okefenokee Swamp. In an attempt to save a friend from ruin, she organizes an illegal operation that makes a credible alibi impossible just when she needs one most: She's indicted for attempted murder. If the victim dies, the charge will be murder one.

Mystery in the Sunshine State edited by Stuart Kaminsky. Offers a selection of Florida mysteries from many of Florida's notable writers, including Edna Buchanan, Jeremiah Healy, Stuart McIver, and Les Standiford. Follow professional investigators and amateur sleuths alike as they patiently uncover clues to finally reveal the identity of a killer or the answer to a riddle.

CPSIA information can be obtained at www.ICGtesting.com
Printed in the USA
BVOW071952170613

323556BV00002B/2/P